Danger on the Atlantic

Books by Erica Ruth Neubauer

MURDER AT THE MENA HOUSE

MURDER AT WEDGEFIELD MANOR

DANGER ON THE ATLANTIC

Published by Kensington Publishing Corp.

DANGER ON THE ATLANTIC

ERICA RUTH NEUBAUER

KENSINGTON
PUBLISHING CORP.

www.kensingtonbooks.com

KENSINGTON BOOKS are published by

Kensington Publishing Corp.
119 West 40th Street
New York, NY 10018

All Kensington titles, imprints and distributed lines are available at special quantity discounts for bulk purchases for sales promotion, premiums, fund-raising, educational or institutional use. Special book excerpts or customized printings can also be created to fit specific needs. For details, write or phone the office of the Kensington Special Sales Manager: Kensington Publishing Corp., 119 West 40th Street, New York, NY, 10018. Attn. Special Sales Department. Phone: 1-800-221-2647.

The K with book logo Reg. US Pat & TM Off.

Library of Congress Control Number: 2021949979

ISBN: 978-1-4967-2591-2
First Kensington Hardcover Edition: April 2022

ISBN: 978-1-4967-2593-6 (e-book)

10 9 8 7 6 5 4 3 2 1

Printed in the United States of America

For Gunther and Mandi,
Tim and Carrie.

Thank you for being solid ground
while the earth is shaking.

CHAPTER ONE

The metallic groaning of the giant ocean liner pulling away from the dock at Southampton was nearly drowned out by the frenetic calls from both ship and shore. White handkerchiefs waved gaily from hands all around us—tiny flags of surrender, giving themselves over to the voyage—and long, multicolored streamers decorated the railings and the sky over our heads. I could see the stout figure of my aunt Millie on shore, standing next to her trim fiancé, Lord Hughes, and their daughter Lillian. Millie had offered only a perfunctory gesture before becoming impatient with the ritual, but Hughes and Lillian were still waving gaily as we pulled away.

Redvers and I found ourselves in an orderly crowd on the first-class deck, each of us offering a few waves to my cousin and her father before dropping our hands. I surveyed the wealthy travelers around us, doing my best to make my interest look casual.

"What does a spy look like, I wonder?" The question was muttered from the corner of my mouth.

Leaning against the teak railing, one leg hitched onto the lower rung, Redvers merely shot me an amused look. He looked handsome in his charcoal wool coat and tweed cap—a bit informal, but I noticed many of the male passengers wore similar attire. Rather than ogle the man's broad shoulders, I hitched my coat collar a little higher against the chill off the water and looked over the railing at the crush of people on the second- and third-class decks below us. I had been informed that they were no longer called "steerage," an improvement in terminology if not quarters. It was only due to the generosity of the British government that I was traveling in first class on this voyage, or I would have found myself in the human chaos below. And I was intent on fulfilling my obligations—which meant keeping my eye out for a German agent.

I turned back to the upper-crust travelers around me, looking over our fellow passengers, when I found my eye drawn to a tall woman swimming in a luxurious coat of silver fox. I cringed a bit—I always felt badly for the animal, despite the beauty of the coat. She was standing just a few people down the railing from us, so I could see that the woman's features were a little too sharp to be traditionally beautiful, but her makeup had been artfully applied and her green eyes were luminous and striking against her dark red hair. She was clutching the arm of a bearded man who was nearly the same height as she was, and from the way they were clinging to each other and murmuring in one another's ears, I guessed they were in the throes of a brand-new relationship. The man was nattily dressed, although his trousers were just a shade too short and his shoes were overdue for a shine. He turned his head slightly in my direction and I was able to take him in more fully—I didn't typically care for a man with facial hair, but his beard was close cropped and worked well with his strong, dark features. When the open display of affection between the two became too intimate, I turned back to Redvers.

"Shall we head to our quarters, Mrs. Wunderly?" Redvers offered me his arm and I paused for only a moment before I took it. The ship had pulled far enough from the quay that people were slowly drifting away from the railings and off to their own devices, and it was time to face our living situation for the upcoming voyage. We made our way down the long promenade before pushing through a door and entering another world. Once inside the ship, it was easy to forget you were traveling on what amounted to a floating city—the interior resembled a grand manor house with gorgeous oak paneling lining the walls and plush carpet beneath our feet. We moved toward the grand first-class staircase at the front of the ship—one of two such staircases—and my eye was immediately drawn upward toward the glass dome arching overhead, allowing light to filter in and illuminate the area. The rich wood balustrades framing the space were accented with intricate bronze and iron scrollwork, and the heavy oak banister was smooth beneath my hand as we descended one level to the B-deck. Three elevators were available to take passengers to the various decks below, but I doubted I would be using them. I preferred to soak in the beautiful décor—like the elegant clock bordered by a handsomely carved panel on the opposite wall.

We didn't have far to travel to our cabin, where Redvers produced a key and opened the door to our suite. Through the connecting door I could see that both of our trunks had been delivered and set up in the adjoining bedroom.

I paused inside the doorway, letting my senses soak up the richness of the room. A small desk occupied one corner beside what I could only assume was a false fireplace with an elaborate oval mirror hanging above the carved wooden mantel. I eyed the mirror with some reservation—I hoped it was firmly secured to the wall, since in the event of a squall it could do some serious damage to any occupants of the room. Two windows with gray silk curtains framed the fireplace, letting in more light than I would have imagined possible on board a ship. A modest table was positioned to one side with several seats pushed in, and the rest of the space was occupied by two comfortably upholstered chairs. The walls were paneled in oak with tastefully decorative molding framing out spaces on the walls. All in all, it was a small space, but every inch of it was used well, and far more spacious than I had anticipated.

My eyes flicked toward the bedroom, and the reality of our traveling arrangements began to set in now that we were alone in our quarters. Together. "Ehrm. Are you absolutely sure we need to travel as husband and wife?"

Redvers' eyes lit with a teasing light. "Is the idea of being alone with me so repulsive?" He knew very well that it was not, but I was glad he had left the marriage issue alone—even pretending wedlock was a touchy subject for me, due to my disastrous marriage to the late Grant Stanley.

"Well, I'm not physically ill at the thought, but these are rather close quarters."

A small smile played on his lips, but then he quashed it. "It's rather late now to change our minds. And it really will be easier if we play the part of a married couple on board. There will be fewer questions about us spending so much time together that way."

He was correct there, at least. We had discussed the situation at length when I agreed to help Redvers with this investigation. Ultimately, I had agreed to the plan since a married man traveling with his wife was much less conspicuous than a single man traveling alone. Or a single woman, for that matter. Of course, we had kept the entire matter from my aunt, who believed that we were occupying separate cabins for this trip. What Millie didn't know wouldn't hurt her.

Redvers cleared his throat and clasped his hands behind him. "And I'll be sleeping out here in the sitting room, so you needn't worry about that."

"Oh," was all I could muster. I eyed the two upholstered chairs and glanced back at Redvers. I wondered how he planned to make things work—the man was far too tall to do anything but sleep on the floor out here, and I was struck with a pang of guilt. He was attempting to protect me and prove himself as a gentleman, but it wasn't necessarily Redvers I was worried about. The more time I spent alone with him, the more I found myself rethinking my hardline stance on never marrying again, despite my terrible past experience. Plus, the man kissed like heaven.

No, Redvers wasn't the one I was worried about.

We were interrupted by a knock at the door, and Redvers went to meet with the steward who had come to introduce himself. While they spoke, I wandered about, inspecting the rest of the suite we had been assigned. The bedroom attached to our sitting room had a double bed along one wall with a brass sconce overhead for reading. A small table and chair occupied the corner near the window, while yet another door led to the attached private bathroom. The bedroom walls were lined in a rich damask silk with decorative wood insets breaking the patterns into panels. Glancing up, I noticed the intricately carved molding creating a circular pattern on the ceiling—it appeared that no detail was overlooked in creating an atmosphere of luxury.

I poked my head into the bathroom and found a partially enclosed spray shower above the bathtub occupying one wall. I walked forward and inspected the various knobs it took to operate the thing, and hoped it would prove easier than it appeared at first glance. A marble sink with a large mirror graced the opposite wall, and I ambled over and picked up the Vinolia Otto toilet soap that had been provided, taking a sniff of the light rose and lemon scent before replacing it in the soap dish.

"Jane?" Redvers' low voice carried in from the sitting room to where I was standing. I passed through the bedroom once again and joined the two men. Redvers gestured to the steward in his sharp blue uniform, with its gold buttons marching smartly down the front of the military-style coat. "This is our steward, Francis Dobbins. He'll be working with us."

I shot a questioning look at Redvers and he nodded. I didn't know how they managed it, but apparently Her Majesty had contacts working everywhere. For my own curiosity's sake, I would inquire later as to whether the man was an existing employee on the ship and had simply been tapped to help, or whether he had been planted here by Redvers' employers. Of course, regardless of how he had come to be on board, it was going to be helpful to have someone on the inside. I reached out and shook the man's soft hand, worried for a moment that I might hurt him with my firm handshake. He was young, and had yet to lose the baby fat in his round face—as well as the rest of him.

Redvers invited the steward to have a seat while we discussed matters, but Dobbins refused the invitation, standing with his hands clasped behind his back.

"We suspect there is a German spy on board this ship. Our sources confirmed his presence, but not his identity. We've narrowed the field to three possible suspects," Redvers said.

I was all attention. This was the first time I had been officially included on one of Redvers' cases, and I wasn't going to miss this opportunity to prove myself to his employers. Whoever they were. He'd never been terribly specific on that front.

Dobbins spoke up. "One of the men is a passenger. Heinz Naumann. He's staying in cabin C48, and I've arranged for Mrs. Wunderly to have the deck chair next to his."

I raised an eyebrow at Redvers. I was bemused that we appeared to be traveling under my last name instead of Redvers'—which was Dibble—although I knew that he used his surname as little as possible. "Redvers Dibble" didn't exactly command respect, so I could understand his reluctance to use it, yet I suspected there were also more personal reasons at play. I hoped to someday learn what those were.

"It's common for the first-class passengers to reserve their deck chairs. We've arranged for you to have the one next to Mr. Naumann so that you can chat him up." Redvers turned back to the soft-spoken steward. "Excellent work, Dobbins."

"Do you want to be seated at his dinner table?" Dobbins asked.

Redvers shook his head. "I think that would be overly conspicuous. This is an excellent start. With our first suspect, anyway. What about the other two?"

"They are both employed here on the ship. The band leader, Keith Brubacher, and the man who runs the photography office, Edwin Banks."

"Have you learned anything about either of them?"

Dobbins shook his head. "I haven't had the opportunity, sir. I just received word of the names. Although I do know they are both new on board for this voyage."

Redvers nodded, and I wondered if this was the first time he had heard those names or whether he was simply checking Dobbins's work.

"We'll start looking into them immediately," Redvers said.

Dobbins inclined his head. "I'll leave you to dress for dinner then. It starts promptly at six, but you should hear the bugle call before then."

Dobbins left the room, closing the door silently behind him, and I turned to Redvers. A little tingle of excitement flashed over my skin—I was excited to get underway with this investigation. It was a refreshing change to be consulted rather than left in the dark until the last minute. "So, we have three suspects." All Redvers had told me before we got on board was that we were looking for someone passing information to the German government, but he hadn't shared any particulars with me beyond that. I wasn't even certain the person we were looking for was a German citizen, or just someone working for them. "Which person do we want to investigate first?"

Redvers looked amused at my eagerness. "I think our first step is simply for you to become friendly with Naumann, while I start looking into the other two men."

I could feel my forehead puckering in annoyance, but I quickly smoothed it out. We had a little more than a week on board this ship before we reached New York, and I would be at my most charming.

Heinz Naumann didn't stand a chance. For that matter, neither did the others, once I went to work on them.

CHAPTER TWO

When it came time to dress for dinner, I locked myself in the bedroom and changed into a forest-green silk evening gown, adding my favorite pair of silver kitten heels. An entire wardrobe of beautiful gowns and day dresses had been provided for me especially for this trip since I needed to look the part of a first-class passenger. Nothing I owned was quite so fine, and I briefly wondered who had picked up the bill for my trousseau. Shrugging, I pulled out a beaded black shawl and added it to my ensemble, along with an Egyptian scarab brooch. Even if we weren't going above-deck, I suspected I would need the extra layer in some areas of the ship, and the brooch was a lovely reminder of where Redvers and I first met.

I paused for a moment inside the bedroom door and attempted to hear whether Redvers was still moving around changing into his evening wear, but the only sound I could make out was the gentle thrum of the ship's engines below us. Redvers had dragged his trunk into the sitting room as soon as Dobbins left; it was fortunate that our steward was aware of our situation, because otherwise eyebrows would be raised at the unusual arrangement in our suite.

I knocked on the inside of the bedroom door. "Are you ready?"

Redvers' low, rumbling voice answered me. "I'm ready." I stepped out into the sitting room and my mouth went dry. The man was stunning in a simple black dinner jacket with matching tie and starched white shirt, the jacket accentuating his broad shoulders and dark hair. I almost missed the appreciation in his chocolate-brown gaze, but his eyes sparkled as he greeted me.

"You look lovely."

"Thank you."

We stood awkwardly for a moment, feeling the tension of being left to our own devices for once, with no meddling aunt or other family members to interrupt us.

At least I was feeling the tension. I couldn't be certain why Redvers was behaving awkwardly.

After the silence had stretched on for a beat too long, Redvers cleared his throat, a light flush on his neck stark against the brightness of his white shirt. "Shall we?" I nodded and hid a smile as I came forward and took the arm he offered me.

Redvers locked our suite and we made our way to the dining room two levels below on the D-deck, falling into the steady stream of well-dressed passengers heading that way. Before we made it to the reception room, the raised voice of a woman drew my attention and I slowed to a stop. I cocked my head, then pulled Redvers by the arm in the direction of the corridor where the voice was coming from.

"I would think it's easy enough for you to have your people search for him." The woman's voice was high and sharp, but it probably had more to do with the obvious tension in her words rather than her natural speaking voice.

"Madam, I'm sure your husband will turn up in an hour or so. There's no need to fret." The man's tone was obviously meant to be soothing, but instead came across as nothing short of patronizing.

I popped my head around the corner and recognized the tall redhead from on deck during the ship's departure. She was no longer wearing the fur coat, but it was unmistakably the same woman. She was speaking with a ship officer, obvious in his smart cap and impeccable uniform with its gold stripe running along the cuff of his coat. Another man in uniform stood with them, hat tucked under his arm, and as I watched the two men exchanged a loaded look.

The woman practically growled now. "I know you think he's just disappeared with some sheba, but I assure you that isn't the case. We're newlyweds, and my husband isn't a heel. He was supposed to meet me for a drink and he didn't show."

The officer looked uncomfortable. It was obvious where he believed this woman's husband was, and her argument wasn't swaying his opinion. "Perhaps you should check the common rooms again. Or have your steward look in the gentlemen's lounge. It's entirely possible he simply got caught up in a conversation." He gave a forced chuckle. "And you know, more than one husband has been 'lost' to a card game there—perhaps he's just forgotten the time."

The woman huffed, spun on her heel without another word, and started in our direction. I quickly turned to Redvers, who was patiently waiting for me to finish eavesdropping, and took his arm again. "Shall we?" We started moving toward the dining room just as the redhead came around the corner and brushed past us, her heels clacking angrily down the hall. Within moments she was out of sight.

"Curiosity killed the cat, you know." Redvers' eyes twinkled, and I gave him a soft jab in the ribs.

"I recognize her. From the deck this morning."

"Do you?" Redvers shrugged. "I didn't notice her, I'm afraid. I was busy watching the young man with his camera."

I had missed that individual entirely. "I guess we're even then."

* * *

Down on the D-deck, the *Olympic* had a reception area where guests could meet and have a drink before going into the dining room for their evening meal. The white paneling in this room was delicate but just as detailed as elsewhere on the ship, and I noticed the decorative molding on the ceiling here as well, a pattern of alternating squares and swirls. Small groupings of wicker chairs with comfortable pads and small tables were scattered throughout the space, the occasional potted palm adding some warmth to the busy room. A huge tapestry hung at the entrance directly opposite the staircase, and its rich detail and coloring drew the eye immediately. I stopped and stood to one side to take in the scene while Redvers checked in with the steward at the entrance to the dining room.

"Mr. and Mrs. Wunderly, excellent. If you'll follow me to your table, I believe your tablemates have already begun their dinner, but that shouldn't be an issue." He gestured for us to follow him, and we fell into line behind him.

The dining room was enormous, extending nearly the entire width of the ship, and although it was only one level, the high ceilings gave it a feeling of spaciousness. The patterned ceiling from the reception area was repeated here, with decorative wood pillars running in a line down the center of the room. It seemed there were perfectly set tables and elegantly dressed passengers as far as the eye could see. Our seating assignment was centrally located with a decent view in both directions—I was certain that was no accident. Redvers would be able to casually keep an eye on the entire room from here. I then turned my attention to our table, finding three people already seated, and the steward gave an apologetic smile before turning on his heel and hurrying away. I wondered for only a moment what he was sorry for.

"Well, you're a bit late, but sit yourselves down." The owner of the booming voice that greeted us was a buxom woman wearing a dress entirely covered with silver sequins, and the overhead light playing over them was nearly blinding. She half stood as we approached to rearrange herself in her chair, and I could see that her height was matched only by her width. We only just managed to introduce ourselves and take our seats when the woman continued on in the same projecting volume even though we shared a table. "I'm Miss Eloise Baumann and this is my sister, Margret Gould." She gestured to the thin woman sitting quietly at the table sipping a glass of water. Then she turned to the gentleman who had stood when we approached and was seated at Margret's left. "And this is Douglas Gould." Her lip curled a bit as Douglas nodded briefly at us and went back to his soup. It looked as though Douglas was determined to ignore any further interruptions to his meal.

"Where are you both from?" Eloise didn't wait for either of us to actually answer her question before continuing on. "We hail from New York, and were just spending a little holiday in England. Well, these two were. I was interviewing with organizations to do some overseas missionary work. We must bring the good word to the savages overseas, you know, and with England over in India just now, it seemed like a good time to make the trip."

I tried to keep my lip from curling at her characterization of the Indian people as "savages," since I knew full well they were no such thing. From the corner of my eye I could see Redvers' eyebrows creeping further up his forehead the more the woman talked. It was an onslaught of information, and every time I opened my mouth to answer a question she moved on before I could make a sound.

The waitstaff brought our soup quickly and just as quickly hurried away. I imagined it hadn't taken them long to figure out that the best way to deal with our table was to keep their distance from it. I could hardly blame them. All through our soup course Eloise talked—I was amazed to see that she had somehow managed to finish her own, but I wasn't sure when she'd had time to do so. Her nonstop monologue ranged from the quality of the food on board the ship to the suitability of her suite to what Mr. Gould did for a living—he was a hospital administrator.

"I live with my dear sister and Mr. Gould, and I have to say I don't quite know what they would do without me." This bold statement finally sparked a response from Margret, who looked to the heavens but quickly went back to the entrée that had just been delivered to her. I sighed as I realized that salvation was not going to come from either Mrs. Gould or her husband, although I wondered if even her relations could stop her. A quick glance around showed me that all the tables within earshot were quiet and being held captive by our tormentor as well. "I mean, it's such a large house and the staff will take advantage if you don't have a firm hand with them. That has never been Margret's strong suit."

"You never married then, Miss Baumann?" I finally popped a question in when the woman filled her mouth with a large bite of steak. Redvers shot me a dirty look, but I simply shrugged. If she was going to talk nonstop, I might as well hear things I was curious about.

"Heavens no. I could never find anyone who could match our dear father, Walter. And once he died, I came to help Margret."

"I wonder if Walter died just to get some quiet," Redvers muttered under his breath, and I stifled a giggle.

"What was that?" Eloise cast a sharp look at Redvers, who coughed once.

"I was just wondering what Walter did for a living." Redvers looked completely innocent as he spun this lie. "You speak so well of him."

Eloise seemed gratified and I gave Redvers' leg a little kick under the table. He hid a smile behind his wineglass.

"Well, you know our father was a house painter. But I

don't want you to think he was common. No, he put himself through school and became an associate professor at a university that is quite well respected."

Here I tuned out and nodded vaguely at the woman while I took in the wider room behind her. I scanned the tables but caught no sight of the redheaded woman or the man she was married to.

"Any sign of him?" Redvers asked under his breath. I wondered how he knew that the woman's missing husband was still on my mind.

"What was that? You must speak up." Eloise had to be nearing seventy, but there was nothing wrong with her hearing.

Redvers smiled politely. "I was just asking if Jane had seen some old friends of ours."

"It's such a treat to see old friends, isn't it? I was just writing to my friend Ethel—her husband is blind you know, so she reads my letters aloud to him. It really brings him joy to hear from me, and it's the least I can do. I've known them since, well, since at least 1899, yes, it must be that long. . . ."

I wished Ethel all the best, mentally of course, since there wasn't a chance to say as much out loud, but I couldn't help wonder how enthusiastic the woman truly was about her verbose friend Eloise.

As soon as our dessert plates left the table, Redvers was grasping my arm and making our excuses to the table. Mr. Gould seemed to think this was a brilliant idea, and stood as well.

"Are you heading to the smoking lounge, Mr. Wunderly?"

"I was not—" Redvers was cut off by the suddenly enthusiastic Gould.

"Well, I'll just accompany you there, then. Ladies, I'll see you later this evening."

Margret gave her husband a look that shot daggers, but Eloise simply rolled her eyes. It seemed that as far as she was concerned, her brother-in-law was not necessary to her evening's pleasure. "Mrs. Wunderly, would you like to stay with us? We were going to head to the reception room. I know some delightful arias that I can perform if they have a piano player that is any good, that is. . . ."

I just smiled and shook my head, feigning regret while I let Redvers lead me away. "It was a pleasure," I called behind me. It was a lie, but a well-intentioned one.

Mr. Gould was suddenly Mr. Congeniality, now that we had left his sister-in-law behind. "Good lord, that woman never stops talking." He shook his head, but didn't stop moving at the quick pace that took him out of the dining room and up the stairs to the next deck. "Thank you for giving me an out, Redvers old man."

"My pleasure. But I must admit that I'm planning to accompany my wife to the lounge."

My stomach gave a little jolt at Redvers' referring to me as his wife. I knew it was the part we were playing, but it hadn't been said aloud until now, and I felt myself growing warm in the face. I also couldn't help but wonder what it would be like if it were true. What kind of husband would the secretive man next to me make? Surely a much better one than my last.

Gould paused his escape and slapped Redvers on the back, effectively interrupting my wayward thoughts. "Oh, that's fine, that's fine. I'm just glad to have shaken myself free." The man bid us good night and was gone a moment later.

"That was certainly not how I intended the evening to go."

I paused and regarded him. "And just what *did* you intend for this evening?"

Redvers winked and said nothing, smoothly maneuvering me toward the lounge instead.

CHAPTER THREE

We pushed through heavy oak doors and moved toward the large fireplace dominating one wall of the lounge, the stunning oak panels decorated in floral scrollwork flanking either side of the rich gray marble. A large mirror hung above the heavy mantel. I could see that a coal fire was ready to be started in the grate, and I was astonished there was an actual working fireplace on board the ship. My heels sank into the velvety carpet as we crossed through the low hum of chatter and cigarette smoke swirling to the ceiling. The entire room was paneled in carved oak and, with the upholstered couches and chairs scattered about, had a distinctly French feel to it.

As a nearby couple stood and vacated their small table, Redvers held out a hand toward the newly empty arrangement. "Shall we?" We sat in the plushy chairs and I surveyed the crowd. I didn't see the redheaded woman, nor could I spot her husband. I wished that I knew what Heinz Naumann looked like, but without a detailed description I had no idea how I would pick him out of the crowd. At least with Banks and Brubacher, we knew their roles on board the ship. It would make them easy to identify and keep an eye on.

A sudden moment of panic had me searching the room for

a piano, and I breathed a sigh of relief when I realized there wasn't one.

"What is it?"

"For a moment, I was worried that there was a piano and we were going to be joined by our new friend Eloise."

Redvers chuckled and signaled a nearby waiter. "No, there isn't one here. I believe there is a piano in the reception room we were just in, and possibly in the lounge down on the D-deck. Aft of the ship."

I had no idea what direction that was in. All I knew was that it was an area I would be avoiding.

The waiter had hurried across the room at Redvers' signal, and we placed a drink order—a gin rickey for myself and a neat whiskey for Redvers. As we waited, I continued inspecting the first-class passengers around us, but Redvers' attention was focused on me.

"The investigation can wait until the morning, you know."

I looked at him in surprise. "Don't we want to start immediately?" He shrugged carelessly. Since it was the first time I was actually being included on a mission, I didn't want to make a hash of things—I wanted to prove I was worthy of the trust both he and his employers had placed in me. And if I was honest, I wanted to excel. Because if I did, perhaps I would be included on missions in the future. Not that I was ready to admit that aloud, of course. It was just that nothing made my blood sing quite like diving into an investigation.

Well, that and the man sitting across from me.

"What will you do once you're home in Boston?" Our drinks arrived and Redvers took a sip.

"Check in on my father," I replied. "It's been several months since I've seen him."

"He can't function without you?"

"Oh, he can, but since my mother died I like to keep an eye on him, make sure he hasn't burned the place down, that sort of thing. He's rather absentminded." I gave a chuckle. "I found his eyeglasses in the ice box last time I was home."

"I imagine they're difficult to find if you can't see without them."

"I'm not sure he even noticed they were gone." I smiled at the memory, then cocked my head. "How long are you planning on staying in the States?" I wondered if Redvers would ever have occasion to meet my father in person.

His smile widened, crinkling the edges of his dark eyes. "I guess that depends."

"Depends on?" I held my breath, unsure what I wanted his answer to be.

He paused and surveyed the room casually. "Would you care for a smoke?"

My mouth squeezed into an irritated line. "What terrible misdirection. You know very well I don't smoke."

He chuckled. He was tormenting me and enjoying it. "It depends on what happens during this investigation. And with some other matters I'm attending to." His dark eyes held mine.

"Dare I ask what those matters are?"

"I think it's best they remain a secret for the time being."

My heart fluttered and I inspected the last few sips in my drink for a moment. I realized I was dearly wishing that I was one of those matters. Recalling our close quarters, I was suddenly unsure how our evening would end and how we would navigate the inevitable awkwardness when we retired for the night. As comfortable as I had grown with the man, I was still just the tiniest bit uneasy about what would happen behind those closed doors. And I was also unsure what I *wanted* to happen.

"You know, I think I'm ready for another drink."

Redvers' look was a little too knowing as he put a hand up and signaled to the waiter.

*   *   *

Any potential awkwardness was soon forgotten when our waiter returned with our second round and Redvers started asking me numerous questions about my life back in Boston.

"What about your mother?"

"What about her?"

Redvers gave me a pointed look. "What kind of person was she?"

I took a sip of my drink and thought about the answer to that. "She was an early suffragist back in England. Believed firmly in women's independence." I felt a pang as I thought about how disappointed she would have been in my choice of husband the first time around. "She passed when I was fairly young—she never got to cast her own vote." I shook my head. "I'm afraid my memories of her are fading."

Redvers patted my hand and gave me a moment before turning the conversation to lighter topics. I was soon laughing and chatting away, and it wasn't until we were standing before the door to our suite that I remembered my earlier trepidation about the night's arrangements.

"I feel terribly letting you sleep on this floor," I said as soon as he shut the door behind us. I could see that Dobbins had already provided extra blankets and pillows for him, stacked neatly on the opposite chair, but it still didn't seem like enough.

He chuckled. "Don't worry. I've slept much rougher than this." He waved a hand at the stack of blankets. "And Dobbins has left me plenty to cushion myself with."

I shifted from foot to foot. "Well, I'm awfully tired. It was an early start this morning. I think I'll try to get some sleep." But I stayed standing where I was.

Redvers stifled a yawn, then sat on the edge of one of the upholstered chairs. "I'm done in as well." He began loosening his tie and my eyes darted around the room before landing back on what his hands were doing.

"Erm . . . Do you need to use the washroom?"

His eyes twinkled. "I should be fine for the evening." He removed the tie entirely and folded it neatly, placing it on the low table at his elbow, and began removing his shoes.

I cleared my throat. "Well. Then. Good night, Redvers."

"Good night, Jane."

I turned quickly and headed for the bedroom. I cast my handsome companion one last glance before I shut the door quietly behind me.

And spent quite a restless night.

CHAPTER FOUR

Sometime during the night our ship moved into stormier seas, and one of the many times I found myself tossing in my bed, I awoke and found that we were rolling quite a bit. Not enough to send me out of bed, but enough for me to worry about the sturdiness of the ship we sailed on. It had been many years past, but I remembered that the RMS *Olympic* was in fact the sister ship to the ill-fated *Titanic*, and while I doubted we would meet the same demise, I couldn't help but feel a bit nervous all the same. Especially as my stomach was now doing figure eights in the dark.

Despite the stormy seas twisting my stomach and the worry racking my brain, I managed to snatch a few solid hours of sleep just after dawn and I woke a bit later than I had intended. I rushed through my morning routine and knocked on the inner door to the bedroom, fully expecting Redvers to be gone already.

"Come in." Redvers' voice was cheerful.

As I entered the room, I could see that he was already fully dressed and buttering some toast. A full breakfast tray was laid out on the low table before him.

"I thought you might appreciate breakfast in the room before you headed up on deck." He frowned a bit and gestured toward the window with a tip of his head. "Although the weather changed overnight and it might be a bit unpleasant out there."

"Thank you. That was very thoughtful of you." I appreciated not having to face a full dining room of people quite yet. I was also grateful that Redvers was avoiding mention of how long I had slept in. "I'm sure I'll be fine." I glanced toward the window where quite a bit of light was coming through—hopefully it meant rain wasn't accompanying the stormy seas.

Without another word Redvers poured a bit of cream into a cup and added some dark coffee before handing it to me. I inhaled a deep breath of the delicious aroma and murmured my thanks. It didn't escape my notice that he recalled exactly how I took my coffee—or that I preferred it to tea in the mornings. This was a lifestyle that I could easily get used to.

After breakfast Redvers accompanied me as far as the top deck, mostly to ensure that the weather really was decent enough for me to sit outdoors, but I was also grateful for the help in navigating the ship. I was still struggling to get my bearings on the overwhelmingly large vessel—it seemed that every passageway looked incredibly similar to the one before it. Once on deck, we looked out over the railing at the white-caps surging around us.

"I've seen worse," Redvers said.

I gulped at the thought, but put on a brave face. It really wasn't so bad as that, especially once the body got used to the constant rolling motion. It did make walking a straight line difficult—the corridors were full of passengers looking as though they had imbibed a few too many cocktails. But up here in the fresh sea air, I could watch the horizon as it bobbed. I gave a firm nod of my head. "I'll be fine." There was a brisk wind and overcast skies, but it was blessedly dry.

Redvers looked at me, then gave a nod of his own before leading me to where Dobbins waited for us. Redvers disappeared back down the stairs as the steward took over and led me to my deck chair. I'd had the foresight to bring a book, just in case our suspect decided not to take fresh air at the same time, although I wasn't sure I would be able to read it given the motion of the ship.

The wind was chilly and whipped the ends of my hair around my face. I was glad I had securely fastened my hat, although even with the pins, I was worried I might lose it in a good gust. Dobbins provided me with a fur rug, thick and warm, and I draped it over myself and settled in for a wait, watching the waves that tossed us gently about. We had already left the shores of England long behind us, and the vast expanse of water and overcast sky stretched before me. It made me shiver; I didn't like the feeling of being so isolated in the middle of a great ocean of water. It was rather surprising given how much I had loved taking flight lessons and soaring through the open sky. But even without the swelling waves, this felt more dangerous somehow—perhaps because I had no control over the ship or the water that carried it.

I was so distracted by the overwhelming view that I almost didn't register when the seat next to mine became occupied, and I nearly jumped when a voice addressed me.

"*Guten Morgen.*" A handsome man with neatly slicked back brown hair and snapping blue eyes greeted me as he settled himself into his chair, draping his own rug over his lower legs. Unless this man was an interloper sitting in someone else's seat, I was looking at Heinz Naumann.

"Good morning! I apologize, I was just taking in the view." My heart was racing a bit from the scare, and from the uneasiness of being alone with a strange man. Fortunately, a discreet glance around assured me that it was far from the case—there were numerous other passengers within calling distance.

"Quite overwhelming, is it not?" Echoing my thoughts exactly from only a moment before, Naumann gazed out over the railing to the roiling ocean beyond before turning back to me. "Is this your first time at sea, Mrs. . . . ?"

It was not, but the first time we had crossed the Atlantic, the weather had been much fairer and we had been headed south to Egypt. It was a far different experience than this brisk and stormy trip.

"Wunderly. Jane Wunderly." Naumann introduced himself as well, confirming my initial assumption about his identity. Introductions made, I answered his question. "And it is not my first time at sea, but I'm afraid this is my first time taking this particular trip. It's much . . . brisker than I had expected."

Heinz laughed. "It is true. I find myself very thankful for these warm rugs. And even more thankful for some inner warmth." He pulled a flask from his coat pocket and poured something into the cup of tea he had perched on the table between us. He held the flask up in offering, and when I shook my head, he dipped his in acknowledgment before he capped the little silver container and returned it to his pocket. His eyes twinkled. "I find that a little brandy helps settle the stomach. Some medicine for all these waves."

I smiled and briefly wondered if that was true. Although I was fortunate that my own stomach had not yet revolted against the constant motion.

Conversation continued easily between us. We chatted about the book I was reading and novels in general. In the back of my mind I was aware that I needed to ingratiate myself with the man, but what I hadn't expected was to actually *like* him. He was charming and pleasant, not at all what I expected from an enemy spy. I found myself hoping that the man we sought was one of the other two suspects.

"I should really return to my husband," I said at length, glancing at my watch. My cheeks were cold, and I didn't want to seem too obvious by waiting until he excused him-self—it was far better for me to leave first. Besides, it felt like I had already made great strides in befriending the man.

"If your husband has sense, he will be missing you." Heinz's bright eyes sparkled. "It was very much a pleasure, Mrs. Wunderly. I hope that we can chat again soon."

"I hope so too, Mr. Naumann." I folded my rug and headed back for the middle of the ship, keeping far away from the railing. I knew there was little chance of my going overboard, but the swelling water and my unsteady gait made me uncomfortable. Better safe than sorry.

I had nearly reached the door leading back inside when I was met by Redvers opening that same door.

"Successful?"

"I think so."

He offered his arm and we headed toward the staircase when Redvers paused.

"It's nearly time for lunch. Shall we head into the dining room? Or would you like to eat in the à la carte restaurant?"

My stomach rumbled and I realized I had been on deck for far longer than I had thought. But the prospect of sharing a table with Eloise Baumann and her put-upon relations had me thinking we should try a new venue for dining.

"Let's do à la carte."

Redvers led me down the stairs to the next deck, and even though I had questions about what he had accomplished while I was busy with Naumann, I kept my mouth shut. There would be time for that later when we were behind closed doors. No sense in broadcasting our conversations about the investigation when anyone could be listening.

We were nearing the entrance to the restaurant when we came upon a trio of people blocking the hallway. I immedi-ately recognized the wealthy redheaded woman from the pre-vious day, although she had traded her full fox coat for a smaller black mink stole draped over an elegant gray suit. Her green eyes flashed angrily at the ship captain and another man in uniform.

"I'm not crazy. I have a husband and he was with me when we boarded yesterday. You refused to look for him last night, and now his things have disappeared as well."

CHAPTER FIVE

The man standing beside the captain put his hands up. "Now, we aren't saying that you're crazy. No one has said that, madam. Just that you might be confused."

"I am not confused." The woman was gritting her teeth. "And I demand that you search the ship immediately."

"Why are we getting involved in this?" Redvers hissed into my ear as I moved closer.

I didn't answer him as we joined the small group. "Excuse me, I couldn't help but overhear. Did you misplace your husband?"

The woman shot me an assessing look, then went back to glaring at the two men before her. "I didn't *misplace* him so much as he's *missing*. And for whatever reason, these two fools don't seem to believe me."

I looked at the men, only one of which had the grace to look slightly abashed. He was a tall man with thinning gray hair and sharp blue eyes. "It's just that husbands often go missing. Seaboard romances and such," he said.

I had to wonder about the "such."

"But what about his things? Do those often go missing as well?" The woman's voice hadn't lost a bit of its edge.

The captain turned to Redvers and me. "Nothing to worry

about. You two should just continue on to where you were going, and we'll see this sorted out." Redvers lifted one eyebrow in amusement at our dismissal, but the woman snorted in derision.

I could feel Redvers about to move away, but I wasn't going to be sent off so easily. "I did see this woman's husband with her yesterday as we left Southampton. They were standing near us on the deck." I wasn't sure if my information was helpful, but it was true.

Captain Bisset's lips twisted. "But have you seen him since?"

"And do you know Miss FitzSimmons?" The other man gestured to the redhead. "Perhaps it was someone else that you saw earlier." It didn't escape my notice that he'd neglected to address the woman as "Mrs.," as though he didn't believe she was even married.

I wasn't sure whether these men thought she had fabricated a husband entirely or still believed that he had found another woman to occupy his time with. Either way, I was incensed that they refused to take her concerns seriously. I said nothing but stared at the captain, arms crossed.

Redvers cleared his throat. "Captain Bisset, if my wife says she saw them earlier, then she saw them." It was a relief that he at least believed me, no questions asked.

The captain gave a huff of annoyance. "Well, it seems unlikely that a man could simply vanish off this ship." He looked at Mrs. FitzSimmons. "Perhaps he disembarked before we left shore."

Hands on hips, Mrs. FitzSimmons gritted her teeth. "He was with me as we pulled away from the dock. So unless you took this hulking piece of metal back while we were in our quarters, he is still on board. He has to be."

Captain Bisset huffed again, his grizzled gray whiskers

bristling in indignation. He was a man who was used to being obeyed, not argued with. "And I still say that perhaps he is spending his time somewhere else on this boat and he just doesn't want you to know about it. We've already done a sweep for stowaways and found no one. I expect we would have found your husband then."

Mrs. FitzSimmons and the captain locked eyes, and it was difficult to say which one was more put out. Looking between the two, the tall man took a step forward and interjected in a calming voice, "Captain, it wouldn't hurt to have the crew take another look around." He turned to Mrs. FitzSimmons. "Do you have a picture?"

At this the woman's haughty stance slumped a bit. "I don't. We were only recently married. But I can give you a thorough description."

"Fine," the captain said. "But you take care of this, Montgomery. I have other matters to attend to." With a glare that encompassed all of us, Captain Bisset stalked off.

Redvers cast an amused look at me, then leaned in. "I guess we can forget about dining at the captain's table this trip," he murmured.

"It would have been bad for blending into the crowd anyway," I muttered back.

Mrs. FitzSimmons ignored our side conversation, put out her hand, and briskly shook mine. "Thank you for your help, Mrs. . . ."

"Mrs. Wunderly," I said. "But call me Jane."

"Vanessa FitzSimmons. Of the New York FitzSimmonses."

I smiled politely even though I had never heard of the family, New York or otherwise. It did make me curious as to why she hadn't taken her husband's name, since she was obviously a FitzSimmons from birth, but perhaps the marriage was still too new.

Vanessa looked over at the tall man in our midst, a wary look in her eye. "And this is Dr. Montgomery." The doctor and Redvers murmured their greetings to one another, then fell silent as Vanessa continued on.

"Now, Jane. Did you actually see my husband with me yesterday, or are you merely being helpful?"

Ordinarily I might have been offended by the woman's question, but I liked her matter-of-fact tone. "No, I really did see the both of you on deck as we were leaving. I noticed because you were wearing a lovely fur coat." I didn't mention that I had also noticed the pair because of how openly affectionate they had been with each other in public.

She nodded. "Of course. The silver fox. I do get compliments on that piece." She looked at Redvers. "And you, Mr. Wunderly? Do you have anything to add?"

It still amused me to hear Redvers being referred to as Mr. Wunderly, and I wondered how he was able to answer to it with such equanimity.

"I didn't happen to notice, but my wife is very observant and I believe her."

Vanessa turned back to the doctor. "Well, at least now you know that my husband isn't a figment of my imagination." She gave Montgomery a description of the man I had seen with her the day before. "What are you going to do about it?"

Montgomery looked uncomfortable, but he was resolute. "I'm going to circulate a description among the staff and see that we search the entire ship. If he was still on board when we pulled away from the dock, it's unlikely that he was able to leave. Unless he went overboard."

"He didn't do that," Vanessa said firmly. And when the doctor didn't move, she flapped her hands at him. "What are you waiting for? Get a move on. I've already told you what he looks like. And his trunks are clearly marked with his name—they have to be somewhere on board as well."

With as much dignity as he could muster, the doctor took his leave of us, and Vanessa FitzSimmons heaved a sigh.

"Unbelievable that this should happen. We haven't even been married a week and the man disappears. Typical."

"How long have you known . . . Mr. FitzSimmons." I realized I hadn't heard anyone refer to him by name.

"His name is Miles. Miles Van de Meter." She sighed again. "We met in Monte Carlo two weeks ago, and I admit it was a bit of a whirlwind romance. He just swept me off my feet. I haven't had time to consider taking his name yet." Her mouth puckered. "I do hope he's all right. We haven't even gone on a honeymoon or had time to plan one. We were supposed to travel home to New York and meet my family first."

It seemed Redvers had tuned out of our conversation, but here he finally stepped in. "When was the last time you saw your husband?"

Vanessa put her wrist to her forehead and thought for a moment before flicking it back down to her side. "Oh, it must have been not long after we went belowdecks. I took a bit of a nap—too much champagne, you know—and when I woke up, there was no sign of him. His luggage was unopened, and no Miles." A grimace crossed her face. "And then this morning his things were gone as well. Trunk and everything."

"Was it gone when you woke up?" It was possible that someone had collected it while she slept.

Vanessa shook her head. "I don't recall. I think it was there when I got up this morning, but perhaps it was gone when I returned from the lounge. I'll have to ask my maid."

I raised my eyebrows a bit. I couldn't help it. The woman had gone to the lounge even though her husband was missing.

As though she knew exactly what I was thinking, she put a fist on her hip and gave me a steady look. "I wasn't truly worried until I came back and saw that his things had gone as well." She shot a look at Redvers before turning back to me. "I didn't want to admit it to the captain, but men really are predictable."

So, she *had* considered the possibility that her brand-new husband had already strayed. It was a dim view of her marriage and men in general, although my own experience in the field hadn't been any great success either. And I didn't blame her for keeping her views from the captain; it wouldn't have helped her case in the slightest to admit that he might be correct. The man was already reluctant to mount a search— confirming his suspicions would have done nothing but ensure there was no search at all.

"Would you like us to come have a look around your room?"

Vanessa's look of skepticism spoke volumes.

"I have some . . . experience looking into things like this." I paused, trying to decide how to convince the woman that I knew a thing or two without explaining anything explicitly. I didn't want to risk blowing my cover for our actual investigation, so I quickly made up a vague story. "I helped my aunt out with a similar situation. I was able to figure things out for her."

Surprisingly, Redvers held his tongue, and simply nodded his agreement.

"Hmm." Vanessa gave me a long, speculative look but didn't ask for further details. Which was a relief since I wasn't sure I could make them up for her. "I just may take you up on that, but for the time being I think I'm going to have a lie-down. I have a dreadful headache." Her green eyes flicked to Redvers, then back to me. "Perhaps we can meet later in the lounge."

With that we were dismissed. Vanessa went on her way, and we continued on to lunch.

I hoped that my instincts were wrong, but I suspected even a thorough search of the ship wasn't going to turn up Miles Van de Meter.

CHAPTER SIX

Redvers led me to the restaurant, saying nothing. I was lost in my own thoughts and it wasn't until we were seated at our table that I realized how quiet he had been.

"What are you thinking?"

"I'm not certain why you want to get involved in this woman's troubles."

I couldn't hide my surprise, but an immediate answer didn't roll off my tongue either. "Um, well, because . . ." I sat for a moment and tried to find a way to explain. "She's in trouble. And if there's a way I can help, I will."

"But she's a complete stranger. We know nothing about her." Redvers sounded adamant, his strong jaw set.

I studied him for a moment. "Do you not believe her?"

Redvers shrugged. "The captain is most likely right. The man is probably off catting around on board with some other woman." He picked up the menu that had been left by the steward. "And we have other matters to concern ourselves with."

I picked up my own menu, but I could hardly concentrate on reading the words. Redvers had immediately backed me up when I vouched for the existence of the woman's husband, but it was quite obvious he didn't want me getting involved. Was it simply because he thought I couldn't manage two issues at the same time? I had no doubt that I could help this woman look for her husband and continue investigating our case.

"I'm quite sure I can handle both things at once, if that's what you're worried about."

Redvers shook his head and I could tell he was finished with the topic, but I felt a familiar fissure of doubt. I'd been forced to silence myself and become as small as possible during my marriage to Grant. It wasn't possible that I had misjudged Redvers so badly, was it? Especially given all that we'd been through together. After a few moments I squashed the little voice—surely, he wouldn't do the same thing to me. I knew him better than that.

We sat in charged silence waiting for the waiter to arrive and take our orders. To avoid meeting Redvers' eye I took the time to study the room since I hadn't taken it in when we entered. I gave a little sigh. Every time I thought we'd seen the finest room the ship had to offer we entered a new one even more stunning than the last.

This room also had a French flair to it, with fawn-colored wood paneling, the molding intricately carved and gilded. The plush carpet had a delicate vieux rose pattern complementing the embroidered design on the silk draperies hanging over the large bay windows that illuminated the space—I noticed the expanse of the windows was broken into squares by thin metal ornamentation, a detail that added to the Gallic feel of the room. To the right of the entrance was a large counter with a marble top supported by the same gorgeous wood paneling, the carvings reflecting those found on the walls. There were several well-placed gilt metal and crystal light fixtures hanging from the ceiling; our own table had a small crystal lamp with a rose-colored shade. Altogether the room came together in a warm and entirely harmonious way.

Once our orders were placed and the waiter had gone,

Redvers folded his hands on the tabletop. "Tell me about your conversation with Naumann."

I looked at him in surprise. "Here? Now?"

He looked around and I did the same. We were at a somewhat secluded table, and a quick glance around told me that no one was paying us any mind. I shrugged and recapped our conversation and the various topics we had touched on.

Redvers eyed me shrewdly. "You liked him."

I shifted in my seat. "I did like him. But I can remain objective."

Redvers didn't respond to that.

"I'm hoping to run into him again later tonight, perhaps at the lounge," I said after a moment. "He seemed open to further conversation."

"Excellent." It was quiet for a few moments, then the waiter returned with the items we had ordered—a hearty stew with crusty bread for myself and a steak and mushroom pie for Redvers.

Once I was certain our waiter was out of earshot, I asked what I'd been wondering all morning. "How did you occupy yourself while I was on deck?"

"I started making inquiries into our other . . . subjects." He wasn't short with me, but he turned his attention back to his meal, and I decided it was a topic best discussed behind closed doors. Hopefully that was the reason he was refusing to elaborate.

The attentive waiter stopped once more to top off our water glasses. This time once the man left, Redvers steered the conversation to more neutral topics instead of letting the silence overtake us. I was grateful for the exchange, but I couldn't help but wonder why he didn't want me involved with Vanessa FitzSimmons.

After lunch Redvers announced that he was going to take advantage of the squash court on board, and went to get some exercise. I hoped that he was able to sweat out whatever was bothering him, since his behavior was decidedly off.

Vanessa hadn't exactly asked me to look into things, but I figured it couldn't hurt to seek out our steward and talk with him. As someone who resided with the rest of the crew, Dobbins might have picked up some gossip about the search for Vanessa's husband that could prove useful.

I called the switchboard to request that Dobbins come by my suite and I was assured by the voice on the other end that he would be notified and sent to me directly. I waited in our sitting room—Redvers' bedroom—on the remaining upholstered chair and glanced around. I noticed that his trunk had been moved into a corner of the room where one of the chairs had previously resided and I idly wondered where the missing chair had been taken to. With the exception of the trunk, and the blankets and pillow piled beside it, you could hardly tell someone was sleeping here. All Redvers' personal effects had been tidied away as well as our trays from breakfast. Dobbins was at the very least a very effective steward.

When the knock came at the door, I called "come in" and Dobbins quietly entered the room, closing the door behind him.

"Dobbins! Excellent. Please come sit down." I moved to the table where there were still two wood chairs and took a seat.

The man looked extremely uncomfortable, but came and perched lightly on the edge of the chair opposite me.

"How can I help you, Mrs. Wunderly?"

"What can you tell me about the search for Miles Van de Meter? I ran into Mrs. FitzSimmons and learned that she is looking for her husband—the crew is supposed to be searching the ship."

Dobbins nodded. "There was some reluctance, but the crew are having a look around now."

Given the captain's reaction to Vanessa's demand, reluctance was hardly surprising. His staff would certainly follow his lead.

"Do you know if they've found anything yet?"

Dobbins shook his head. "Nothing yet, but it's a large ship. It will take some time." He paused. "And I'm not certain how seriously anyone is taking it. Plus we'll be docking in Cherbourg soon."

I groaned. "And will anyone be disembarking?"

"Not this voyage, ma'am. We'll only be taking on a few new passengers and some cargo."

That was a positive at least. Hopefully the crew would be attentive to anyone trying to leave the ship who shouldn't be. "Do you know who the steward is for Mrs. FitzSimmons's suite?"

"I do."

I waited a beat to see if he would volunteer anything else, but he simply sat and regarded me quietly. "Could you talk with him? See if he's seen anything unusual?"

"If you like."

"I do like. And perhaps you can ask when the steward noticed that Miles's luggage disappeared from the room. It would be helpful to know approximately when that luggage went missing from her suite."

Francis nodded. He was obviously a man of few words, but I was beginning to feel like I was pulling teeth.

"And then you should ask if he knows where it might have gone to."

He nodded again and we regarded each other in silence for a few moments. "Will that be all, Mrs. Wunderly?"

I allowed myself a tiny sigh. "That will be all."

Francis Dobbins gave a shallow bow and left the room as quietly as he had entered. If you were looking for someone inconspicuous, you couldn't have found a better steward. But I was looking for someone who could also do a decent interrogation. I wasn't sure I had found my man.

Stymied for the moment, I decided to take a walk—but while keeping to the inside of the ship. I'd had my fill of sea wind for the day. I went up to the A-deck and walked down the inner corridor toward the front of the ship. There I found the rug room where passengers could hire one of the lovely thick rugs that I had used on deck—I hadn't known that they weren't automatically provided. Dobbins must have done this little service for me, renting the rug so that I didn't have to take the time to do so. I made a mental note to thank him for it later.

Directly opposite the rug room, I noticed that there was a door labeled PHOTOGRAPH DARKROOM. With a start, I realized that it was probably run by one of our suspects. For a moment, I couldn't remember his name, then I managed to pull it up. Banks. That was it. I hesitated outside the door, conjuring up a reason to go inside and talk with him. I decided I could pretend to have some film that needed to be developed, and simply wanted to know how long it would take. A perfect excuse.

I recalled that Redvers had seen a young man with a camera on deck as we pulled away from Southampton. Was it possible that the passenger had captured a photo of Vanessa's elusive husband?

CHAPTER SEVEN

I tried the door, but it was locked. A spark of excitement about those photos had me knocking on it a little more enthusiastically than was strictly necessary.

"Just a MINUTE! Cripes." The voice came from behind the door, and I looked abashed when a neat little man in a dark suit opened it a moment later.

"I had to get the darkroom closed up first. Where's the fire, lady?"

I peered past the man and I could see a small reception room with a counter. Beyond that was another door leading to where I assumed this fellow did the film developing.

"I had some questions about photography. And getting film developed." The last statement came out almost like a question, but the man didn't seem to notice.

"Come in then. But close the door behind you."

I nodded and did as he said, pulling the door shut as I followed him into the room.

The man went behind the counter and stood there, looking at me expectantly. He wasn't wearing one of the standard ship uniforms—I decided it was likely that he was a photographer hired specifically for this job. A little silver tag above his breast pocket read "Banks."

I nodded. "Do you develop film here on board?"

"Right in the back room there." Banks gave his head a little tip at the door behind him, then pushed his wire spectacles back up his broad nose.

"Does it take a long time? To develop the pictures?"

Banks gave that a moment's thought. "It depends on how many people have turned their film in before you, I guess. But I can usually get them all done by the next day."

I nodded. That was a great deal faster than I had expected. "Have you already had quite a few people turn film in?" Banks gave me a strange look and I hurried to explain. "I have a roll of film to be developed. I'm just wondering if there is a queue."

He gave a shrug. "Only one or two. They're soaking now."

"Could I see them? I would love to see the process of how you develop the film." I did find the process interesting, but what I really wanted was to snoop through the photographs he was developing. Chances were good that there would be at least a few of the ship leaving Southampton if the rolls had been turned in already. And perhaps I would get lucky and find a photo of Vanessa's husband. Then at least the crew would have a better idea of who they were looking for.

"Can't do that, lady. The only one allowed in the back room is me. And it wouldn't be right letting you see other folks' pictures. Sometimes they're . . . well, personal." He flushed a bit and I wondered what exactly he had seen while developing other people's photographs.

But I gave a polite smile. "Of course." I was already making mental plans to return at night when the room was sitting empty. Assuming this fellow didn't work all night long, of course.

Then I switched my brain to our other objective. Since I was here, I should try to find something out about this man, prove to Redvers that I could in fact balance this investigation with the one about Miles Van de Meter's whereabouts.

"You're American?" I asked Banks. It was obvious what the answer to that was, but I needed to start somewhere.

Banks narrowed his eyes slightly. "Yeah. I'm from Brooklyn."

I nodded. "And how are you enjoying your post here on the ship? It must be tiring, just going back and forth across the ocean."

Banks gave me a long look, as though he couldn't figure out why I was trying to make small talk, but with a tiny shake of his head, he answered me. "This is my first voyage. So it's too soon to tell whether I'll tire of it. What's your interest?"

"Oh, I'm just wondering how it would be. To spend so long out at sea. I'm afraid my stomach is still a bit unsettled—I'm wondering if you ever get used to it."

Banks seemed to accept this flimsy explanation. "I'm told it gets better. You just gotta hold out a few days."

"Were you a professional photographer on land?" I asked.

He nodded. "But I had . . . ah . . . personal reasons to want to get out of town for a little bit."

I hoped that my eyes didn't light up. Could his personal reasons be that he was spying for someone else's government? I waited for long moments, but Banks busied himself with some items behind the counter. I decided he wasn't going to elaborate, and it would be suspicious for me to push the issue.

I changed the subject. "I was just wondering. . . ." I looked around and noticed that there were several cameras on shelves. "Do you rent cameras here, Mr. Banks? And give lessons? In case I was interested in learning how to use one."

This time Banks's eyes narrowed noticeably. "I thought you had a roll of film to be developed."

I almost cursed out loud. Instead I ducked my head and played the part of a shy little woman. "Well, truthfully, my husband took the pictures. But I would love to learn how to do it myself."

"It's not that difficult, ma'am. And we do in fact rent them by the day." He paused. "Your husband won't show you how to do this?"

I shook my head. "I just don't want to bother him with it. He's so busy." I wanted to choke on this story, but I had committed to it.

With another shrug, Banks pulled one from the shelf, the device nearly dwarfing his neat little hands. "I can give you a few instructions here before you take it out. It really isn't hard—you just point and push the button."

Banks spent a few more minutes showing me how to load film and advance it after every photo, and I left with the warning not to drop the thing overboard ringing in my ears.

Once I was safely on the other side of the door, I allowed myself a smile. I might not have learned anything earth shattering, but at least I had come away with a small clue. We needed to look into the "personal reason" that forced Banks to leave the solid ground of the U.S. for a stint on a transatlantic cruise ship.

CHAPTER EIGHT

Walking away from Mr. Banks's domain, I realized that the ship was no longer moving at all, and that we must have docked in Cherbourg, France, while I was renting the camera. Since I was already on the A-deck, I decided to walk out to the promenade and have a look.

The port here looked similar to the one in Southampton, with numerous workers bustling about an area of the city that was dedicated to ships and cargo—human or otherwise. I leaned against the railing, mindful of the camera in my hands, and watched as they pushed the gangplank out onto the dock. A few members of the crew headed down the narrow gangway, but it didn't appear from where I stood that any passengers were disembarking here, just as Dobbins had reported. Craning my neck to look down the long length of the ship, I could see that there was no other reasonable way to get onto the dock, so Vanessa's husband was still on board unless he had suddenly learned to fly.

I braced myself against the railing and snapped a photo—I needed to use some film since I'd gone to the trouble of having Banks explain it all to me, and he would be expecting at least one roll of undeveloped film. I would come up with an excuse later as to why all the photos were of the cruise, and not the roll I'd mentioned earlier. As I idly watched the activity on the dock, a ship's officer began checking in the few passengers who were joining us—there looked to be only a handful. Past where that little group had gathered, I saw Captain Bisset standing on the dock speaking with another man. I frowned and aimed my camera at them, looking down through the viewfinder just as I saw Bisset reach his hand out for an envelope in the other man's hand. I quickly snapped the photo and looked back up in time to see Bisset secure the envelope in the inner breast pocket of his uniform coat. I quickly advanced the film and, without looking down, I clicked the button again, snapping another picture.

The envelope could contain anything; there was no real reason to think it was anything suspicious, but I couldn't shake the feeling that I was watching something unsavory happen. Perhaps it was the appearance of the man bearing the envelope—he wore a dark suit and a kerchief around his neck, and while it should have made the man look polished, the fine clothes only served to underline his otherwise disreputable appearance. Even from a distance I could see this was a man who was used to getting what he wanted; arrogance came off him in waves. I snapped yet another photo of the two of them together, then turned my attention to where the crew were loading the luggage.

A second gangway had been pulled out, and numerous trunks were being loaded on board. The first metal plank was strictly for passengers, and this one appeared to be strictly for luggage and cargo. I snapped another photo of the crew members at work before lowering the camera, frowning again. For the number of passengers I had seen getting on board, this seemed like an extraordinary amount of luggage. Of course, it was possible someone was moving their entire household, although I couldn't imagine what the cost of that would be. Then I wondered where the crew would store all these trunks. Surely the luggage room couldn't hold them all.

Captain Bisset turned and headed back up the gangway

and I left the railing to head down the stairs to the B-deck. I had seen enough, and I needed to stop by our suite to drop off the camera. Now that I had the thing, I needed to use it, and I was glad I'd taken the time to snap a few pictures—it would look awfully suspicious to return it to Mr. Banks without having used any of the film. But I would save the rest of the roll for later.

I pushed open the door and found the outer room empty. Closing the door behind me, I put the camera down on the table in the sitting room, then walked through to the bedroom. Also empty. With a sigh I sat on the edge of the bed; I had hoped that Redvers would have returned by now in improved spirits so we could get back on better footing. This would be a miserable trip closed up in this cabin together if we couldn't resolve things quickly.

I stood and made my way into the sitting room. I needed to break into the photography office tonight, and to do that I would need some tools. I eyed Redvers' trunk, and with a silent apology to the man, began rifling through his things, careful not to disturb his neat folding. I found the leather case I was looking for under an assembly of socks and secreted it in my handbag. That done, I tidied up the stacks, hoping he wouldn't realize that I had been through them. I'd been careful, but Redvers was terribly observant.

I crossed to the small desk where the telephone sat. When the operator spoke, I asked for Dobbins to be sent to my room once again. Then I settled into the upholstered chair and gazed out the porthole at the gray sky overhead. Before long I heard a knock at the door, and I ushered Dobbins in.

"Thank you for coming again, Dobbins. Did you have a chance to talk to Mrs. FitzSimmons's steward?"

Dobbins nodded. "He definitely saw the trunks in her room the night we sailed, ma'am. And when he brought her breakfast the following morning they were already gone."

I mulled that over. That meant the trunks were removed

sometime during the night. I would have to get a better idea of when Mrs. FitzSimmons had gone to bed that night in order to narrow the window.

"Thank you, Dobbins. That's very helpful. Did he say anything else?"

Dobbins shook his head and said nothing further, so I pressed him a bit. "Did he say whether he had seen Mrs. Fitz-Simmons's husband?"

"He clammed up and he wouldn't say, ma'am."

I thought that was interesting. Why would the steward refuse to admit he had seen one of the passengers under his care? Especially after having just admitted to seeing the passenger's baggage. Was it possible he was being paid by that passenger to keep his mouth shut? But that begged the question of why Vanessa's husband would disappear on purpose. And where on this ship had he gone?

"Thank you, Dobbins," I said.

"Will that be all, ma'am?"

"For now, thank you." Then my memory sparked. "But, Dobbins. Thank you for renting the travel rug for me this morning. It was very kind of you to make sure I was taken care of."

The young man's round face pinkened a bit. "It's my pleasure, Mrs. Wunderly."

I smiled at him, and he turned and went out, the door closing a little less quietly than it did normally. I hoped I hadn't embarrassed the young man, but I really did appreciate his thoughtfulness.

I was still pondering the issue of Vanessa's steward when Redvers returned, not long after Dobbins left. I glanced at him warily, wondering if he was still in an ill temper, but he smiled as soon as he saw me, the edges of his dark eyes crinkling.

"Did you have a good afternoon, Jane?" he asked politely.

Then his gaze fell on the camera, one eyebrow raising slightly. "Taking up a new hobby?"

I was heartened by the good humor in his voice. Perhaps this little storm had blown over. "I stopped by the darkroom and was inspired to check one out. And I took the opportunity to talk with Mr. Banks." I said this last part carefully—I didn't want to ruin the mood, but I did want to share with him what I'd learned.

Redvers stilled, and I braced myself for what would come next, but he simply cocked his head at me. "Did you learn anything interesting?"

I breathed a silent sigh of relief. "I asked why he'd left the States for this job, and he said he had 'personal reasons.'"

"Not much to go on," Redvers said, and I found myself slightly irritated.

"Well, it's something." I could hear the edge in my voice.

Redvers nodded. "I'll mention it when I wire to shore. It would probably have come out in the investigation into his background, but it's interesting that he mentioned it to you at all."

I was slightly mollified and watched as Redvers crossed to the table and picked the camera up, aiming it in my direction and taking a quick snap before I could react. "This actually might come in handy, to tell you the truth."

"That's what I was thinking." Very well, that was a lie. I'd rented it as an afterthought. But I was glad he thought it might be useful to have around.

"I assume it's a rental," Redvers said.

I nodded. "We're to pay when we return it. I wasn't sure how many days I would want it for."

"Excellent." Redvers put the camera back down and looked at his watch. "It's nearly time to dress for dinner."

With a glance at the clock on the mantel I realized it had gotten much later than I'd thought. I'd meant to tell Redvers what I had seen on the dock in case he thought any of it out of the ordinary, but that would have to wait until dinner. I stood and went into the bedroom to get dressed, feeling relieved that the tension in the room had dissipated, and that by the end of our discussion Redvers had seemed more like his usual self. I dressed quickly, and we headed toward the à la carte restaurant, an extra little spring in my step since we would have another meal's respite from Eloise Baumann. We couldn't avoid her forever, but I would take what quiet I could get.

CHAPTER NINE

After dinner we retired once again to the first-class lounge where we immediately snagged a table and a waiter hurried over to take our drink orders. Once I had a gin fizz in hand, I studied it sadly. "I'm going to miss these once we get back to the States." I took a sip and savored the refreshing goodness.

"You don't necessarily have to stay there, you know."

I looked up from my drink to find Redvers studying me intently.

"Good evening, Mrs. Wunderly." I looked up to find Heinz Naumann standing beside our table. "This must be your husband."

Redvers and I stood as I made the introductions between the two men, both of us quickly slipping into our roles. Learning everything we could about our list of suspects was our primary purpose here, after all. But I tucked away Redvers' ambiguous statement to take out and examine later.

"Would you care to join us?" I indicated the empty chair.

Naumann hesitated for a moment before agreeing. "Well, perhaps for just one drink."

I smiled at Redvers and gestured to our guest. "I met Mr. Naumann this morning. He has the deck chair next to mine."

"Ah, lovely. I'm glad you could keep my wife company."

"I'm the one who should be thanking you." Heinz's eyes glowed with appreciation as he turned to regard me. "I enjoyed our conversation this morning, Mrs. Wunderly."

It was the second time he had mentioned his enjoyment of our chat, and his mildly flirtatious tone set me back a bit, since he was using it in front of the man he believed to be my husband. I kept my own smile in place, but inwardly I was a little unsettled by his demeanor. Not to mention the fact that he kept referring to our conversation—did he think there was something suspicious about what we had discussed?

"You'll have to let me borrow her for a dance this evening once the band starts."

"Oh, no," I started to protest. I had no rhythm and stepping on the man's toes would do nothing to further our cause.

But Redvers' eyes took on a wicked gleam. "I'm sure I can spare her for one dance."

I tried to kick the man under the table but merely succeeded in kicking a table leg, causing our drinks to slosh precariously.

"What was that?" Heinz reached for his drink and held it off the table.

I shrugged innocently. "Boats are so unpredictable."

I could tell Redvers was choking back a laugh, so I redirected the conversation back to Heinz, asking him how he was enjoying the ship.

"I have always found that it is the company that makes sea adventures worthwhile." Heinz gave a little wink.

I cocked my head at him. Naumann was definitely flirting with me—there was no mistaking that little wink. In my peripheral I could see Redvers' eyes narrow a bit as I smiled back at Heinz. It took some effort to make sure that smile looked natural, and I could only hope I was pulling it off.

Truthfully, I didn't know how I should react, but smiling seemed the safest bet. The man's flirtatiousness in front of

Redvers—mild though it was—made me uncomfortable, despite the fact that I had liked the man quite a bit just hours before. Was it simply his nature to flirt with women? With his easy good looks, it wasn't hard to assume this was the case. Or did he have the wrong idea about me based on how friendly I had been with him up on deck? Was that why he kept bringing up our conversation?

Of course, it was probably better for him to believe I was flirting with him as well rather than have him suspect I was here to gather information about him. I assured myself that I could step outside my comfort zone and do a little flirting if it was necessary for the good of the investigation.

Redvers cleared his throat. "Have you taken many sea voyages, Mr. Naumann?"

With a final glance at me, Naumann turned his attention to Redvers and the two men began discussing their travels. Redvers made it seem that he traveled only very infrequently, which I knew to be an outrageous lie. At the Crown's disposal, Redvers investigated issues all over the world. It was how I'd met the man in Egypt.

"And what do you do, Mr. Wunderly?"

This time, instead of finding it amusing for Redvers to be addressed by my last name, I found that I liked the sound of it more and more. Redvers never used his own last name, so he may as well borrow mine.

Redvers launched into his explanation of how he was a banker, and I hid a smile behind my drink. It was the same story the man had fed me when we first met, but unlike Heinz Naumann, I hadn't believed it for a second. At least, it looked like Heinz believed him. For both of our sakes, I hoped that was the case—nothing would blow our cover faster.

At the far end of the room I could see that the ship's band was setting up, and I watched the various men as they bustled about, eager to determine which was the band leader, our third suspect on the list. I spotted a likely candidate—a tall, lanky blond with a thin baton in his hand who seemed to be directing the mild chaos of the players finding their seats. I studied the good-looking man for a moment, and nearly missed Heinz's return explanation of what he did for a living.

"I am a restaurant manager." He went on to describe the restaurant he worked at and how long he had been there. According to Heinz, he had been sent specifically on this voyage in order to study the large-scale restaurants on board and their ability to turn out such renowned meals.

Redvers looked completely at ease and totally absorbed in what our companion was saying. "Really? And how have you found the cuisine on board?" Heinz went into a detailed description of the pluses and minuses he had discovered so far, and Redvers followed up by asking him a series of questions related to the industry, which Heinz parried easily. If this was nothing but a cover story, Heinz was doing a remarkable job selling it.

Their conversation finally petered out, and draining his glass, Heinz stood. I glanced over to where the band had begun playing, although there were few couples on the floor yet. I fully expected Heinz to ask for his dance, but instead he executed a short little bow and, with an engaging smile, excused himself.

"I'm afraid I'll have to ask for that dance another evening, Mrs. Wunderly. I fear my bed is calling to me."

I nearly looked at my watch since the hour was still quite early, but instead I smiled and graciously told the man that I was looking forward to it.

As soon as Naumann was out of earshot, Redvers leaned forward slightly. "You dodged a bullet there."

I frowned. Instead of feeling relief at escaping my fate on the dance floor—I really was the most terrible dancer—I felt slightly anxious. "Why do you think he changed his mind?"

Redvers leaned back and gave a small shrug. "It could be that he's tired. Or he's heading to the gaming tables and didn't want to admit as much to you."

I puzzled over that. "I suppose. I just hope he isn't suspicious of us." And the litany of questions that Redvers had thrown his way.

Redvers didn't say anything, but the pucker in his forehead told me that he was worried about the same thing, despite his reassurances.

"I'll give him a head start, but perhaps I should follow after him. It's likely that he's headed to the gentlemen's smoking room."

I tipped my head toward the band. "What about Mr. Brubacher?"

Redvers' eyes swiveled in that direction. "I think he'll be busy for the next few hours waving that baton." He then gave me an apologetic look. "If I leave you here, will you find our room all right?"

I thought about the darkroom and lock picks awaiting me and gave Redvers a bright smile. "I'll be perfectly fine."

CHAPTER TEN

That brief conversation had given Heinz enough of a head start, so Redvers left immediately to follow the man. I sat in my seat for a while, both to observe Brubacher for a few minutes and to give Redvers his own head start. I sat through a few songs before I decided that Redvers was right—Brubacher would be busy with the band for the next few hours, and nothing of interest was likely to happen, so I left my table and headed up to the A-deck.

I walked slowly, keeping an eye out for any of the men I needed to avoid. A sudden bump made me realize that I was already getting used to the rolling gait of the ship—I had stopped noticing it even though I still walked with something of a sway. Of course, it helped that the large, swelling waves from the night before had subsided; the ship now simply rocked gently front and back.

I made it to the corridor at the front of the ship and headed toward the photography studio. Passing the rug room, I saw that it was abandoned—no sensible person would be looking to sit on the deck at this time of night. I crossed my fingers that the photography room was equally as deserted.

With a glance around I knocked on the door and listened carefully. I was greeted by nothing but silence, so I tried the door handle and was not surprised to find it locked. I shrugged to myself and pulled Redvers' lock-pick kit from my bag. I had never used the picks, but I had watched Redvers handle them on numerous occasions and I hoped I would be able to mimic what he had done.

I quickly learned that it wasn't nearly as easy as the man made it look. Nearly twenty minutes passed while I tried to get the tumblers in the lock to click into place while also keeping an eye out for passengers who might wonder what on earth I was doing. It was terribly nerve-racking and I was about to give it up as a lost cause when I finally heard the last click. I twisted the metal tools in my hand and the lock popped open. I wiped sweat from my forehead and slipped through the door, closing it, then leaned back, heart pounding. I would need to practice a great deal before I tried this again on my own. Hopefully Redvers would be willing to show me his tricks at some point in the future.

The room was completely dark, and I groped along the wall until I found the light switch. I flicked it on for only a moment—long enough for me to get a sense of what obstacles were in my path on the way to the darkroom door before flicking it off again. I put my hands out and walked carefully across the room, the slight sway of the ship slowing my progress in the dark without a fixed object to guide me. I reached the door on the other side and groped until I found the knob, letting out a relieved sigh when it turned easily.

I stepped carefully into the room and felt on the wall for a switch. I hoped that turning it on wouldn't ruin any of the photos Banks might have left behind—I didn't know much about photography, but I did know that it needed to be done in darkness or it would destroy the film. I breathed a prayer that Banks had already finished developing that day's photographs.

When my fingers found the switch, I squinted my eyes closed and flipped it on, reopening them to find that a red light had turned on above me. I glanced up at it, then around at the room. It was not bright, but there was enough light that I could see fairly clearly. Counters ran along either side of the closet-like space, with large basins on one and a collection of supplies on the other. I assumed the basins were where Banks put the developing chemicals needed for processing. Beyond that, I had little idea of how the whole operation worked. A quick peek inside told me that the basins were empty, so I moved to the other counter. A few envelopes had been set aside and looked fat with pictures, so I picked up the top envelope and opened it.

This envelope held nothing interesting, simply a series of photos from London—Big Ben, the Tower, and other tourist attractions. As I thumbed through, I could see that these most likely belonged to an older couple, but there was nothing from the ship. They had obviously used this roll before boarding the *Olympic*.

The next two packets proved as equally boring. And there was nothing as salacious as Banks had suggested there might be—I wondered if that had been an excuse to keep me out of the darkroom or an abundance of caution on his part.

Either way, the mundanity was a little disappointing.

I picked up the last packet and closed my eyes briefly before opening the flap, hoping this would be the winner. On seeing the first few photos my spirits immediately perked—this had to be the roll taken by the young man Redvers had seen on deck. I thumbed through the pictures slowly, reliving the morning we'd set sail. It already seemed like ages ago, even though it had only been the previous day.

I startled when I came to a photo of Redvers and I standing against the railing. I hadn't even noticed it was being taken, but Redvers was looking directly at the camera. I sighed; Redvers always looked so handsome. I, on the other hand, was gazing off to the left—probably at Vanessa and her husband—and had a strange expression on my face. With a shrug I kept flipping. Several pictures later I finally came upon what I was looking for—a photograph of Vanessa and her husband on deck. Unfortunately, his face was buried in her shoulder and it was impossible to make out his features. Furthermore, Vanessa was turned toward him, obscuring what little of his face might have been seen. With a frustrated sigh, I turned to the next photograph. Here too the man's face was completely obscured—this time turned away from the camera, while Vanessa's was fully in frame. It didn't look as though Vanessa had been aware that her photo was being taken, but from the way Van de Meter was angling his head, it seemed possible that he had known. And he was ensuring that his face wasn't captured on film.

I looked through the rest, but those were the only two where Vanessa and Miles appeared. I flipped back and looked at them one last time, then replaced the stack in their envelope with a shake of my head. After tidying the pile, I opened the door and flipped off the light switch, bathing myself in complete darkness once again. Closing the darkroom door, I shuffled back across the outer room and paused, considering, before I switched the light on. I didn't have a flashlight with me, which would have been ideal for conducting a search, but it seemed a waste not to take a quick look around since I was already here. I could only hope no one would see the light beneath the door and wonder why someone was inside this late at night.

With that thought, I made sure the door was bolted before I went about my business.

There wasn't much to search, so I was able to finish up in just a few minutes. Another stack of envelopes initially looked promising, but turned out to be unclaimed packets of pictures from the previous voyage, when Banks wasn't even employed on the ship. Going through them showed me nothing more interesting than photos of a border collie and a summer garden. The garden was quite lovely, but not what I was looking for. A hunt through the records kept beneath the counter only revealed receipts for passengers who'd rented cameras, just as I had done. Other than those items, there was nothing to find but unused film and camera equipment. It appeared that Mr. Banks didn't keep anything even remotely personal in the room, which wasn't necessarily a surprise, but disappointing all the same. A damning piece of evidence would have been nice to uncover, however unlikely.

I shut the light back off and waited a few minutes, ear pressed to the door, to make certain I wouldn't be seen before I let myself back out into the quiet corridor. I softly shut the photography door, and after giving myself a moment to let my eyes adjust to the light, headed down to my room on the deck below.

I hadn't learned anything about Edwin Banks, but my little expedition had raised some more questions about Miles Van de Meter. Why would the man have gone out of his way to avoid having his photo taken? Especially since he was with his brand-new wife on deck—a newly married couple normally loved having their picture taken. Not to mention the fact that Miles and Vanessa had been awfully caught up in their . . . affections. One would expect that Miles had been entirely too busy to notice the photographer.

And yet, he had. And he'd made certain to obscure his face every time.

CHAPTER ELEVEN

I let myself back into our suite and found Redvers laying out his blankets. He wore a set of blue and white striped pajamas and I reminded myself that I really needed to remember to knock before entering—it would look strange if another passenger saw me knocking on the door to my own suite, but this outer room *was* Redvers' bedroom.

Redvers stopped what he was doing and turned, one eyebrow raised.

"I didn't think you'd be back so soon," I said.

"Naumann really did go to bed. I decided I might as well do the same."

I nodded. "Well, good night, Redvers."

The eyebrow went a little higher. "And where were you?"

"Nowhere in particular."

"Mmm-hmm. Do you want to give me my lock picks now, or would you prefer to wait until the morning?"

"I suppose I can give them to you now. I have no further need of them." I reached into my handbag and handed over the neat leather case.

"Did you find what you were looking for?" Redvers asked.

I sighed. "Yes and no. It wasn't nearly as fruitful as I'd hoped."

"Well, I am sorry about that." Redvers put the case back in his trunk. I waited for a further lecture about going through his things, or even another question about where I had actually been, but it seemed Redvers had said as much as he was going to on the subject.

"Good night, Redvers," I said again, uncertainly this time.

"Good night, Jane."

I went through and closed the door. His voice had been warm enough, but I was left feeling unsettled just the same. Why hadn't he bothered to push me on where I had been? And why hadn't he asked about what I had or hadn't learned?

The next morning proceeded as usual. By the time I woke up and entered the sitting room, Redvers had tidied away his night things and had breakfast waiting for me. I sipped my coffee and regarded him over the edge of my cup.

"What are your plans for the morning, Redvers?"

He leaned back in his chair and folded the napkin that had been in his lap, placing it on the table. "I need to send some messages back to shore, and see if any new information has been sent to us about our suspects." I was glad he was still using the inclusive term "us" when it came to this investigation. It made me feel a bit better.

"Aren't you concerned about all these messages going back and forth through the operator?"

Redvers flashed me one of his smiles, the kind that made my insides fluttery. "I've already won that young man over. And the messages are in code, anyway."

I coughed once and steadied myself. "He isn't suspicious that you're receiving all sorts of coded messages?"

"I've explained to him that I have an elderly grandfather who likes to play games and experiment with ciphers." Redvers gave a casual shrug. "Even though it's costly to send the messages back and forth to the ship, it's really what keeps the old man going. McIntyre seemed to buy it."

"McIntyre?"

"John McIntyre. Nice young Irish lad. No interest in the German government."

I nodded. An unlikely additional suspect then.

Redvers continued on. "And I got a note this morning that Heinz would like to play some squash. I'm going to take him up on the offer."

That took some of the wind out of my sails. If Heinz was otherwise occupied, I wasn't needed on deck. And I couldn't exactly join the men, so I was rather at loose ends. "Is there anything I can do to look into either Banks or Brubacher?" Well, more than I had the night before when I'd broken into the photography studio. For some reason I was still reluctant to admit to that, especially since I hadn't learned anything useful about Banks.

Redvers shook his head. "We're waiting for background information on all three of the men. And I will search each of their quarters."

I felt a flash of irritation—he was going to conduct those searches without me, was he? But I quickly smoothed my own feathers since I fully intended to conduct my own inquiries anyway. And if I was honest, it would be difficult for both of us to sneak into the crew quarters undetected. It would be easier for Redvers to do it alone.

"And what will you do?" Redvers asked.

"I'll probably just take some air. Do a little exploring around the ship perhaps."

Redvers nodded and excused himself, assuring me that he would be back to meet me for dinner. Once he had gone, I looked around the room, then eyed the boxy camera that had been relocated to the desk. I decided to leave it for now. A brisk stroll sounded like just the thing to clear my head and I didn't want to be weighed down by the contraption.

I walked several of the ship's upper decks, getting a feel for where things on board were located. Today's weather was much calmer than the day before, and I reflected that it was a shame I didn't need to meet Heinz in our chairs—it was a pleasant enough day that I would be happy to sit on deck and enjoy the fresh air. On the other hand, if I kept to the inside corridors it was easier to forget we were powering through a seemingly unending ocean surrounded by nothing but water for hundreds of miles. The vastness was still quite unnerving if I let myself think about it for too long.

At the end of my stroll, I found myself back on the A-deck and, passing through a set of revolving doors, I entered one of the two cafés that flanked either side of that level. The room was fitted out with summery wicker chairs and a profusion of lush green plants climbing strategically placed trellises. The gracefully arching windows lining the room had decorative bronze metalwork, designed to give the illusion of an actual café—if one could ignore the gray ocean stretching out beyond them. I decided it would be pleasant to spend some time here, perhaps enjoy a cup of coffee. It wasn't until I saw the piano parked in the corner that I realized my mistake.

"Mrs. Wunderly! You must join us for tea." Eloise's voice boomed across the room and most of the chattering conversations stopped. I felt numerous eyes on me as I briefly closed my own. My mind shuffled through a number of possible excuses, but I finally shrugged and gave myself over to my fate. I crossed over to the table occupied by Eloise Baumann and her sister, Margret, and managed to eek out a greeting before Eloise started in. Margret gave me an apologetic smile over her teacup.

"I hope you're enjoying your time on board, Mrs. Wunderly. I know we are, although the lunch they served in the dining room did seem a little dry today. I told the steward that he needed to inform the kitchen to use more sauce in the future. And I wasn't sure he actually conveyed the message, so I tried to go back there myself. Do you know they stopped me at the door?" She paused for a breath. "But they brought the chef out, I assume it was the head chef. . . ."

I tuned out, nodding politely and accepting the cup of tea from the waiter, who hurried away before I had the chance to request a cup of coffee instead. Smart lad.

It looked as though Margret employed the same tactic that I was using—tuning out her sister's droning voice and interjecting the occasional "mmm-hmm" while sipping her tea and staring into space. I supposed Margret had quite a rich inner life to be able to live with Eloise and I wondered what she spent her time thinking about.

"Don't you think, Mrs. Wunderly?"

I snapped to, realizing that I was expected to give a response for once. Eloise was looking at me quite expectantly and I felt a little flush start up my neck. I was being quite rude, regardless of how intolerable the woman was.

"I'm sorry to interrupt."

I could have kissed whoever it was, but I was especially pleased to turn and find Vanessa FitzSimmons standing beside me.

Eloise looked delighted to have a new victim, her earlier question to me entirely forgotten. "Please join us, Miss . . ."

Vanessa looked at Eloise. "I'm afraid I don't have time for that. And I need to borrow Mrs. Wunderly."

"Well." Eloise huffed. A quick glance at Margret told me that the woman was amused, her sparkling eyes a dead giveaway, but she hid it well otherwise. I supposed she had a lot of practice in that department.

I made my excuses to Eloise and Margret and joined Vanessa in promptly leaving the café.

"I apologize if they were friends of yours, but I couldn't bear the thought of sitting at a table with that woman." She shuddered dramatically. "I could hear her clear across the room. What was she even talking about?"

"I haven't the faintest idea, to be honest. But thank you for rescuing me." I hadn't wanted to join the ladies, but I'd felt compelled by social graces to do so. I admired Vanessa's ability to completely flaunt convention without a trace of guilt; she seemed to do precisely what she wanted—or didn't, as the case may be.

I admired it, but I also knew it wasn't me.

"You're entirely welcome. Now, I thought I would take you up on that offer to look at my suite. I don't see anything unusual, but perhaps you will."

"It never hurts to have another set of eyes," I said.

CHAPTER TWELVE

Vanessa led me toward the grand staircase at the front of the ship and we traveled below to the C-deck, breaking off to head down a corridor. Vanessa's suite was nearly twice the size of our own suite and much grander. It was also closer to the center of the ship where the movement of the ocean was much less noticeable—she would be even better off if we encountered rough seas on our voyage.

As I looked around the room, I could feel Vanessa's gaze on me. "What exactly did you help your aunt with?"

I paused for a moment, deciding how best to convince her that I had some experience doing some amateur sleuthing without giving too much away. "A young man was killed on the estate of a family friend last year. I looked into it for my aunt, and helped the police determine who killed him." Turning back to Vanessa, I braced myself for follow-up questions, but judging by her disinterested look, her attention had already returned to her own problems.

Vanessa flopped into one of the upholstered chairs and gave a wave of her hand. "Have at it then. Work your magic, Jane."

I didn't say anything, but took my time inspecting the room. There was nothing amiss in the sitting room as far as I could see. The desk looked unused, and aside from a long wool coat and a velvet clutch lying on one of the chairs, both of which I assumed belonged to Vanessa, there was nothing to examine. I moved into the bedroom. The oak paneling complemented the rich red of the upholstered sofa and chair, as well as the silk curtains pulled back from the twin portholes. I took in the room for a moment before crossing to the dressing table, which revealed nothing but strictly female items. Hands on hips, I looked around—there were two beds, and it was clear that the smaller of the two had not been slept in, while the covers on the larger bed had been casually pulled up. The steward had obviously not been in to clean the room yet, or it would no doubt be impeccably made. I crossed to the wardrobe occupying one full wall of the room, fully expecting to find it chock-full of clothing, yet found nothing but empty hangers. I frowned.

"Where are your clothes?" I called to Vanessa. I heard her push herself up and she came into the bedroom. Turning to look at her, I could see that she was suddenly quite uncomfortable.

"Well, that's the strange thing. I don't know."

I raised my eyebrows, incredulous that she wouldn't have mentioned this before now. "What do you mean you don't know?"

"When I got up this morning and went to find something to wear, there was nothing in the closet except this dress." She waved a hand down at herself. "I don't know where the rest has gone to. I was planning on asking my maid what on earth she's done with my things." Vanessa glanced at the delicate jewel-encrusted watch on her wrist. "She should be here any moment. Then I can clear that little issue up."

It hardly seemed like a "little" issue, but I shook my head and closed the wardrobe doors again before I resumed my inspection of the room, finding nothing else in the bedroom out of the ordinary. But neither was there any hint of a man having ever been there.

I moved into the bathroom. Vanessa's cosmetics and beauty products were spread across the small countertop, but there were no men's products in sight. Not so much as a stray whisker. I shook the small trash bin and found nothing there either. There was not a single thing to indicate that Miles Van de Meter had ever stepped foot in the room.

I came back into the sitting room just as the phone rang. Vanessa made no move to answer it.

"Do you need to get that?"

Vanessa's face pinched and she shook her head. "There's never anyone there." It was impossible to miss the tension in her voice although she was doing her best to cover it up.

"Vanessa. What aren't you telling me? I can't very well help you if you don't tell me what's going on."

A series of emotions flashed over the woman's face before she smoothed it over entirely. "I'm sure it's nothing serious. The phone just keeps ringing, and when I answer there's no one on the other end."

"Have you asked the switchboard operator? Surely they can tell where the call is coming from?"

"A common area of the ship. Every time, and always a different one." She shrugged, but I could tell it was costing her to remain so casual. "There's no way to tell for certain who it is, unfortunately." She gave a hollow little laugh. "Pretty soon I'm going to leave the damn thing off the hook entirely."

I sank into one of the three comfortable chairs in the room, looking around once again. It occurred to me that if our suite was as large as this, Redvers would be much more comfortable sleeping. He could nearly fit on the sofa along the far wall. With a little shake of my head, I turned my mind back to the issue at hand.

"Do you think it could be your husband?" I asked slowly.

Vanessa gave another shrug. "I don't see why he would do something like that. Why call but never say anything?"

"Can you hear anything on the other end? Sounds of breathing, or people talking in the background?"

She shook her head and looked toward the windows where the overcast gray sky was visible, but didn't say anything more.

We sat in silence for several minutes while I puzzled over the strange phone calls and her missing clothing. I couldn't imagine why the woman would invent either story. It didn't seem there was anything for her to gain by admitting to either. Which left the questions of where her clothes had disappeared to, and why someone would repeatedly call her suite only to hang up and never say a word.

My musing over the issue was interrupted by a knock at the door. Without bothering to rise, Vanessa called for the person to enter. A young woman in a muslin dress with a small floral print and a wool coat over the top came through the door.

"Rebecca! Excellent. Mrs. Wunderly and I both have some questions for you." Vanessa turned to me. "Jane, this is my maid, Rebecca Tesch."

Rebecca gave a small curtsy. Her straight blond hair was cut in a severe bob that complemented her attractive features. Wide green eyes studied me from beneath her straight fringe of bangs.

"First of all, where on earth have my clothes gone to?" Vanessa's voice was harsh, but she hadn't changed her lounging posture in the slightest.

"Your clothes, ma'am?" Rebecca's voice was hesitant.

"Yes, you foolish girl. My clothes. What have you done with them?"

I watched Rebecca's face during this exchange and her expression alternated between fear and confusion. The confusion looked genuine; I wondered if the fear was because the girl was concerned about losing her position or if there was some other cause behind it. Either way I could hardly blame her—the tone of Vanessa's voice made me uncomfortable as well.

"They were just where I left them in the closet last night, ma'am."

"Well, they aren't there now." Vanessa's voice was granite.

Rebecca shook her head, and her eyes now threatened to spill unshed tears. I was left with the impression that the poor girl really had no idea what had become of Vanessa's clothing.

"Did you happen to take some of her things to the cleaners?" I asked the girl gently.

Rebecca nodded, blinking rapidly. "I put the dresses and things into the laundry bag just like she asked me to and left them to be picked up. But it was only three or four things, ma'am."

I nodded, deciding that my next stop would be the laundry room to see just what had been taken from the room to be cleaned.

"We'll look into that later. Now, Rebecca, do you remember seeing Mr. Van de Meter's luggage here the other night?" I asked. "The night we sailed from Southampton?"

Rebecca looked between Vanessa and me before answering. "Yes, ma'am."

"And when did you realize it was missing?"

"I couldn't say for sure. I just knew it was missing once Mrs. Vanessa noticed it was."

"I see." That wasn't helpful in the slightest. "When was the last time you saw Mr. Van de Meter?"

The maid shifted uneasily and didn't quite meet my eyes. "I've never seen him, ma'am."

I couldn't help my show of surprise. I looked between Vanessa and her soft-spoken maid, who was now studying the floor, hands twisting in front of her.

"I'd given Rebecca a few weeks of vacation while I was

playing in Monte Carlo, and her passage is booked in second class. I'm afraid I told her I would only call her when I needed her. I figured Miles and I would want our privacy." Vanessa frowned. "I suppose it's true that they've never crossed paths."

Newlyweds. I nodded my understanding of their desire to be left alone, although it was quite inconvenient at the moment. Rebecca might have been a valuable witness if she'd actually seen the man.

"When were you in the room to see the luggage, Rebecca?"

"I was instructed to come in while Mrs. Vanessa was at dinner to take care of her things last night and make sure everything was hung up properly." The girl glanced at Vanessa, then back to me. "I saw several trunks, but I only took care of Mrs. Vanessa's things. And then I came this morning after Mrs. Vanessa sent for me. Only her trunks were here."

"Do you remember what time that was?"

Once again Rebecca glanced at Vanessa and back at me. "About eleven, ma'am?"

She sounded as though she wasn't sure whether it was a statement or a question. I thanked her for her time and Vanessa dismissed her until the evening. As Rebecca left the room, I followed her to the door, catching it before it closed.

"What are you doing?" Vanessa was twisted in the chair to watch me.

"Just checking something." I bent down and looked at the lock of the door. There were some marks, but they were old and worn. There were no shiny new scratches to indicate that anyone had tried to open it with anything but a key. It didn't mean much, but it was something. And I would grasp at anything at this point, since Vanessa's room had offered up no other clue besides the missing clothing.

I closed the door and came across the room. "It doesn't look like the lock has been tampered with at all."

Vanessa looked mildly impressed. "I wouldn't have thought to look."

I shrugged. "Have you heard any news on the search for Mr. Van de Meter?"

The elegant woman rolled her eyes and tapped her fingers angrily on the arm of the chair. "Dr. Montgomery has stopped by to reassure me that they're looking, but other than that, nothing. I have my doubts about whether they're doing anything at all." A look of hurt crossed her face as her fingers stilled. "Especially after our stop at Cherbourg yesterday. There's nothing to say he didn't simply get off there. Although I can't imagine why he would want to." This was said airily, as though she didn't care one way or another, although the hurt I had seen moments before told another story entirely.

Unfortunately, I was inclined to agree that little was being done on board to find her missing husband. And I didn't bother to mention that I'd been on deck and watched the comings and goings at Cherbourg since there was every chance I had missed something. There was no sense in giving the woman false hope that Van de Meter was still on board when I couldn't say with absolute certainty that he was.

"I need to get back to my . . . husband." The word still wasn't rolling off my tongue, and I hoped it wasn't as obvious to others as it was to me. "But I'll check in with you again this afternoon. See if anything has turned up."

"Lovely. In the meantime, I think I'll head to the tennis court."

I gave my head a little shake and headed out.

The first place I went was the laundry service to see exactly what from Vanessa's wardrobe had been sent for cleaning. The walk there gave me some time to think.

I didn't quite know what to make of Vanessa FitzSimmons— at times she seemed genuinely upset that her new husband was missing. But at other times she was completely cavalier about the entire affair. I wondered if her devil-may-care attitude was merely a front—if I was pressed to make a guess, I would say it was.

Vanessa's maid hadn't been especially helpful, and I thought it was very strange that Rebecca had never laid eyes on Miles Van de Meter. Although, Rebecca had seemed uncomfortable when she answered my questions about the man—was she hiding something? Or just worried for her job? The only thing I could say for certain was that the girl did seem legitimately confused about where Vanessa's clothing had disappeared to. I would wager money she wasn't involved in whatever had happened there.

I would never admit it to Redvers, but he may have had a point about my not getting involved with a woman I knew nothing about. On the other hand, I felt my blood run hot remembering the dismissive attitude of the captain and the crew toward Vanessa. I had seen her husband with my own eyes and I knew he existed—he wasn't a figment of anyone's imagination, although I didn't have any answers about where Van de Meter might have gone. The whole affair made me think back to my marriage and how things had turned terribly wrong not long after the vows were said. Grant was so charming and likeable on the surface, I worried people wouldn't believe what a monster he was in private.

I still feared no one would believe me, all these years later, even with Grant long dead and buried.

Pushing those memories back, I thought more about Van de Meter and wondered if he could be the spy we were seeking. We knew nothing about the man, and now he'd mysteriously disappeared on board a ship. Could he have gotten wind that someone was searching for him and gone into hiding? I liked it as a possibility, although I wasn't sure *how* he would have suddenly learned we were looking for him. Especially since he'd disappeared so soon after we left the dock at Southampton. All the same, I made a mental note to not only ask Vanessa about her husband's past but to also suggest to Redvers that he request a background investigation on the man. He might not like us getting further involved, but we couldn't ignore the glaring possibility that the two matters were related.

I turned my mind to the business with our other suspects. Even with the addition of a missing husband and the strange goings-on in Vanessa's cabin, I was certain I could fulfill my obligations to Redvers' shadowy employer. I had no doubt that I could juggle both cases at the same time, regardless of what Redvers thought I was capable of. Besides, right now I was simply filling my free time with another matter—Redvers was the one who was currently spending time with Naumann and had plans to search the other suspect's rooms. I pushed back any hurt over the idea that I was being edged out of the case—it wasn't helpful, and the only thing that truly mattered was that we learned what we needed to. Not who accomplished what.

I found the laundry facility down on the C-deck and cautiously entered the small reception room. It didn't look as though many guests visited this particular area of the ship— their clothes were picked up and dropped off at their cabins, so there was little reason for wealthy tourists to stop by the actual facility. There was no one in the small reception area to greet me and I waited a few moments before calling out a tentative "hello?"

"Yes!" I heard the response from behind the door at the back of the room, and when it opened moments later, I could hear the sounds of chatter and hard work being done. A little steam escaped into the room where I stood, and a young woman wearing a uniform with a smock-like apron over the front bustled in. "Can I help you, ma'am?"

"I'm wondering if Vanessa FitzSimmons's clothes are ready yet?" I asked, deliberately not mentioning that I was not in fact Vanessa herself.

"Just one moment . . ." The young woman stepped behind the counter and began shuffling through one stack of receipts before she frowned and picked up another stack.

She paused when she reached what she had been looking for. "Oh, Mrs. FitzSimmons. Yes, you had quite a few items, so they're not all ready yet. We can deliver what is done so far, of course."

"That would be lovely." I decided to continue the charade that I was Vanessa FitzSimmons. "Could I see the receipt, please?"

The young woman nodded politely and passed it over to me, and even before it was in my hand I could see that the paper had been written on both front and back. I looked it over—there was an enormous amount of clothing listed, and the box had been checked for it to be picked up and cleaned. I looked at the very bottom of the long list and found Vanessa FitzSimmons's signature. Of course, I had no idea how to tell whether the signature was authentic or not—but even if it didn't belong to Vanessa, someone had gone to an awful lot of trouble to make it look as though it was hers.

"Could I take this? There's something I need to check on back in my suite," I said.

The young woman tucked a strand of brown hair behind her ear and shifted on her feet. "Well, we really need the slips, ma'am."

"Perhaps I could copy it out for you," I offered.

"Oh!" she said. "That would be fine, I suppose. But I will do it myself. And it will take me a few minutes, since there are . . . well, so many items here."

I nodded. "That's fine. I can certainly wait."

And wait I did while the poor young woman meticulously copied down a list of nearly every item of clothing that

Vanessa had brought on board. It took more time than necessary since she was obviously doing her best to be completely thorough, but I was feeling impatient by the time I left the laundry with the original slip in hand. I would show it to Vanessa later and ask if it was her signature on the bottom. I very much hoped that it wasn't—if Vanessa had in fact sent all her clothes away, she had done a disturbingly convincing job lying about it. But why spin such a story? Or could Vanessa actually be losing her grasp on reality? Neither option was an appealing one.

I turned down the corridor to our suite and unlocked the door, pushing inside while still ruminating. I closed the door behind me when I heard an exclamation.

I looked up and saw Redvers standing in the doorway between the two rooms in nothing more than a bath towel. It was a large bath towel, but a bath towel nonetheless. He was dripping wet, and absolutely glorious.

CHAPTER THIRTEEN

"I'm so sorry! I should have knocked or . . . I'll go!" I said the words, but I didn't move. I could feel my face turning a shade of scarlet from the neck moving swiftly upward, but my mouth was suddenly dry and I couldn't seem to make myself turn around. Redvers cleared his throat once and I finally whirled about, facing the door instead of leaving, which was probably the more appropriate course of action. I caught the twinkle in his eye before I did so, and I rolled my eyes at the door.

"There's no need to knock; this is your room also. I just wasn't sure where you had gone to, and I thought I should bathe after spending so much time in the gymnasium this morning."

"Mmm-hmm. Yes. That was an excellent idea." And I wasn't *upset* I had come in when I did—I now had a picture burned onto my brain that I wasn't distressed to have. The man obviously spent a fair amount of time staying fit.

I heard rustling of clothing behind me. "Just give me a moment."

To distract myself from further mental images of what was happening behind me, I began chattering away. "I ran into Eloise Baumann in the Veranda Café. I was strong-armed into having tea with her and Margret."

"I thought you were going to avoid the lounge for that reason." His voice held a note of amusement.

"They weren't in the lounge, were they? They were in the café. And I stumbled onto them by accident. I was just out walking." I heard a zipper and started talking faster. "I haven't the foggiest idea what Eloise was talking about, but then Vanessa FitzSimmons came and rescued me. Thank heavens for her. I'll make a point to avoid Eloise in the future, you can be sure of that."

"You can turn around now." Redvers' dark eyes twinkled and he ran a hand over his damp hair, attempting to smooth the waves into place.

"That was quick."

"I had extra incentive."

"Mmm."

"You could have gone into the bedroom, you know."

My mouth opened and closed a few times—I was doing a more than adequate imitation of a fish. I could not admit that the sight of him had completely suspended all thought, and that to get to the bedroom I would have had to pass too closely by him. No, I wouldn't admit anything—he was already having too much fun.

I finally came up with a response. "I'd hate to make things too easy for you." Not my best quip, but these were trying times.

His next words were chosen carefully as he added a tweed tie to the collar of his crisp white shirt. "And did you learn anything from Vanessa?" In asking it seemed he was offering a truce. It wasn't necessarily an apology for earlier, but it was close. I decided to take it.

"Not much. They haven't turned up anything in the search. I spoke with her maid, who was not in the least bit helpful. She hasn't even met the man, which I find strange."

"That is odd." He left the ends of the tie dangling and turned his attention to his cuff links, fiddling with his right cuff. He seemed to be struggling, so I came forward to give him a hand.

"Thank you," he said as I pushed his other hand away and set my fingers to fastening the link. This close I was nearly overwhelmed by the smell of clean soap and pine. If I had been the swooning type, I might have done so. As it was, it took me a couple tries to finish my task, and I resolutely turned to the next one, trying to remember what I had been talking about.

"I think we need to ask your contacts to do a background on Van de Meter. What if he's our spy?"

I could feel skepticism radiating from him but I didn't look up from my task. Why were my fingers suddenly like large sausages? Surely it wasn't this hard to fasten one cuff link.

"It's unlikely." There was a pause and my fingers slowed. "But it would be best to be completely thorough." His head was slightly bowed as he watched me work. I shot him a quick glance, then turned back to my task, my fingers now able to quickly finish up. I took several large steps back, out of range of his delicious smell.

I was relieved that he had agreed to the background request, so I decided not to mention the strange phone calls and the laundry.

"Well." He looked at me steadily. "Do you want to join me for lunch?"

I looked down at myself. I was perfectly presentable, but perhaps I should freshen up a bit. "Yes, but I need just a moment." I headed for the door to the bedroom. "Are you done in here?" I called behind me.

"For the time being."

"Excellent." I shut the door, and after a second's thought, turned the lock.

I came out a few minutes later having given myself some time to gather my wits and splash some water on my face. I'd also combed my hair and freshened my lipstick before head-ing back out.

"That was quick."

"I had extra incentive," I tossed back, using his own words from earlier.

Redvers laughed and offered me his arm. We left our room just as the bugle call announced the lunch hour.

"Perfect timing."

"Indeed. Shall we do the à la carte restaurant again? It sounds like you've already had your fill of Eloise Baumann."

"I have indeed. But won't we pay extra if we dine at that restaurant?"

Redvers shrugged. "Neither of us will be footing the bill."

When we arrived, we were immediately escorted to a small, private table hidden away behind a large palm plant. Lunch passed pleasantly, neither of us mentioning the awk-ward interlude in our room earlier, or my interest in Vanessa FitzSimmons's missing husband. Instead, we stuck to safer topics. Such as Heinz Naumann.

"Did you learn anything this morning?" I tucked into my beef Wellington.

"Just that Naumann is a fierce squash player." Redvers' eyes turned speculative. "He mentioned again how much he enjoyed conversing with you. In fact, he said he regretted missing the opportunity to see you on the deck this morning."

I studied his face, but it seemed that Redvers was simply relating information. I would have been secretly pleased if he had seemed a bit jealous of Heinz's attention, but I didn't de-tect any. Of course, his face was very carefully neutral, so perhaps he was covering it well. I mentally shrugged.

"That's very . . . kind of him," I said.

Redvers cocked a brow. "I'm not convinced it's kindess. But it does look like you might be our best bet for learning anything useful since he enjoys your company so much."

My heart lifted at the thought that I was necessary to the

case after all. I'd been more troubled at being left out than I'd been willing to admit even to myself. But I certainly didn't need to tell that to Redvers. "What about our other two suspects?"

"They will be more difficult since they are crew members. It's unlikely you'll be able to strike up a conversation with Brubacher; from what I can tell he only leaves the crew deck when he's directing the band. He's probably best left to me."

"And you're just going to wander into the crew area to strike up a conversation?"

Redvers smiled. "I have my methods."

I rolled my eyes.

Redvers ignored it. "You've already spoken to Banks."

I nodded. "Have you heard anything back about him?" I was desperately curious about what his "personal reasons" for leaving New York were.

Redvers shook his head. "I need to stop by the office and see if there are any messages for me. There weren't any when I checked first thing this morning."

I reflected that it was a good thing he'd befriended McIntyre if he was going to be checking in to that office multiple times a day.

"I suppose I can find another reason to stop by the photography office."

Redvers tilted his head. "You don't want to go by too often and seem obvious. But perhaps take the camera out this afternoon. Start using up the film so that we can drop it off to be developed."

I nodded, and Redvers eyed me. "Just be careful."

I wasn't sure if he was referring to something in particular or if this was just a general advisement. "I will," I assured him.

After lunch I stopped by the room to grab the boxy camera and headed onto the deck. I could snap a few photos and then retire to my chair and see if Heinz decided to join me. It seemed a good possibility after what Redvers had reported about their conversation.

I snapped a photo of the long deck with the passengers making their way along it as though it was a promenade in fashionable Mayfair. I then pointed the camera out over the ocean and snapped one photo before giving a little shiver and dropping the viewfinder away from my face. There was nothing but water and waves as far as the eye could see, not even a bird to break up the monotony. I decided I didn't need any more photographs of that particular view.

I settled in to my deck chair, resting the camera on the small table between my seat and Heinz's. Unfortunately, now that I wasn't moving, I realized I needed a travel rug. The winds had died down, but there was enough of a nip in the air that if I sat too long I would become chilled. I was just about to head to the rug room when Dobbins appeared, carrying that very item.

"Dobbins, you're a dear. Thank you."

The young man's face blushed pink, but there was no other change to his demeanor—he took his professionalism quite seriously, and I had yet to see him crack a smile. "Can I bring you anything else, Mrs. Wunderly? Some tea perhaps?"

"If it's not too much trouble, Dobbins."

"Not at all." He disappeared back inside the ship.

Since I was watching Dobbins's retreat, I happened to notice Vanessa's maid scurrying my way. She was dressed in the brown wool coat from that morning and a matching cloche that she clutched to her head. She was glancing around furtively and was slightly breathless when she reached me.

"I've been looking for you, Mrs. Wunderly."

"What can I do for you, Rebecca? Would you like to have a seat?"

The girl looked horrified at the offer. "That wouldn't do at all, ma'am. I shouldn't even be seen up on this deck." She looked behind her again; it gave me the feeling she was being followed, but I didn't see anyone paying either of us any attention.

"We can always pretend I've called you here if anyone asks."

She gave a nod, but it didn't relieve much of her obvious anxiety. She opened her mouth, but then closed it again, biting her lip.

"What is it? What did you want to talk to me about?"

Rebecca set her face resolutely. "I wanted to tell you that I lied to you earlier."

My eyebrows went up in surprise. "About what?"

"I didn't want to say so in front of Miss Vanessa, but I never saw any extra trunks in her room." She shook her head and looked miserable. "I did tell the truth when I said I'd never met her husband. But I'm not sure there ever was one, Mrs. Wunderly. A husband, that is."

The girl's eyes were still darting about anxiously, and I couldn't tell whether it was about the story she was telling me, her fears about being found on the first-class deck when she was obviously dressed for the lower classes below, or something else entirely. My own thick wool coat had been provided for this trip and was of the finest quality—I was grateful that I would be allowed to keep something so well made once the cruise was over. It was far more than I could have afforded on my own, and I understood a little about how underdressed Rebecca must feel on the first-class deck. Yet her shifting gaze and nervous posture suggested it was something much more than that.

"Do you think Mrs. FitzSimmons is making it up?" I asked.

Rebecca shrugged. "Or maybe she's just confused? It seems Miss Vanessa does like a certain amount of attention."

I studied the young woman. "How long have you worked for her?"

"Not long. I needed a job quite badly a few months ago, and she took me on just before she began her trip over here."

She frowned. "This is my second time on a boat, and I don't like it any more than I did the first time."

"And the first time was with Miss Vanessa on your way over to the continent?"

"Yes, ma'am. And then she dismissed me for a few weeks right after she hired me. I thought it was very strange."

If what Rebecca was saying was true, it was indeed strange. It would be unusual to hire a maid, immediately take her to Europe without knowing a thing about her, dismiss the girl for several weeks only to bring her back across the water. It didn't make any sense.

"She gave me funds over there, ma'am. She left me with some money and told me to enjoy myself until she needed me again."

At least Vanessa hadn't completely abandoned the girl after taking her halfway around the world. She had been generous with her.

"And you didn't do that?"

Rebecca looked horrified. "Waste all that money? I wired most of it back to my ma so she could feed my brothers and sisters. I only kept a little so I could hire a cheap room and buy myself one good meal a day."

"I understand," I reassured Rebecca, and she shifted uneasily on her feet, glancing around before twisting nearly her entire body to take in the deck behind her. From my seated position, I couldn't quite see around her, and the girl was making me nearly as nervous as she obviously felt. Was someone watching us? Or was Rebecca's anxiety making *me* paranoid now? I considered grabbing the camera and taking a photograph of the deck behind her, but I didn't want to spook the young maid even further.

"Have you met the steward that is assigned to Mrs. Fitz-Simmons's room?" The steward's story was different from the one I was hearing from Rebecca Tesch. He'd seen Van de Meter's trunks but then refused to talk about the man—leading me to believe that he knew exactly who he was. And I already knew that Van de Meter did, in fact, exist. I'd seen the man with my own eyes, and had also seen the photographs of him entwined with Vanessa on deck. He may have been hiding his face, but he was real. So why was Rebecca now suggesting that he hadn't existed at all?

She shook her head, one hand clasping her felt cloche. "I heard Miss Vanessa griping about that steward. He drinks too much and isn't doing his job—he's barely been in her room. She said she was going to complain to the captain."

That was interesting. Vanessa had mentioned nothing of the sort to me, and it was the sort of detail I would expect she would share since she asked me to take a look at her room. Of course, she had left out the hang-up phone calls as well as the disappearance of her clothing. Perhaps she wouldn't have told me about the steward after all.

"But I saw Mr. Van de Meter, Rebecca. On deck when we left Southampton," I said gently.

She sagged for a moment, then stiffened, her mouth pressing into a little line. "Maybe that was someone else, ma'am. I'm just saying I don't think she was ever married. And there were no trunks in her room."

I decided that whatever Rebecca's reasons for relating this story—and I was beginning to suspect that it wasn't her idea to relate it to me—I wasn't going to make any headway in learning why she was insisting that her version of events was true.

Instead, I pulled the laundry slip from my pocket. "Have you seen this before, Rebecca?"

The girl's eyes widened as she took it in her hand. "No, ma'am. This isn't the slip I filled out. The one I did only had three or four items on it."

I nodded. "And the signature?"

Rebecca turned the paper over and looked at the bottom. She shook her head. "It looks like Miss Vanessa's signature, but I can't be sure." Rebecca looked troubled and passed the paper back to me. "I haven't seen her write many things, ma'am."

That was reasonable—the girl had only been with Vanessa for a short time, and it sounded like most of that hadn't even been spent with the woman. I would have to confront Vanessa directly about the laundry slip.

"But why would she send all her clothing?" Rebecca's brows were creased in confusion. Gone was her earlier anxiety and skipping gaze. Her clear green eyes held mine and I felt this was the first time during our conversation that the girl was being entirely truthful.

"I don't know, Rebecca. But I intend to find out."

I thanked Rebecca for coming to find me and she went scurrying back to the door leading to the lower decks, still clasping her cloche to her head despite the lack of wind. There were only a few other passengers out this afternoon— a scattering in their chairs and a couple here and there taking a leisurely stroll in the reasonable weather. But none of them had any interest in myself or Rebecca. Yet I was still left with the feeling that we had been observed—and that Rebecca had been aware of it too.

I went back to contemplating the ocean and the gray sky above it, rubbing my fingers absently on the dried sea salt coating the arm of my wooden chair. Rebecca's story was at odds with what Vanessa's steward had reported to Dobbins, yet her anxious behavior had me feeling as though we'd been watched. I thought that over. I hadn't seen anyone observing us, but if someone *had* been watching, I would lay odds that whoever it was had convinced Rebecca to come to me with her story about the trunks and the idea that Vanessa's husband didn't exist. Could that person have been Miles Van de Meter? Or had someone else put Rebecca up to it?

And what did the girl have to gain by bringing me a set of lies? It was possible that she was telling the truth about the trunks—she might not have noticed them—but to suggest that Vanessa's husband didn't exist? Rebecca had to realize that if I related her story to Vanessa, Vanessa would have good reason to let her go. And the girl genuinely seemed to need the position. If she was helping to support her mother and siblings, it was unlikely she could afford to lose this job.

I started to get out of my seat to follow her, but I saw Heinz pushing open the door leading to our deck. I settled back into my chair with some reluctance. Chatting up Heinz was a higher priority, so Rebecca and my questions about Miles Van de Meter would have to wait.

I didn't have a clear picture of what was going on, and Rebecca had done nothing but muddy the waters. The only thing I knew for certain was that nearly everyone was lying.

Chapter Fourteen

"Good afternoon, Jane!" Heinz said cheerfully as he reached me, giving a little bow before taking his seat. I saw that he had brought his own travel rug—I supposed it meant that he was prepared to settle in for a bit. I wasn't sure whether to be pleased about that, since I would have the chance to talk with him longer, or frustrated that I couldn't follow after Rebecca. I decided it was a little bit of both.

"Good afternoon, Heinz. I'm so pleased you decided to join me out here."

"I am as well." He looked very serious. "I enjoyed my morning squash game with your husband, but I did not like that I had to skip the opportunity to spend time with you." He gave me a sunny smile. "But here you are! I have the best of both worlds."

I smiled back at him, then caught sight of Dobbins in my peripheral. He stepped to the little wooden table between our chairs and put down a cup for both Heinz and me. Dobbins then poured the tea and set down the little pot for us.

"Can I get you anything else?" Dobbins looked directly at me.

"No. But thank you, Dobbins." Confusion tinged my voice—why had he brought a cup for Heinz as well?

"Yes, thank you, young man." Heinz smiled and reached into his inner pocket for his flask, adding a liberal dash to his cup. He held it aloft in question, and I shook my head before watching Dobbins retreat once more. I looked back at Heinz, who caught the question in my eyes. "I caught him just as he was coming out and I recognized him as your steward." Heinz flashed a winning smile at me that twisted my stomach instead of achieving its desired effect. "I talked him into getting an extra cup for me."

I smiled back and picked up my porcelain cup, taking a small sip, but I felt a little uncertain. How had Heinz known who our steward was? Or perhaps more to the point, why had he registered that information? Was Naumann simply observant, or did he have a reason to be watching us? I could feel my shoulders tensing up around my ears.

With a deep breath, I forced myself to relax. Right now, I had a part to play. Any other questions could be discussed with Redvers later.

Heinz was as urbane and charming as he'd been the day before, and it didn't take long before his easy manner and genuine interest in my opinions had me relaxing into my role. It also helped that his inclination toward flirtation subsided when he was involved in direct conversation—especially about music. The man became awfully long-winded once we came to that topic. But at least he had the grace to realize it quickly and apologize.

And yet by the time we parted, I still hadn't learned anything useful and I returned to our suite feeling frustrated by my lack of progress. I wasn't sure exactly what I expected him to tell me, but I certainly wanted to learn something more helpful than the man had an undying passion for American jazz.

This time when I reached our door I remembered to give a soft knock before walking in, and I heard Redvers' response giving me clearance to enter. He was seated in the upholstered chair staring absently at the clouds scudding across the sky beyond the porthole.

I closed the door behind me and regarded him. "Are you just sitting here staring out the window?"

He chuckled. "I was thinking."

"So that's how you do it."

Redvers gave a little shake of his head, but he was smiling. "Did you learn anything from Naumann?"

I gave a frustrated sigh and took a seat in one of the wooden chairs at the small table. "Nothing useful. Although don't get him started on the topic of jazz. He'll never stop." I removed my cloche and put it down before me. "I have some concerns though, especially after last night." I related to him how he knew who our steward was and had requested an extra cup from him.

Redvers frowned. "It's possible that he saw Dobbins showing you to your deck chair yesterday."

"But it feels unlikely since Heinz joined me some time later." I'd been staring off into space myself, so I couldn't say exactly how long after Dobbins had left that Heinz had joined me, but it had been longer than a few minutes.

Redvers nodded. "We'll have to continue to be quite careful. Perhaps we should give him some breathing room tonight and focus on Brubacher."

It was gratifying that Redvers seemed as concerned as I was—it was good to know my instincts were correct. "What about Banks?" I asked. "Or Van de Meter, for that matter." I hadn't forgotten that I'd asked for information on Miles's background in case our disappearing husband was in fact the spy we were seeking.

Redvers shook his head. "Nothing yet on Van de Meter. But I did receive a response on Banks."

I looked around but didn't see any messages on the tables near the man. I wondered what he did with them once he decoded them. Ate them?

Instead of asking that impertinent question, I simply prompted him to continue. "And?"

"It looks like his 'personal reason' for leaving the city is a messy divorce."

"Oh." That was an entirely disappointing motive for fleeing and not at all close to what my imagination had conjured up.

"His in-laws, and apparently there are many, were making it unpleasant for him to live there. Might have to do with the fact that he had an affair with his photography assistant."

I could feel my lip curling but could do nothing to stop it. "It serves him right then."

"It does at that."

It was hard to imagine the neat little man that I'd met as a womanizer, but it just went to show that you never could tell about a person.

A useful reminder.

Redvers checked his watch. "We have a bit of time before we need to dress for dinner. Would you like to take a stroll with me?" He tipped his head at the camera I carried. "Perhaps use up some more of this film? Unless you've finished the roll already."

I shook my head. "I only managed to snap a photograph or two. There's still quite a bit left to use."

I stood, picking up my cloche and replacing it on my head. I was relieved that we seemed to be back on solid footing, and that whatever had been bothering Redvers earlier appeared to have resolved itself. Redvers pushed himself up elegantly and took the camera from me before leading me back out.

We meandered about, taking the occasional photograph of the grand ship we were living on, and the various passengers enjoying themselves on deck. The sky was now overcast, but the seas were calm enough that there was a small crowd enjoying a lively game of shuffleboard, and I snapped a few photos of the spirited competition. As we continued on, a smiling older gentleman in a bowler hat asked if he might take a photo of Redvers and me and we obliged. Standing against the railing with Redvers' arm around my waist, I thrilled a bit at the notion of having that particular photograph developed later.

I kept an eye out for Vanessa since she seemed to enjoy sports so much, but I didn't catch sight of her in our wanderings. I thought about asking Redvers if we might stop by Vanessa's suite so that I could ask her about the signature on the laundry slip, but we were getting on so well that I didn't want to break the spell by bringing it up. Instead, I simply let myself enjoy Redvers' company.

When the film on our camera was finished we stopped by the photography office. Redvers paid for the rental, chatting Banks up about photography in general and his former studio in New York while I pretended to inspect the wall of cameras available to rent. I could sense rather than see when Banks glanced over at me, then dropped his voice nearly out of my hearing. From the snatches I was able to catch, he was confirming that his soon-to-be ex-wife was his reason for getting out of town. Redvers dropped his own voice and offered his sympathies; it took an effort to stop myself from shooting them both a dark look. Instead, I returned to Redvers' side, and Mr. Banks told me I could pick up the photographs the next day. I thanked him, and we took our leave.

Once we were far enough away from the little studio, I asked my question. "Did he confirm what you learned about his divorce?"

Redvers nodded. "He says his ex-wife went off the deep end and he had to escape the city."

I pursed my lips. "You got that out of him quite fast."

"The man's an open book. I doubt he'd be able to pull off

any sort of espionage. And I'm not surprised he couldn't pull off an affair without getting caught." Then he grinned. "Besides, I'm entirely charming."

I gave him a small slug to the arm. The man could also be entirely irritating at times.

By the time we made it back to our room, it was time to dress for dinner.

CHAPTER FIFTEEN

I donned a black velvet number with a plunging neckline and fluttering sleeves that—for once—set off my curves nicely. The dress had a bit of a cut-out in the front, showcasing my new black and silver shoes with their metallic gleam, but brushed the floor in the back. Fortunately, the back was cut high enough that I didn't have to worry about whether the scars there would show.

When I reappeared in the sitting room, Redvers was struck speechless for a moment before taking a step forward and pronouncing me lovely. I knew the glow from that one compliment, and the tone of voice in which it was delivered, would keep me warm for days to come.

Redvers was resplendent as usual in his black tuxedo, his wavy dark hair very neatly contained tonight. I was so taken with the picture he presented, despite the fact that I had seen it numerous times before, that I almost didn't realize we had descended to the D-deck and were entering the reception room. It appeared we were eating in the formal dining room this evening.

I gave a little sigh when I realized what we faced. "Must we?"

Redvers gave a little chuckle. "I'm afraid so." He glanced over at me. "I'm no more thrilled than you are, but we do need to keep up appearances. In the evenings at least."

I nodded and braced myself for the onslaught of chatter from our tablemate Eloise, who started in as soon as she spied us approaching our table.

"I must say, Mrs. Wunderly, your friend was quite rude this morning taking you away from us. At the very least she could have joined us at our table instead of announcing that you were needed elsewhere."

I nodded politely, but before I could apologize for Vanessa, Eloise was already onto another topic. From the corner of my eye I saw Redvers frown at the mention of my "friend" Vanessa. I'd told him that she was the one who rescued me from my morning tea with Eloise, so I wondered why he was frowning now. I turned to face him more fully and saw that his expression had already smoothed and he shot me a warm smile. I returned it, and went back to studying the menu, tuning out whatever it was that Eloise was currently lecturing us on. When the waiter returned to learn which entrée selection each of us wanted that evening, Eloise informed the young man that nothing on the menu suited her palate and she insisted that they find her a nice piece of prime rib instead.

"Really, Eloise," Douglas Gould interjected. "Do you have to be so difficult? The selections are quite nice this evening." I mentally applauded Gould for finally challenging his difficult sister-in-law. Margret kept conspicuously quiet, studying her quickly emptying wineglass with enthusiasm.

Eloise glared at him. "Douglas, you know I have a delicate constitution." I didn't think anyone at that table, the waiter included, believed that assertion. "And I am quite sure that my special needs can be accommodated. We've certainly paid enough for the privilege."

Douglas rolled his eyes but declined to comment further, and our waiter scurried away with his special instructions to the chef. I was curious to see what would actually be served to the woman, since her "delicate constitution" apparently required a bloody piece of beef.

*   *   *

Dinner took an interminably long time. None of us made eye contact with one other, focusing instead on eating our food and suffering through what was another painful meal listening to Eloise hold court. She didn't seem to notice, only requiring the occasional noise from anyone in order to keep going. I'm not even sure that much was necessary. It was incredible to me that Margret and Douglas were subjected to this day in and day out—but judging by the amount of wine they both consumed, they had found their own manner of coping.

The waiter did in fact bring Eloise a piece of prime rib for dinner, as she had demanded, but it was nearly sent back for being not rare enough. Eloise finally consented to eat it, but only after an absurd amount of bellyaching at the poor waiter. I nearly tried to tell her that it wasn't the young man's fault, but Redvers' restraining hand on my arm stopped me from attempting to reason with the woman. As soon as we slurped down our post-meal coffees, Redvers and I made our escape, Eloise calling after me that I must promise to join them again in the morning, this time without interruption. I didn't bother to respond—I felt a bit like an animal caught in a trap. I would gnaw off my own leg to escape the woman's company.

Redvers and I made it to the deck above where we paused and shared a loaded look before we both dissolved into laughter.

"That was painful," Redvers said.

"Entirely," I agreed, taking his arm as we headed to the first-class lounge on the A-deck.

The room was already busy, and I could see that the ship's musicians were setting up near the stage. I caught sight of Keith Brubacher, blond hair gleaming in the lights, as he patiently waited for his band to finish putting their instruments together and find their seats. I made a note to ask Redvers whether he'd had an opportunity to talk with the man, and how he intended to explain his transition from crew member to passenger if he was noticed by the band leader. That was assuming Redvers pretended to be crew in order to access the restricted deck where Brubacher stayed—I had no idea what his actual strategy was, of course, since he failed to share it with me.

Casting my eyes around the room, I noticed Heinz Naumann was absent from the growing crowd. I wasn't upset that he was missing since I didn't particularly want him to claim his dance and give me the chance to embarrass myself on the dance floor. I did, however, see Vanessa. She was standing near the bar at the other end of the room, nursing a drink and chatting with a pair of young men. I gave my head a little shake and followed Redvers into the fray, looking for a table where we could set up for the evening. There were none that were unoccupied, but we eventually spotted an older couple who had two empty chairs at theirs. They politely invited us to join them and went back to their conversation, something about a bridge game they had engaged in that afternoon. With the bustle of the after-dinner crowd, Redvers decided to go to the bar instead of waiting for a waiter to find us, and I smiled at his retreating back.

As I watched him, my gaze moved back to where Vanessa stood, and she turned at that moment and caught my eye. She arched an eyebrow, then placed her drink on the bar, apparently instructing one of the young men to keep an eye on it. She threaded through the bodies and then draped herself in the chair next to me.

"Really, this is all too much, but I'm dying for a turn on the dance floor," she said by way of greeting. "Luckily I found those two and they seem quite willing."

I didn't quite know how to respond to that, so I changed course. "Are you still getting the strange phone calls?" I glanced at the older couple, but they were paying us no mind.

She shook her head. "I wouldn't know. I've been busy out and about. Staying out of my suite." Vanessa shrugged. "I'm more concerned about where my clothing is. I couldn't even dress for dinner!" She gestured at the same day dress she'd been wearing that morning when I had seen her.

It surprised me that she hadn't bothered to find out about her clothing herself if she was that concerned about it, but perhaps she was simply used to things being done for her. "Well, I happen to have some information about that."

"You do? That's simply the bee's knees. Do tell."

"All of your clothing is at the laundry. They should be bringing back the pieces that are finished." I wondered if they had already done that and she simply hadn't bothered to go by her suite to look. It seemed likely. "But there's a further issue. It appears that the slip was signed by you."

Vanessa looked at me for a long moment. "It couldn't be. Why would I send all my clothing at once?"

"I don't know, but the signature at the bottom is your name. I have no idea if it's your handwriting though. It's back in my room—I can show you later."

Vanessa shook her head and gazed off into the distance for a few moments. I watched her closely, but her face was completely devoid of emotion. I couldn't begin to tell what she was thinking.

"Well, thank you for finding my things," Vanessa said stiffly, rising to leave.

"I can stop by later to show you the slip."

"That won't be necessary," she said. "I'll see you some time tomorrow." Vanessa gave a vague wave of her hand and walked straight out of the lounge, not even returning to the drink she'd left with the young men at the bar.

I stared after her, completely bewildered. I hadn't been suggesting that it absolutely was her signature, just that her name was on the slip. We needed to take a look at it together and decide what was going on, discuss whether someone else had signed her name, but Vanessa had abruptly left instead. I couldn't understand the woman at all.

I looked at the older couple on the other side of the table, but they were completely uninterested in the drama that was unfolding on my side, so I returned to my musings.

"I see your husband was foolish enough to leave you unattended."

CHAPTER SIXTEEN

Heinz's voice came from just behind me and I jumped in my seat before turning to find the man smiling at me. He had approached so quietly I hadn't heard the slightest sound.

"It does look like he's been caught up in something." I looked back to the bar and located Redvers—he was engrossed in a conversation with a middle-aged man who was slightly balding at the crown and rounding about his middle.

"But it works in my favor since I can claim that dance I had the misfortune to miss out on last night." Heinz held out his hand just as the band started up with their first number.

It was on the tip of my tongue to decline the offer since we were supposed to avoid suspicion by giving Heinz his space, but I closed my mouth and forced a smile instead. It was foolish to waste an opportunity, and frankly it might look more suspicious to decline and send him away. His hand was still extended, and I paused for only a moment longer before putting my hand in his and allowing him to pull me up. We walked over to the dance floor, and I sent another quick look behind us to where Redvers stood, but he seemed completely oblivious to what I was doing. With a tiny shrug I allowed myself to be pulled into Heinz's arms. Luckily the band had started in with a slower song, "How Am I to Know?" and I wasn't required to jitterbug. Of course, we hadn't even done a full turn around the floor before I stepped on the man's toes—I grimaced and gave a sincere apology. He was quite gracious but also careful to keep his distance after that. I did my best to give the appearance that I was having a good time, but I was truly just short of miserable. I didn't enjoy dancing as much as some women did—rhythm just didn't come naturally to me, and I spent the majority of the time concentrating on not making a fool of myself.

Mercifully, the dance ended and, with a little bow, Heinz escorted me from the floor.

"You look flushed, Mrs. Wunderly. Perhaps a quick turn on the deck would do you some good."

My smile froze in place. Going on deck with the man—alone—was a terrible idea, but it was also my job to earn his trust and learn as much information as I could. So, against my better judgment, I allowed Heinz to lead me out of the room, stopping by my table briefly to grab my shrug and make my excuses to the older couple, who barely paused long enough in their conversation to wish me a good night. I wondered if they even noticed I was leaving with a different man than I had come with. But I made certain to tell them that I was going for a walk on deck all the same.

I looked behind us as we pushed through the heavy wooden doors, but whatever conversation Redvers was embroiled in must have been a doozy, because he didn't appear to be aware of me leaving the lounge at all. I hoped the older couple would repeat what I had told them when Redvers decided to return to the table we had shared. But it was possible they might not even remember I'd been there in the first place.

Heinz and I made our way down the corridor and stepped through the metal door leading to the outside promenade. I shivered and pulled my shrug tighter around myself. The wind had picked up and it was chilly, especially now that night had fallen—although it was not just the cold that made me shiver. For all his solicitude, Heinz didn't seem to notice my discomfort.

Misty gray fog shrouded the ship, our path illuminated by the occasional yellow light glowing feebly overhead. I found the vastness of the ocean unsettling during the day, but it was even more disturbing in the dark now that we were unable to see anything at all. I fervently hoped the officers on deck knew what they were doing—it was all too easy to imagine an obstacle suddenly popping up out of the fog. Like the iceberg that had sunk the *Titanic*—the sister ship to the one we were currently on.

"You seem . . . distracted this evening, Mrs. Wunderly." Heinz was obviously trying to give me an out for my poor dancing abilities.

I gave a chuckle. "I wish I could blame my rotten dancing on something else, Mr. Naumann, but I'm afraid I can't. I've just never been a very good dancer. Did I hurt you terribly?"

He shook his head and gave me a winning smile. "Not at all." But he also didn't try to argue the point any further, which, despite my current feelings of discomfort, made me like him more. It would have been utterly insincere for him to press the point otherwise. I knew where my talents lay—and didn't.

I sighed. "But I must admit, I am also somewhat distracted."

Heinz cocked his head attentively as we slowly made our way in the foggy gloom. My heels clacked against the wood—now slightly slippery in the damp—and sounded louder in the fog, as though my footsteps were trapped in the same pocket of cotton that we were. Heinz kept a respectable distance, but I hugged the inside track nearest the ship just the same. Being alone in the dark with a strange man had my nerves more than a little on edge; I was definitely reconsidering the wisdom of having accepted his offer to step outside, despite my assigned mission.

"I met a woman on board who is having some troubles. She can't seem to find her husband," I said.

Heinz cocked an eyebrow as I sketched the very basics about Vanessa FitzSimmons and her situation. I figured it couldn't hurt to give a bit of the truth to the man—after all, it would give me that much more subterfuge. If I was worried about my new friend, and trying to help her find her husband, I was much less likely to be investigating Heinz. Or anyone else, for that matter. And giving a little bit of truth might allow him to forget himself and do the same. I also found it soothing to concentrate on something other than the sound of our lonely footsteps in the dark. If something happened to me out here, no one was around to witness it since we had yet to pass another living soul.

"It does not sound very good for this woman. But why should you concern yourself with her problems?"

I shrugged. There was no way I was going to explain my personal reasons for getting involved. "She reminds me of my sister." I didn't have a sister—or a brother, for that matter—but it seemed the easiest explanation, and a believable one.

Heinz nodded wisely. "Ahh, yes. It is hard when the family becomes involved, is it not?" I gave him a vague smile. "It is because of my own sister that I do everything that I do."

I cast a sideways look. "Your sister?" A sudden swell caused the boat to tip just enough that I stumbled on my next step. Heinz reached out and steadied me, one hand on my upper arm and the other landing somewhere near my waist.

"Careful," he said. "The water is unpredictable."

I thanked him, but pulled away from his hands, and they dropped back to his sides.

I paused for a few beats before trying again; I didn't want to seem too eager. "What did you mean about your sister? What is it you do for her?"

But the moment had passed and Heinz's smile was now

tight. "She is not always well. That is all. It is not a cheerful topic." I wanted to ask more, but from the tone of his voice I could tell the matter was closed. I felt frustration rising—my instincts told me he had been close to telling me something that could have been important.

I cleared my throat and began walking again. Heinz fell into step beside me as we continued our circuit around the deck. "I can't think of anywhere Vanessa's husband could be hiding that the crew wouldn't have thought to look. Do you have any suggestions?"

"It's hard to say. It does not sound like the crew did much searching and it would be very easy to get lost on a ship like this." Naumann looked out over the railing into the murky distance. "Or even go overboard. No one would know he was gone."

Heinz's voice was utterly conversational, so I didn't get the feeling that the man was threatening me, but my skin crackled with dread all the same—stepping outside into the dark with this man had not been a smart decision. We were nearing a set of stairs leading back to the deck below when I heard the metal door creaking open. I held my breath, teetering between fear and relief, unsure who would be joining us.

"I was wondering where you had taken yourself off to." Out into the gloom stepped Redvers. I let out my breath, more than a little relieved to see him.

"Your wife seemed a little warm. I was just helping her cool off." Heinz's voice was the tiniest bit defensive.

"I appreciate that." Redvers smiled widely, but I could see the strain behind it—although only because I knew the man so well. I didn't think it would be obvious to anyone else. "She does have a tendency to get overheated."

I stepped forward and took Redvers' arm, smiling at both men. "Thank you for the turn around the deck, Mr. Naumann. It's always a pleasure."

He gave me a genuine smile. "And I hope your friend's troubles sort themselves out."

I inclined my head. "I hope so too."

"Until tomorrow, Mrs. Wunderly. Mr. Wunderly." Redvers and Naumann shook hands and Naumann disappeared behind the door and down the same stairs Redvers had just come up.

We waited a few beats before Redvers started in. "Was that wise?"

One shoulder went up. "Perhaps not, but no harm came of it."

"It would have been entirely too easy to push you over the side. Please don't go off alone with him again at night." Redvers' voice was strained and he pulled me into a tight hug against his chest.

Despite the warmth now flooding my body, I shuddered. A cry and a splash were all that stood between me and an icy ending in the Atlantic should someone get the idea. I knew Redvers was right, and for once I didn't argue with the man. I couldn't help but wonder if Miles Van de Meter had met that fate.

Redvers released me from his embrace, but his hands stayed anchored on my upper arms. "Did you learn anything interesting?" he asked.

I immediately missed the lack of bodily contact, but concentrated on the question he'd asked. "Heinz mentioned his sister. He said she was the reason for everything that he did."

"Did he explain what that meant?"

I shook my head sadly. "No, we were interrupted by a sudden wave. And then he wouldn't say anything more about it."

Redvers nodded slowly. "But perhaps you can come back to it."

"Of course." Heinz had shown a chink in his armor, and I

had every intention of prying it open. I still had several days in which to do so.

"And I'll do a better job of keeping watch," Redvers said.

I didn't argue that point. "Did you learn anything from your conversation at the bar? You seemed terribly interested in whatever the man had to say."

"No, unfortunately. It was utter drivel, but I was trying to be polite. The man is a minor politician in New York, and it never hurts to foster connections."

I hadn't recognized the man, but then, I was a Boston girl, born and bred. From what I understood, the New York political machine was another animal entirely.

"How about Brubacher?" My voice dropped as I said his name even though we were standing close and there was no one around to hear me. "Did you speak with him today?"

Redvers shook his head. "No, but I'm expecting something back about the man's background very soon."

I nodded and was about to ask how he intended to go about talking to Brubacher, when Redvers briskly rubbed my upper arms. "You're cold. Let's get you inside." He held the door for me as I passed through. "Frankly, I can't believe he brought you out here with nothing but that wrap."

I shrugged, but I was grateful that Redvers had noticed how poorly I'd been prepared for the outdoors.

We returned to the lounge where the dancing was now in full swing. A table near the back was being cleared of its empty glasses and Redvers and I took a seat, placing an order with the harried-looking waiter for a round of drinks. I could see Heinz across the room chatting with a small group of well-dressed people. I didn't think he had seen us, and even if he had, I thought he would probably keep his distance for the remainder of the evening. Our stroll on the deck had been innocent, but there had been some tension between the two men when Redvers had appeared.

When I turned to him, Redvers was gazing at me intently. I flushed a bit. "What is it?"

"Nothing." A small smile touched his lips as he took a sip of his drink. "Are you warming up?"

Between the man's proximity and his hands on my arms, I hadn't been truly cold, but that wasn't something I was going to share. "I am, thank you." I took a sip of my gin rickey. "What are your plans for tomorrow?"

"Well, I don't think Naumann and I will be playing squash." He gave a rueful chuckle.

"No, I don't think you will be." They'd shaken hands after Redvers had reclaimed me, but I didn't think they would be playing sports together any time soon.

"But I was thinking I might try to engage with Mr. Gould."

I looked at Redvers in interest. "Any particular reason?"

Redvers gave a casual shrug. "The man seems like he could use an outlet."

That was certainly true, and I said as much before I went back to surveying the crowd. I spotted Heinz making his way over to the band just as they finished their song. He stopped at the band leader's small podium, then bent and spoke to Brubacher for a moment.

I nodded in that direction. "What do you think that's about?"

Redvers shook his head, but a tiny crease appeared between his dark brows.

Brubacher, in his pristine white tuxedo, cocked his head, then gave Heinz a quick nod before turning back to his band. There was a shuffling of papers before the band started in on the next tune.

"Perhaps he was making a song request," I suggested. But then Heinz casually strolled across the lounge and exited through the wooden doors. "Or not."

"It does seem unlikely that he would request a song and then leave."

I looked back at the band leader, now enthusiastically waving his baton in time with the upbeat tempo being played. "What other reason would our two best suspects have to talk with one another?"

"I don't know," Redvers said. "But we should try to find out."

Once Heinz had gone, it felt as though both of us were able to relax a bit and we found ourselves in a lively argument about the merits of American jazz. It reminded me of the early days of our acquaintance when the two of us would argue about politics—Redvers often taking a stance simply to provoke me—but the evenings ending in a great deal of fun for both of us. I looked down and realized that both of our drinks were empty, but before I could suggest we have another round, Redvers stood and held out his hand. I stared at him in shock for a moment, before slowly putting my hand in his, not knowing what I was agreeing to.

"It's my turn for a dance."

I let him pull me to my feet. "You know what I'm capable of," I warned.

He chuckled. "I'm well aware."

Redvers led me onto the dance floor just as the band switched to a slow waltz. I breathed a small sigh of relief; I would still trample his toes, but it was far better than my trying to do something like the Charleston or jitterbug. Dances like those usually led to far greater bodily injuries for my dance partners. Or victims, rather.

Redvers pulled me close—a little closer than was strictly proper—and when I was about to object for his own safety, he leaned down and whispered in my ear. "We're supposed to be married, you know."

I sighed a little and released the muscles I'd been holding. I gave myself over to the feeling of being in his arms, and managed to step on his toes only once. The evening took on a dreamlike quality, and before I knew it I was swept up in the romance of it all. We may have been pretending at marriage, but in that moment, our relationship felt awfully real. I didn't even object when he leaned in for a quick kiss at the end of the first number.

The spark I felt from being so near to Redvers hadn't been replicated at all in my dance with Heinz earlier. Dancing with Heinz had been pleasant enough, but Redvers' mere proximity set my skin on fire, let alone what happened when his lips touched mine. When we first met that attraction had scared me silly, but the unseen wounds from my marriage had finally come a long way in healing, and Redvers had proved himself worthy of my trust. Sure, there were bumps in the road along the way—such as his reaction to my desire to help Vanessa FitzSimmons—but Redvers always proved himself in the end. It occurred to me that I should leave the past where it belonged, and let myself enjoy the present.

It was time to drop those final barriers. Which meant Redvers wouldn't be spending the night in the sitting room. Not if I had any say in the matter.

CHAPTER SEVENTEEN

I awoke the next morning, momentarily startled that I was alone in the double bed, but then I stretched contentedly. If I were a cat, I would have purred. I could hear Redvers in the outer room, and from the sounds of things he had once again ordered breakfast to be delivered. I wasn't surprised the man was already up and out of bed—he seemed to sleep very little as a general rule. Although it would have been nice to wake up next to him after the evening we had shared.

As I became more awake, I felt some stirrings of panic as I replayed the night before. Intimacy was difficult for me, but upon reflection nothing about the night had reminded me of my past horrors. If anything, it had helped to erase some of those bad memories. And Redvers hadn't been disgusted by the scars on my back—reminders of Grant's cruelty—nor had he ignored them. He simply accepted them as part of me. Recalling his tenderness, I was able to dispel my doubts about the wisdom of opening up to him. With a smile, I pulled on a silk robe, splashed some water on my face to freshen up, and went out to meet the day.

Redvers greeted me with a kiss on the cheek and a hot cup of coffee. I beamed at him and took a seat at the table where breakfast had been laid out. I was lifting the lid on a silver server when there was a knock at the door.

"Yes?" Redvers called out.

"It's Dobbins, sir."

Redvers looked at me and I shrugged as I pulled a piece of toast from the basket and began buttering it. Dobbins was our steward, after all. I decided it didn't matter to me if the man saw me in my robe.

Dobbins entered, closing the door silently behind him. Redvers looked at him expectantly, but he gave his head a little shake. "I've come to talk to Mrs. Wunderly."

I sat up a bit straighter and put down the toast, swallowing the mouthful I had just bit off. "What is it, Dobbins?" The man came closer and stood awkwardly next to our table as Redvers filled his plate from the apparent feast he'd ordered. I supposed that he *had* worked up an appetite.

"I have some information for you. About where Rebecca Tesch is staying."

"Excellent! Which cabin is she in?"

"D61," Dobbins reported, handing me a small card with the number written on it in a neat square script.

"Very helpful. Thank you, Dobbins. Do you know if there is someone staying there with her?" Glancing over, I saw that Redvers' brow was furrowed and I didn't think it was regarding his eggs.

"I believe there is. Did you want that name as well?"

I shook my head. "I don't think that's necessary." It was most likely someone who had simply been assigned to the cabin with her.

Dobbins turned to Redvers. "Do you have anything for me today, sir?"

Redvers shook his head. "Not at the moment, Dobbins. I'll be sure to let you know if that changes."

Dobbins took his leave and in his wake the silence was a little too quiet. I felt as though I could reach out with my butter knife and cut the tension that had been left by the steward's visit. To cover my anxiety, I busied myself with eating my breakfast before it got cold, but Redvers appeared to be concentrating on his meal instead of consuming it.

Finally, he looked up. "I thought you had let this thing with Mrs. FitzSimmons go, Jane."

I raised my eyebrows. "I'm sorry if I gave you that impression, but no."

"It does not seem worth wasting your time over. Especially when we have something else we are supposed to be focused on."

I felt my temper flare and I folded my arms. "I'm sorry you feel that way, but what about the fact that Miles Van de Meter has disappeared off this ship at the same time we are seeking a German spy? What if that's more than a coincidence? I don't think we can overlook the possibility. And if I happen to help a woman out with her problem while looking into that, all the better." I hadn't raised my voice, but it was heated. I was angry that I had to make excuses for looking into Van de Meter in the first place—I'd hoped Redvers would support my decision to help the woman without needing to tie it to our current investigation. He made it seem as though I wasn't capable of handling both things at once.

"Am I supposed to investigate the rest on my own?"

Now I was truly angry. "That's what you've been doing until now, isn't it? Insisting that you'll do all the searches and interviews with Brubacher and Banks. And you're still leaving me in the dark about everything unless I think to ask. I thought I was supposed to be part of this investigation, but it feels like nothing has changed!"

And that was true. I did feel left out of the investigation yet again. The past several days had made it obvious that Redvers knew more than I did. Which meant he had either forgotten to share things with me, or he'd once again left me out on purpose.

"I took a big risk convincing my superiors that they could trust you with this assignment."

I couldn't even begin to take apart the reasons why that statement hurt so much. But I didn't have time to let it sink in before his next outburst.

"And I don't want you getting involved with her!" This time his voice was loud. But instead of shrinking as I might have done in the past, I felt myself sit even taller in my seat as I quietly folded my napkin and placed it on the table. I regarded him for a moment, taking in how tightly he'd clenched his jaw.

This argument was going nowhere productive. Both of us were entirely too angry at the moment.

I stood up and crossed unsteadily to the bedroom. I could hear his incredulous voice behind me. "You're leaving?"

"You're being unreasonable. When you can think clearly again, let me know." I went into the bedroom and shut the door behind me, locking it. Then I promptly burst into tears.

The panicky feelings I had squashed upon waking came back twofold. It had been years since I had allowed myself to get close to a man, and the first time I did, he changed into a different person practically overnight. Redvers and I had never had an argument before, at least not one this heated, and the echoes of my disastrous marriage rang in my head. How could I have let this happen? How could I let my walls down with someone who wanted to control what I did and with whom I spoke? I felt slightly sick when I thought about just how close we had been the night before, and I drew myself a hot bath as tears streaked my face.

At least I didn't feel physically threatened by Redvers— even when he raised his voice I hadn't felt afraid that he would strike out in any way. It was a small consolation, but a consolation nonetheless.

I immersed myself in the hot water and lay there until the water began to cool. Then I lay there for a while longer, watching the water move with the sway of the ship until I began to shiver and my tears had completely dried up.

The entire time I was in the bathroom there was no knock at the door. Redvers had let me walk away, which was somehow far worse than him trying to follow me and continue our argument. I hadn't wanted to continue fighting, but his indifference was truly devastating.

My eyes were now puffy and red, but I marshaled myself all the same. I dressed in a gray wool sweater with a coordinating pleated skirt and took a few deep breaths. I wasn't ready to face him, but I had to do it eventually. After all, we still had a mission to fulfill—might as well get on with things. I flung open the door with a flourish.

The room was empty.

I stood in the doorway and felt my heart sink to somewhere around my feet—I was truly surprised it could get any lower. Then I gave that heart a good swift mental kick. It hadn't done me any favors before or now.

I went back into the bedroom, careful to lock the door once more, and reclined on the bed with a cool washcloth over the upper half of my face for some time. I didn't sleep, but it gave me time to come up with a plan while I soothed my puffy eyes. As I lay there, I decided I would simply be professional, and keep my distance from Redvers—as much as I could, anyway. I would do the job I had come to do, but I wouldn't let my heart get any more involved with the man. I would simply shut that particular organ down. Immediately.

Although I feared it was already too late.

CHAPTER EIGHTEEN

I looked something close to normal by the time I emerged from the suite and headed up to the deck. I was glad to see that Heinz was missing from his chair. I'd been half afraid he would be waiting for me, but his seat was conspicuously vacant. Taking my own chair, I saw there was a cup of tea on the table that hadn't been cleared yet. Putting my bare fingers to the cup told me it was quite cold. Heinz hadn't been here for at least a little while—although anything hot would cool quickly in the chilly sea air, so it was difficult to guess just how long ago he'd left. Or whether he would return, for that matter. But I was hoping Naumann had had enough fresh air because I'd had more than my fill of men for the morning.

Dobbins had left a rug neatly folded on my chair, and now I pulled it over myself and huddled beneath it for warmth. The temperature had dropped overnight and now cold, salty air whipped my hair around, but I paid it little mind. Instead I stared out over the sea, the gray of the sky nearly indistinguishable from the roiling gray of the water, only a thin line of demarcation between the two at the horizon. Any other day I might have found the view distressing—all that open water empty of other souls, but today I was far too distracted to pay it much attention. It was simply a place for my unfocused gaze to rest.

Every time I thought of Redvers, my eyes welled with tears, and that wouldn't do at all. So I forcibly turned my mind away from that troublesome man and turned it to Vanessa FitzSimmons's missing husband instead.

I could concede that if I hadn't seen Van de Meter with my own eyes, I might struggle to believe he ever existed. The woman's own maid hadn't met the man, and the steward refused to confirm his existence—although he had confirmed seeing the trunks. I shook my head. Between the disappearing trunks, the phone calls, and the missing clothing, it looked to me like someone was deliberately playing games with Vanessa FitzSimmons. Then again, Vanessa herself had reacted strangely to the laundry slip with her name on it. Was it because she thought I didn't believe her story? I needed to talk with her again today.

And Redvers might not like it, but it was entirely plausible that the man Vanessa was looking for and the spy we sought were the very same person. I wouldn't take him off the list of suspects until we had learned something definitive about the man and where he had gone. I caught myself wondering if Redvers had stopped by the telegraph office to check with McIntyre about new messages, then forced my mind away again.

I also needed to spend some time considering what Brubacher and Heinz had to discuss—the scene between them the night before was odd to say the least. Requesting a song from the band leader was one thing, but speaking to him and then walking directly out of the room was entirely another. Was it possible the men were colluding? Could we be looking for more than one person? These were questions I would want to discuss with Redvers if we were speaking to one another.

My face was stinging from the wind, and a dull thrum behind my eyes reminded me that I'd missed out on most of my morning coffee. My stomach rumbled and I realized I hadn't eaten much either. It was time to remedy that. With a sigh I pushed myself up and went back inside the ship, but as I passed by the photography office, I realized that the photographs we'd dropped off were probably ready to be picked up. I paused, then decided that I would stop by on my way back out of the café. I wasn't ready to look through them quite yet, especially since I knew there was at least one of Redvers and me together. My traitorous eyes welled at the thought, and I willed them back under control.

As I turned the corner, I saw Vanessa's maid leaving the café. I opened my mouth to call out to the girl, but something held me back, and I watched instead as Rebecca drifted down the hall and turned the corner. I paused for a moment before following her, despite the grumbling in my stomach. Turning that same corner, I caught a glimpse of her brown wool dress as she strode out onto the first-class deck. Given how nervous she was when she had come to see me before in this area, I was surprised to see her going this way. I waited as she stopped beneath the large funnels, and with a quick glance around, stepped through a doorway marked CREW ONLY. I crept forward and gave her a few moments before following her through.

What was the timid maid doing in the crew area? My foot hit the metal flooring and I could see Rebecca turn another corner. This was obviously not an area where paying passengers were meant to be—the halls were painted white and there was none of the ornamentation or finery that was found in the passenger areas of the ship. This was all utilitarian basics and hard metal.

I peeked around the corner and saw Rebecca knock on a door. After a beat the door opened and she disappeared inside. I was so intent on watching her that I completely missed the sound of footsteps coming up behind me. I felt a hand grasp my elbow just as I took a step forward in the direction of the door.

"Ma'am, you're not allowed in this area." The man's voice was hard and entirely unamused. I looked up to find an officer in uniform gripping my elbow a little harder than was strictly necessary. His brown eyes matched the steel in his voice, and I glanced at his shiny nametag. Benson.

"Oh, I'm terribly sorry. I was just following a friend of mine. I needed to talk with her, and I'm afraid I got a bit turned around." I did my best to appear innocent and lost.

He said nothing, but his unfriendly eyes told me that he wasn't at all taken in by my story. "This area is the crew quarters. You are not allowed in here." He tugged at my elbow, pulling me in the opposite direction from where I wanted to go. I shot a final glance toward where I had seen Rebecca disappear and, with a sigh, allowed the man to physically direct me out of the restricted area. Benson released my arm after a few moments, but followed silently behind me until I was back on the first-class deck.

I threw my act to the wind and simply glared at the man before stalking off toward the café. I was incredibly frustrated that I hadn't learned exactly where Rebecca had gone, but at least I had learned something from Officer Benson— the room she had disappeared into was probably the sleeping quarters for a member of the crew. The question was, who? It may have had nothing to do with Vanessa FitzSimmons, but I was still curious to know whom the girl was meeting.

The café was mostly empty by the time I entered and I was easily able to get a table and a hot cup of coffee. I then ordered a selection of finger sandwiches, which were promptly delivered as well. I inhaled the crustless cucumber and cheese sandwiches, then sat and sipped my coffee, letting the warmth soak into my bones. I felt a little better, although no amount of coffee could touch the chill around my heart. With a sigh I finally put down my empty cup and left the café. I stood awkwardly in the corridor for a moment, not wanting to return to the suite and face Redvers quite yet. I decided to face Mr. Banks in the photography office instead.

"I was beginning to think I would have to send these to your room," Banks said by way of greeting.

"I've been busy," I told the man, watching him shuffle through a stack of envelopes thick with photographs.

"I took a look at what you photographed while I was developing them. You have an eye for this, young lady."

Despite the trials of the day, I felt myself warm a bit at the compliment. I'd never even thought of taking up a hobby like photography, but perhaps it was something to think about for the future.

"I'm sure you say that to all the guests."

Banks snorted. "Hardly." He handed over my envelope and I let it drop to my side. Banks cocked his head. "You aren't going to look at them now?"

"I'd rather do it when I have some time to look at them properly." I couldn't think of a better excuse. But I certainly didn't want to peruse them with anyone around in case my eyes began leaking again.

"That busy, huh?" Banks's voice was wry and I narrowed my eyes at him. He put his hands up. "I'm just asking."

I regarded him for a moment longer before I gave the packet in my hand a little wave. "Thanks for these." We'd already eliminated him as a suspect, so there didn't seem to be any use in trying to strike up further conversation.

He gave me an absentminded salute as he flipped through the other envelopes in the box, before stowing it beneath the counter. I left the office and wandered back out onto the deck, trying to ignore the packet in my hand.

CHAPTER NINETEEN

Icollapsed back into my chair, setting the packet of photographs on the table beside me and pulling the rug back over my legs. I was still turning over the events of the morning when I saw Redvers from the corner of my eye, approaching my chair. My entire body tensed for battle, and beneath my rug I gripped the arms of my seat. I was afraid that I would begin crying again if I looked at him, so I kept my eyes on the unrelenting gray water before me. I felt more than saw him sit down next to me. Neither of us said anything for several minutes, and I could feel the tension building until I was afraid it would explode out of me—probably with my saying something I would immediately regret.

"I've come to explain."

I deflated a little and almost asked if he meant he'd come to apologize, which I felt certain he should be doing, but instead I kept my mouth shut. I gave my head a small nod for him to go ahead without looking at him.

He took a deep breath. "My brother was a liar. A prolific one."

This was not at all what I had expected to hear. My brow furrowed and I forgot my resolve not to look at him. I turned my head slightly and found him staring out over the horizon just as I had been for several hours.

"It began when we were very young, and initially was mostly innocent. Broken vases and who had left the front door open. I always took the blame, and as much as I protested that it was Percival who did it, I was always the one who was punished." I opened my mouth to exclaim, but he continued on. "Not for what had happened, but for lying." Redvers shook his head. "As we got older, things got worse. He got a certain thrill from kicking my dog when no one was looking. Once he started a fire in our cellar and it was only because our housekeeper was so quick on her feet that the entire house didn't go up in flames."

"Were you blamed for all of this as well?" I suspected there was much more to the story that he was keeping back, but I wouldn't press him on it. Not now, anyway.

He shrugged. "Some of it. Not all of it. I had learned by then not to bother arguing. My mother, you see, thought Percival was her golden boy. Her oldest. And in her eyes, he could do no wrong."

As angry and hurt as I was, my heart broke for the little boy Redvers had once been.

"And every time Percival lied, my mother believed him. He had the woman completely charmed."

"What about your father?"

"He was indifferent to all of us. He had his work with . . . well, the government, and that was all he was concerned about."

I turned fully in my chair to face Redvers. "That must have been a lonely childhood."

He shrugged again, eyes still on the choppy ocean. I could tell that he was trying to be cavalier about the whole thing, but it seemed to me that Redvers carried his own scars from the past. "I had my dog. We spent a lot of time outdoors, or hiding in the library."

"Then what happened?"

DANGER ON THE ATLANTIC   123

"I moved out of the house as soon as I was able and I took my dog—Mr. Jones—with me. Percival stuck around, but he finally did something he couldn't deny. He started a brawl at his club and knocked out Lord Wollsey's front teeth. My father told him his only option was to join the military to sort himself out. He did." Redvers grimaced. "And he did well for a time. But the war came about and eventually Percival saw more value in selling secrets to the Germans than he did in loyalty to his men or his country."

I gave a little involuntary gasp and Redvers finally looked over at me, his eyes sad. "I think I mentioned before that my brother was shot by his own men." I nodded. "They learned what he was doing and took it upon themselves to eliminate the problem. He was such an effective liar they didn't want him to go to trial and somehow manage to wriggle out of it."

"That's terrible." Although I wasn't sure which part I was referring to. Truthfully, it sounded as though Percival had gotten exactly what was coming to him. And though I didn't necessarily support such vigilante justice, I could certainly understand the impulse. Especially when someone was an effective liar and managed to get away with things time and again.

Redvers paused for a moment, looking out over the water, then back at me. "I have a hard time with liars. And I thought perhaps you were being taken in by one, like my mother was taken in by my brother for all those years. Vanessa has the same sort of air about her that Percival did when he was spinning one of his tales."

His anger and reluctance for me to get involved with Vanessa FitzSimmons suddenly made sense. And I also had a much better understanding of why he rarely spoke about his family—or used their last name. "Dibble" must have had nothing but bad memories associated with it.

But Redvers wasn't finished. "I should have trusted you,

though. I should have trusted that your instincts are better than my mother's were. And even if Vanessa is lying to you, you won't die of a broken heart."

"Is that what happened to your mother?"

He gave a short nod, and I reached over and grasped his hand, giving it a squeeze. "I'm sorry."

"So am I." His voice was quiet.

It was time for me to do some explaining of my own. "When you didn't believe me," I said slowly, "it reminded me of when I was married to Grant."

Redvers didn't ask the question aloud, but his dark eyes did as he threaded his fingers through mine.

"Grant was so charming on the surface that I thought no one would believe me about what kinds of . . . things . . . were going on at home." I had already explained to Redvers the kind of physical and emotional torture I had survived at the hands of my deceased husband.

Redvers squeezed my hand and murmured, "I'm sorry."

"When I saw that no one would believe Vanessa about what was happening to her . . . I just couldn't let it go. Especially since I did see the man. It reminded me too much of when no one would believe *me*." I shook my head, then turned my thoughts back to Redvers' brother and my deceased husband. "Both of us have had our share of charming liars."

"I hadn't thought of it that way before, but you're right."

We were both quiet for a moment, our fingers still entwined.

Redvers squeezed my hand again. "I promise that I will trust your instincts from now on, Jane."

"Even if they're wrong?"

"Well, we can discuss that when the occasion arises. But it will be a discussion."

I nodded, then took a deep breath. "Well, no time like the present." It was time to tell him everything I had learned and see if he reacted the way he had just promised he would. Plunging in, I explained about the discrepancies between what the steward said he had seen and what Rebecca had come on deck to tell me.

"And she sought you out to tell you this?" Redvers' brow was furrowed with thought.

"Yes. And the steward refused to say whether he had seen a husband—even after he admitted to the trunks."

"Which makes me think he had seen Van de Meter, but is being paid to say nothing."

"Exactly."

Then I explained the rest: the missing clothing, the phantom phone calls, and Rebecca's trip into the restricted crew area.

Redvers was quiet for a moment. "What do you make of Vanessa?"

I thought carefully about my answer, especially given what Redvers had just shared with me about his brother. "I will admit that she is difficult to make out. Sometimes she seems genuinely upset that her husband has gone missing, and sometimes she's very cavalier about it all." This was probably what had bothered Redvers so much about the woman. In part, at least. "But I don't think she's lying. I think much of her attitude has to do with the fact that they didn't know each other for very long before getting married—how attached to a person can you be after only a few weeks?"

Redvers turned his head to gaze into my eyes. "I would say that depends on the people. And what they have gone through together in that time."

I knew he was referring to our escapades in Egypt and again in the countryside of England. My throat tightened up a bit, so I cleared it and continued on. I could examine those feelings later.

Much later. I was already overrun with emotions and needed some time to untangle them.

"I think that's part of it. But I also think she's putting up a very good front. I think Vanessa really is bothered by what's happening, she just doesn't want to show it." I cocked my head, considering. "I don't think she's the type of woman to get hysterical at the first sign of trouble. But I will say her reaction to the laundry slip with her name on it was strange. As well as the fact that she didn't mention it to me immediately—the only reason I discovered that her clothing was missing at all is that I searched her room for her."

Redvers nodded. "It sounds as though something strange is going on."

I agreed.

"And what I learned from the last message I received is only going to add to that," Redvers said.

I barely let him catch a breath. "What is it?"

He smiled at my eagerness before becoming serious again. "They haven't been able to find anything about the man."

I blew out a breath. I'd hoped it was something much more exciting than simply an utter lack of information.

"Will they keep looking?"

"Of course. I instructed them to widen their search."

I always wondered who the shadowy "they" were that Redvers referred to, but I knew better than to ask. "They haven't found anything. But I did see the man. We know that he exists, despite what Rebecca tried to tell me." I frowned and related to Redvers about how I'd broken into the photography office at night and found the pictures of Van de Meter hiding his face. Redvers didn't seem at all surprised about my nighttime exploits.

"You're right. It's strange that a man newly married would hide his face for photos with his new bride. Or that he'd even be aware they were being taken." Redvers squeezed my hand. "Perhaps you were right to add him to our list of suspects. We still need to eliminate Naumann and Brubacher, but a man who disappears on board and is hiding from photographers is suspicious."

"But it's going to be nearly impossible to find out anything about the man if we don't even know where he is," I said in frustration. "It's really too bad the captain and his crew weren't interested in helping. I doubt they actually searched the ship."

"That's also strange, actually. The captain of the ship is responsible for everyone on board. Ordinarily I would have thought a thorough search was the first thing he would have ordered."

I was relieved to hear his opinion on the captain's complete lack of interest in a missing man. "You admit that it's unusual?"

He nodded. "Captain Bisset was very unhelpful, and it's not the reaction I would have expected."

"What do we know about him?"

"How do you know I know anything?"

I rolled my eyes. "I'm certain you've already done your homework."

A little smile teased Redvers' lips and I matched it with one of my own, relieved that things were moving back toward normal. My fingers tightened on his involuntarily, and he gave a little squeeze in return.

"He was commander of a smaller ship during the war. He had an injury to his thumb, of all things, that kept him on-shore for a few days while it was treated. During that time his ship was attacked by a U-boat and the entire thing went down, including the crew."

"That's awful!"

Redvers nodded. "I think he feels a fair amount of guilt that he didn't go down with it."

I considered that. It would explain why the man was a bit gruffer than one would expect—in addition to being in charge of the entire ship, a captain was generally expected to entertain and hobnob with the wealthy guests. To some degree, at least. Captain Bisset seemed unwilling to be that type of captain, but perhaps it was because he had already lost an entire crew of people. It would make anyone want to keep their distance from those around them. Although that kind of tragedy still didn't explain his reluctance to search for Vanessa's missing husband.

With a flash, I recalled what I had seen when we docked briefly in Cherbourg. I reached for the packet of photos and began flipping through them.

"What is it?" Redvers' eyes were alight with interest.

I found the photo I was looking for and passed it over to him. "This."

"When did you take this?"

"When we were docked at Cherbourg. Isn't it odd for a captain to be receiving an envelope from someone on the dock? Not to mention that he was out there himself to supervise the loading of all that luggage. It seems like something he would have delegated to one of his officers."

Redvers studied the photograph. "This is definitely out of the ordinary." He looked up, tapping the photo against his palm. "And it might explain why he's not willing to tear the ship apart."

I cocked my head in question.

"That's an awful lot of luggage." He squinted at the photo again. "And a thick envelope."

I nodded. "That is precisely what I thought at the time. And not very many passengers boarding."

"I doubt it's only clothes in there. Or even household goods."

Realization dawned. "You think he's smuggling?"

Redvers shrugged. "Alcohol is quite the commodity where we are headed. He might just be looking the other way and someone else is shipping it."

It would explain the envelope—probably full of cash. And why Bisset didn't want anyone looking too closely at the ship.

Redvers tucked the picture back into the envelope and slipped it into his jacket.

I raised an eyebrow. "I wasn't finished looking at those, you know."

He grinned. "I'll give them back. But in the meantime, I think we should put them in a very safe space. You never know when we might need them."

I definitely liked the sound of that "we."

"What is our next step with Mrs. FitzSimmons?" he asked.

I held my breath for a moment. Now it was an "our." Things were sounding better and better. "Then you'll help me?"

Redvers' handsome face broke into a smile, his one dimple peeking out, and my heart skipped a beat. "Always."

The feeling of relief that Redvers and I were back on the same team was nearly overwhelming—I could feel it rushing in my blood all the way down to my fingers and toes. I wasn't sure what else might happen between us or where Redvers would spend the rest of his nights during this crossing, but at least we were back in step. That was what mattered most.

Upon further discussion, we decided to divide and conquer. Redvers would hunt down Vanessa's steward and try to get some straight answers from the man. There was no doubt in my mind Redvers would be more persuasive than Dobbins, although just how much more persuasive had yet to be seen. After that task, Redvers would speak with the ship captain and try to get a sense of what the crew had actually done to find Miles Van de Meter. I didn't think he would make much progress in that department.

My plan was to talk with Vanessa and see why she had reacted so strangely to that laundry slip. Then I would try to learn anything she knew about Miles's life before she met him—perhaps there was a clue we could use to find out where he'd come from. I would also try to learn whom her maid was meeting down in the crew quarters—it might be entirely unrelated, but the girl's behavior had raised my suspicions.

Redvers and I agreed that we could not neglect our other duties in favor of chasing this lead, so we needed to figure out what Brubacher and Naumann had talked about the night before and whether we could eliminate either of the men as our spy for the German government. Redvers said he would search their rooms again, and for once, I didn't argue that I should be included.

But I still had no idea how to find Miles Van de Meter. And since we had stopped at the port in Cherbourg, was he even still on board?

CHAPTER TWENTY

Iscanned the common rooms on the ship for Vanessa, feeling one hundred pounds lighter. Redvers and I had parted on a kiss, and it felt as though nothing could bring my feet back down to the ground.

I was wrong.

Seeing Vanessa in none of the cafés or lounges on board, I headed down to her suite. I knew she preferred to spend her time out and about, but before I searched the gymnasium and the Turkish bath, I decided to try her cabin first. And there I found her, standing in the hallway, in absolute hysterics. I almost didn't know how to respond; it was the first time I had seen her upset despite all the unusual things happening to her. Two men stood with her, trying their best to keep her quiet. One I recognized from the other night—Dr. Montgomery. The other was the first mate, none other than Officer Benson. The same Officer Benson who had escorted me none too politely from the crew area just hours ago. His presence didn't bode well for either Vanessa or me.

"But this one is my room. I swear it is. My key won't work now, but this is my room. It's where I've been staying this whole time." Vanessa's voice was choked and her face was a veil of tears.

I stepped up and put my hand on Vanessa's arm and she

looked as though she might collapse in relief. "Oh, Jane," she said on a sob.

Both men flicked a glance at me before turning their attention back to Vanessa.

"Mrs. FitzSimmons, if we could just go inside and discuss this, instead of talking about it out here." Dr. Montgomery's voice was low and soothing.

This made the woman more hysterical. "But we can't! My key doesn't work! That's why I brought you down here in the first place." She was brandishing the key like a sword, and the doctor reached out and gently took it from her. He turned the key over in his hand and brought it closer to his face, examining it. He gave his head a little shake, then walked down the corridor to the next cabin and put the key into the lock. It turned easily and he pushed the door in.

"It does work. Let's go inside."

Vanessa's tears stopped as she looked back and forth in astonishment between the two rooms. I was also surprised— when I had visited her, the door we stood in front of was the room she was staying in—room C41. She looked to me for confirmation.

"No, *this* is the room you were in," I said in a low voice, pointing at the door we stood before. "But let's take a look."

She shook her head but followed me to room C43, where the men had already gone inside. As we stepped into the room, I could see that all of her things were set up just as they had been in the room next door, although this room was the mirror image—all the furniture was placed backward.

"Am I going mad?" Vanessa whispered behind me.

I shook my head, but didn't say anything. It was too bizarre to be believed. I peeked my head into the bedroom and found the same thing there—Vanessa's things were present, but the décor in this room was wildly different than it had been in her previous bedroom. I checked the closet and found a few items of clothing hanging at one end. Not all of her clothes had been returned from the laundry yet, obviously, which made the move that much easier for whoever had done the switch. In fact, I wondered if it was the reason for the trick in the first place.

I returned to the sitting room and found that the men had seated themselves in the upholstered chairs and Benson was gesturing for Vanessa to take a seat on the sofa. Wringing her hands, she was about to acquiesce, but I held her back for a moment. Benson looked entirely irritated, but I ignored him and turned my body to shield Vanessa from his view.

"Where were you today? When did you leave your room this morning?" I hoped my voice was low enough that the men couldn't hear me.

Vanessa reached out and grabbed my hand, her watery eyes red and sad, but no longer leaking fresh tears. "You believe me?"

I nodded.

She blew out a breath in relief but kept her grip on me. "I left after breakfast and spent some time swimming in the pool. I like to swim laps." She thought for a second. "Then I went to the Turkish bath for a few hours to relax." Her eyes welled up again. "When I came back my key wouldn't work."

One of the men cleared his throat and I gave my head a little shake. "Where were your things when you were swimming? Or when you were in the bath?"

"The attendant had them."

I nodded, then gestured with my head that we could join them. I sat next to Vanessa on the small sofa and Benson started in.

"Miss FitzSimmons."

"Mrs. FitzSimmons," Vanessa told him. I squeezed her hand in encouragement.

The officer continued as if she hadn't spoken. "Miss Fitz-Simmons, we're a little concerned. All of your things appear to be here in this room." He gestured at the few personal items scattered around.

"It looks like you were simply confused about your room number. Perhaps you need some rest. The doctor would be happy to help you out with that." Benson gave the doctor a meaningful look that set my teeth on edge.

"Look," I started to say, but was quickly cut off.

"We aren't asking you." Benson narrowed his eyes at me. "And don't think I've forgotten where I found you wandering this morning. You keep turning up where you don't belong—I'm starting to think I need to make a report to the captain."

"What is he talking about, Jane?" When I shook my head, Vanessa became visibly upset again. "Mrs. Wunderly saw me in room C41. That's where my things were. Someone has moved my things."

I nodded my vehement agreement, but kept my mouth shut this time. I inwardly cursed myself for not having taken a picture of her room while I still had the camera. If I had, we would at least have photographic evidence.

Both men looked at us somewhat sadly, as though we'd made up this story—or were living some kind of shared fantasy. "That seems very unlikely, Mrs. FitzSimmons." At least the doctor had extended the courtesy of addressing her correctly. Benson didn't seem to believe that the woman was married at all. "I agree with Officer Benson here. What you need is some rest." He reached into the small black bag at his feet and pulled out a little paper packet. I assumed—or at least hoped—it held a sleeping powder such as Veronal and nothing more nefarious. He stood and crossed to the bathroom, soon returning with a cloudy glass of water that he was stirring with a small spoon.

I looked at Vanessa and shook my head. "You don't need to take that."

The doctor paused before us. "You don't, Mrs. FitzSimmons. But I really recommend that you do. It will make you feel worlds better." He'd obviously honed his soothing tone over the years, because it had the desired effect.

Vanessa paused for only a moment before slowly reaching her hand out and accepting the glass. She turned and gave me a small, sad smile. "I haven't been sleeping well. Perhaps I *should* get some rest, Jane."

I hated the sound of defeat in her voice. It reinforced my spine with steel.

"Gentlemen, I am going to help her to bed. Then could we speak outside?" The tone of my voice brooked no argument, although I wasn't sure either of them would actually comply with my request. Dr. Montgomery at least gave me a nod before both he and Benson left the suite. I followed Vanessa into her bedroom and got her settled into bed, fully clothed. Her bloodshot eyes closed immediately, but not before she muttered a soft, "I'm sorry." I wasn't sure what she was apologizing for, but I felt certain it was the men in the hallway who should be feeling sorry.

When I stepped outside, Officer Benson started in immediately. "Your 'friend' is very ill, miss."

"It's Mrs.," I nearly growled at him, my fists balled at my sides. I was surprised Benson had bothered waiting to speak with me and I found myself regretting that he had.

He seemed unfazed. "Very well, *Mrs.*" He shrugged and continued. "I think it's best if she is confined to her cabin for a few days. We can't have her upsetting the other guests, so we will leave her under the doctor's care." Benson looked at Montgomery, who gave a small nod.

"She wasn't lying. I met with her in the suite next door and all her things were there."

The men exchanged a glance. "I think maybe you're just confused about the numbers. This room, C43, is obviously

Miss FitzSimmons's suite. Maybe you should get some rest too, ma'am." Benson's face twisted with a nasty smirk. "I'm sure the doctor has plenty of powder in his bag."

I had never wanted to inflict physical violence on two grown men so much as I did at that moment. But I also knew that if I continued with my protests, I might find myself drugged up to the eyeballs and socked away in my own bed without any say in the matter. Instead, I smiled tightly and walked away.

This wasn't over. Not by a long shot.

CHAPTER TWENTY-ONE

My fury had barely receded by the time I reached our suite. I pushed inside, closed the door, then proceeded to pace the few open feet in the room, waiting for Redvers to return. There had to be something we could do—someone we could convince—that Vanessa wasn't unbalanced. Because it was obvious to me that someone was doing their best to make her look that way.

I also wanted to know what he had learned from his interviews, but Vanessa's immediate safety had taken precedence in my mind.

It felt like an eternity before I heard the key in the lock. I stopped for a moment and watched him enter before continuing my tiny track. "I'm glad you're back."

He paused inside the room, eyes tracking my movements before quietly shutting the door behind him and leaning back against it. "I take it your chat with Mrs. FitzSimmons didn't go well."

Without missing a beat, I stopped and described finding Vanessa in the hallway with the doctor and Officer Benson.

With a frown he crossed the room and gently took my arm, leading me to the upholstered chair. With a sigh I dropped into it; now that Redvers was here I felt the rage starting to drain from my veins, leaving nothing but a deep sense of weariness in its place.

"Tell me again." Redvers took one of the chairs from the table and flipped it around, then sat facing me. He leaned forward, elbows on knees.

I explained everything again, more slowly this time. I finished with, "I got the feeling that if I stayed much longer, I would find myself drugged and tucked into bed as well." I shook my head. "Not just a feeling. It was definitely a threat."

Redvers leaned back in his chair, looking distinctly uncomfortable. "I don't like it."

"Which part?"

"Any of it. Do you know anything about Vanessa's background? Does she have a history of insanity in her family?"

My face twisted. Was he doubting my judgment again? Just when I thought we had settled the matter? But before I could say anything, he raised a hand.

"No, I'm not changing my mind. And I'm not suggesting she's fit for the asylum either. Not yet, anyway. But I'm wondering if there's a family history that someone might be monopolizing on."

My shoulders relaxed and I nodded. "I don't know of anything, but I'll add it to the list of things I need to ask her about." I grimaced. "Whenever she wakes up. Who knows how much sleeping powder he gave her."

Redvers' face mirrored my own frustration. "I'm afraid I don't have much to report either. I found her steward, but when he realized what I wanted to talk with him about, he abruptly turned and left without a word. I didn't even have a chance to offer him some cash in exchange." He shook his head. "And the captain was occupied with other matters. Almost as though he was trying to avoid me."

"I'm not surprised, I guess."

"But he won't be able to for long. I had Dobbins add us to his table for tonight."

"I doubt he'll be happy to see us." I smiled at Redvers. "But well done. He'll be a captive audience."

We were both quiet for a moment, before Redvers spoke again. "Of course, we can't lose sight of what we originally came here for."

I agreed. As wrapped up in Vanessa FitzSimmons's troubles as I had become, as well as the indignities of being threatened by some crew members, we had other tasks to attend to. "I'll go on deck in a moment and see if Naumann is around."

Redvers nodded. "If he is, I'll take a look at his room. Of course, I'll have to wait until tonight to look at Brubacher's quarters, when he's busy with the band." Redvers' eyes lit with mischief. "And while I'm doing that, perhaps you can get Naumann to dance with you again. If you step on enough of his toes, he just might break and tell us everything."

I stuck my tongue out at him. His response was to throw his head back and laugh.

Since there were still several hours until dinner, I took a stroll around the public areas of the boat, but saw no sign of Heinz Naumann. I also took a turn past Vanessa's room, but there was no answer at my knock there—I assumed she was still out cold.

Frustrated, I went out and paced the decks until it was time to dress for dinner. I didn't find anyone that I needed or wanted to talk to, but I also managed to avoid Officer Benson, so I counted that as a positive. And I felt refreshed after getting some exercise—it had been an excellent opportunity to get my thoughts in order and work off my frustration.

We dressed for dinner, putting on our evening finery, Redvers in his sharp black tuxedo and myself in a fitted navy silk dress with a high-cut back but a plunging neckline covered in lace. It was a little more daring than I was used to, but I could tell from the sparkle in his eyes—and the fiery kiss he greeted me with—that Redvers appreciated how I was turned out.

The captain's table was still empty as we were the first to arrive. Redvers quickly switched the name cards next to the captain's seat with our own while I kept watch. "You're not going to like who our dinner companions are tonight," he whispered as he helped me into my newly assigned seat.

I didn't have time to ask who that might be before a voice boomed out to greet us.

"Excellent! Mr. and Mrs. Wunderly! I'm so glad you're joining us this evening." Eloise Baumann was cutting a path toward our table as her sister and brother-in-law trailed in her substantial wake. My first instinct was to cover my face and moan, but instead I gritted my teeth and greeted our dinner companions with as much equanimity as I had available.

"We aren't going to be able to ask Captain Bisset anything," I whispered testily to Redvers. He simply shook his head sadly and took his seat across from me.

Eloise looked at the seating layout. "How strange. I asked to be seated next to the captain specifically. But they couldn't even get *that* right." I held my breath for a moment, but she took her seat without asking me to move. "It really is hard to get good staff these days. I'm always telling Margret that, aren't I, sister?"

Margret didn't bother to answer, but her husband rolled his eyes and gestured to the nearest waiter. I assumed he was looking for a drink to refill the empty glass he held in his hand, and I regretted that I needed to keep my wits about me tonight—I was already feeling the need for a drink as well.

Captain Bisset joined us just as Eloise was winding up with her next lecture. "My apologies for my tardiness. I had a matter to attend to." His gruff demeanor had been smoothed out and he sounded more like what one would expect from a ship captain. Although when he looked around at all of us, his eyes narrowed slightly as they passed over me. I did my best to smile demurely. "Thank you all for joining me this evening. I hope you all know one another? Mr. and Mrs. Dibble were last minute additions to our party."

Eloise's big voice laughed. "Who are the Dibbles? What a silly name. No, Captain Bisset, I'm afraid you're incorrect. These are the Wunderlys. Mr. and Mrs. Wunderly." She said my last name slowly and loudly, as though she were talking to a small child—it was all I could do not to laugh aloud at the expression on the captain's face.

Bisset looked to Redvers and then to me, clearly expecting one of us to come to his rescue and explain that he was, in fact, correct. But Redvers and I smiled politely and refused to say anything. I was keeping quiet simply to be contrary, but Redvers looked as though he was genuinely enjoying himself.

The captain cleared his throat. "My apologies. I must have been mistaken." This was directed more to Redvers than it was to me, and Redvers shrugged cheerfully.

Redvers never used his last name unless absolutely necessary, and everyone so far had referred to us as the Wunderlys, so I wondered where the captain had seen "Dibble" listed. Had he looked us up in the ship records before coming to dinner? Was Redvers' real name used there? It was something I would have to ask him about later.

Bisset took his seat and Eloise started in on a long diatribe about the entertainment—or lack thereof—on board the ship for such a discerning woman as herself. I knew there were any number of activities for passengers to take part in, from indoor swimming to a gymnasium to the well-stocked library. None of these seemed sufficient for Eloise, however, and she was going to let the captain know. In detail. The rest of us quietly ate our dinners.

"You'll have to distract her if we are to have any chance of asking the captain anything," Redvers whispered to me.

"What's that you're saying over there? Come, come. Share with the table."

I thought quickly. "Redvers and I were just wondering what kind of activities you enjoyed at home, Eloise. You must have many hobbies."

Eloise beamed and focused on me as she began enumerating the many charities she engaged with. Apparently, Eloise was a prolific knitter and provided socks and mittens to a great number of deserving people.

"The colors aren't always the most desirable, but it's whatever is cheapest as far as yarn is concerned." At this, Margret pulled a face that Eloise couldn't see, and I had to wonder just how awful the items were that she was churning out. "They are grateful for whatever they can get, of course," Eloise said.

I had serious doubts as to whether that was true.

In the meantime, Redvers had casually turned to his left and was asking the captain some questions in low tones. He was circumspect enough that Eloise didn't call him out for "not sharing with the table."

He was going to owe me one.

My eyes glazed over as I continued nodding at Eloise. Her relations had plowed through their meals and then through their desserts as if they were being paid to do so. The last bites of a chocolate soufflé were disappearing into Douglas Gould's mouth when Eloise noticed that Redvers was monopolizing the captain's time.

"Well. Captain Bisset, I do hope you'll take to heart everything I've shared with you tonight." Eloise leaned partially across me to ensure she was both seen and heard.

The man scratched his short beard and forced a chuckle. "Of course, of course. But I do hope you'll participate in the on-board activities this evening. I believe there are going to be some parlor games in the lounge."

Eloise reclined back into her seat with a sniff, but said she would attempt to enjoy herself.

The coffee had barely hit the cups when Redvers took the opportunity to cut our evening with the Goulds short once again. "You'll excuse us, but we have some business to attend to with the captain," Redvers said, getting to his feet.

I glanced at the captain, who looked slightly surprised, but quickly nodded in agreement as he pushed back from the table and stood. I suspected he would agree to anything if it meant leaving Eloise behind. I placed my napkin on the table and joined Redvers.

Eloise raised both her eyebrows. "I do hope everything is all right." Douglas looked resigned to their fate, but for once Margret looked aggrieved. I wondered why this time was different.

"Oh, yes. Nothing to concern yourself with." Redvers gave her a bright smile, his hand on my lower back, already ushering me away. "We'll see you again soon. A pleasure as always."

This last was said over his shoulder as we hurriedly followed the captain out of the dining room.

We traveled down the long corridor away from the dining hall and up a stairway to the next deck. Captain Bisset moved ahead of us to take the stairs and I took the opportunity to whisper to Redvers, "How did you get him to agree to talk to us? Did you blackmail him?"

"No, we're saving that."

I was dying of curiosity, but further questions would have to wait.

We went out onto the deck, then made our way through the navigation office, where shiny brass gadgets and gauges adorned every possible space, before we were ushered into the captain's office beyond.

"Well, I'm not sure what that was about, but I do appreciate the out." Bisset crossed the room to his desk. "I suppose I can return the favor."

Redvers nodded briskly.

"As I told you before, Mr. Wunderly, the man isn't on our manifest." There was a pause as a reminder that the captain suspected Redvers' name was something other than Wunderly. But instead of bringing that issue up again, Bisset sat behind his desk and turned, opening a small safe behind him. He pulled out a large docket of papers as I shot a questioning look at Redvers. He gave his head a little shake.

"See for yourself."

Redvers took the packet and flipped through the pages until he came to the listing for Vanessa FitzSimmons. I stood slightly behind him, looking over his shoulder. His finger traced a line beneath her name. It stated that she was traveling solo, but had reserved two full suites: C41 and C43.

Both of the rooms that I had seen her in.

Redvers looked at the captain. "It doesn't say how these were paid for."

Bisset shook his head. "No, but after the issues with her suites this afternoon, I spoke with the purser's office. They were both paid for in cash." That was unfortunate—if it had been a bank draft, we could have tracked whose account the payment had come from.

"Is it usual for one person to book two suites?"

The captain gave me a sharp look, but he answered. "No. Especially not someone traveling alone. And you can see she also has the shared room in second class for her maid, so that is three rooms in total. The only other thing I know is that they were all booked at the same time."

I looked at the next line in the log, and saw that he was correct—the room for Rebecca Tesch was listed as well. My mind was reeling. According to this, Vanessa FitzSimmons was traveling alone and always had been. Why would she have booked two suites for herself? It seemed impossible to book three rooms without knowing you were doing so.

I had a moment of worry that Redvers had been right all along and I was being taken in by an exceptionally skilled liar. But that worry quickly dissipated. The woman's fear and confusion about the location of her suite had been entirely genuine—not even Lillian Gish could have pulled off such a convincing performance. And Vanessa had taken the sleeping draught the doctor gave her without a fight. A woman only playacting would be unlikely to submit to being drugged, wouldn't she?

Which led me to wonder whether her missing husband could have set this up without her knowledge. It seemed the only plausible explanation—although it still didn't explain what had happened to the man, or what kind of game he was playing. And booking the second suite in advance made it seem that this was a game that had been planned out well in advance of the ship ever leaving Southampton.

Redvers had other questions for the captain. "And the search of the ship?"

"We took a cursory look around, but that is normal procedure when we sail to ensure we don't have stowaways." The captain shrugged. "There was no one aboard who wasn't registered on that list."

Redvers thanked Bisset and we took our leave. As soon as the door closed behind us, Redvers pulled me around the corner onto the deserted promenade. I shivered as the cold air hit my skin and I pulled my shrug closer. A light fog drifted around the ship, shrouding us in mist. We stopped and Redvers listened for a minute, but there was no one about.

"Is your last name listed on the manifest?" I asked.

Redvers shook his head. "We are listed as Mr. and Mrs. Wunderly. I'm not sure how he learned about the name Dibble." Redvers thought for a moment. "Unless he was somehow tipped off about our mission here on board."

"I don't know what to think. About any of it." I kept my voice low despite the fact that we were quite alone.

Redvers' eyes scanned the foggy corridor behind me, his mind obviously working. "When you saw Vanessa today and her key didn't work, how did she seem?"

I had already given this question real thought. "She seemed scared and I don't think that was faked. She truly didn't seem to know what was happening. And she took the sleeping draught Montgomery gave her without a fight."

He nodded, hands resting lightly on my upper arms, and gazed into my eyes. "I trust your instincts. Don't you start doubting them now."

I recognized the irony of the tables having been turned, but didn't feel the need to point it out.

"Something very strange is going on here," Redvers said.

"Well, that much is certain. But what are we going to do about it?"

"For now, you and I are going to the lounge for a drink. And later I'm going to have Dobbins do some more poking around, see what he can turn up."

I had my doubts that Dobbins would turn up anything useful, but I couldn't argue with it being time for a drink.

CHAPTER TWENTY-TWO

We headed to the first-class lounge, where I could see that the band was setting up for the evening. Redvers ordered our drinks at the bar while I scanned the crowd. There was no one I recognized—of course, I hadn't met many other travelers other than Naumann and the Goulds, and Eloise and her sister were most likely spending their evening in the dining lounge where the captain had said the entertainment was being held. They were welcome to it.

Redvers brought our drinks to the small table I managed to snag near the back. Even in a large room full of people it felt somewhat private, but perhaps that was because I was the recipient of Redvers' warm and undivided attention. My cheeks flushed a bit under his thoughtful gaze, but I took a sip of my gin rickey and pointed my thoughts toward the issue at hand. I had the opportunity to run through some questions with Redvers and I was going to use it.

"If Vanessa's husband was never on the manifest, how was he on board at all when we left?"

"That's a good question. But I think the first thing we need to establish is who made the travel arrangements. You'll have to ask Vanessa about that when she wakes up. It's entirely possible that Van de Meter made them in her name."

"That would make sense. It would explain her confusion about the rooms." I sipped at my drink. "And it would mean that he planned this from the very beginning. But where is he? Neither she nor I have seen him anywhere on board. I know the crew haven't exactly done a thorough job of searching for the man, but I think he would have been found by *someone* if he was stowed away somewhere."

"I think you're correct there. It's likely he would have been discovered by now."

"Unless he was staying in the other suite," I said. It would have been the perfect hiding place, especially if Vanessa didn't know both suites were in her name.

Redvers and I exchanged a long look. "But now that we know about it, he can't use that room anymore. So where would he have gone?" We were obviously going to search the suite Vanessa had been moved out of, and the man had to realize the room would eventually be looked at once Vanessa's things were moved. To complete the ruse, the other room had to appear completely unoccupied.

"Unless he got off when we docked at Cherbourg. But wouldn't someone have seen him?"

"The docks are awfully busy. It's possible that he could have slipped away. But I agree. It's unlikely that no one saw him disembark."

"And then who moved her things from one suite to another? I can't imagine her maid pulling off such a ruse. And why would she?"

Redvers nodded. "Unless she's being paid to do so. But if he is no longer on board, she would have been paid in advance, with little incentive to go through with such a cruel trick. Not if she wants to keep her job."

I sighed. "And the girl did mention that she needs to send money back to her mother and siblings. I don't think she can afford to lose this position." I considered what else I knew about Rebecca Tesch. "I'm not sure if she'll admit to anything if I confront her—although she's not a terribly good liar. I think I'll be able to tell if she's giving me the truth." I cocked my head. "Perhaps I should take a look around her room as well."

Redvers raised a brow. "That will be difficult since she has a roommate."

I'd forgotten that detail.

"I can add it to the list of things for Dobbins to take care of," Redvers said.

"Poor Dobbins," I sighed. "We're keeping him awfully busy. I doubt he has even a moment to himself between his actual duties and all the things we're asking him to do."

Redvers gave a small shrug. "I think he can manage. And he's being well compensated for his troubles."

"Did your people put him here? Or was he already working on the ship?" I'd nearly forgotten to inquire before.

"He's one of ours that we placed here."

"He seems so young," I mused.

Redvers shook his head without answering that. "I'm hoping in the morning while you're entertaining our . . . friend . . . on deck that I can have a look around that room as well." I knew he didn't want to say Naumann's name out loud on the off chance someone was listening. The bar was noisy and no one was paying us any mind, but better safe than sorry.

"Well, that's one less room for Dobbins to rifle." I sipped at my gin rickey and took the opportunity to gaze around the room. I noticed Heinz standing near the bar and I felt Redvers turn slightly to see what had snagged my attention.

"Speak of the devil."

"And he'll appear," I murmured, still watching Heinz over the top of my glass.

Heinz reached into his inner pocket and I casually put my glass back on the table, keeping my eyes on his hand. After a moment Heinz pulled a small sheaf of folded papers from the pocket, removed one, and replaced the rest in his jacket. I realized I was staring and did my best to casually glance around while still tracking Heinz's movements, although I doubted I was pulling it off. Next to me Redvers appeared to be doing a far better job of pretending disinterest in our quarry. I wondered how he managed it without missing anything.

Heinz tipped his glass back, quickly draining the contents and placing the glass on the bar. As we watched he made his way to the edge of the dance floor where he patiently observed the band play—the paper in his hand was hardly noticeable because of the way he carried it alongside his light-colored trousers. If I hadn't seen the man remove it from his coat, I'm not sure I would have noticed it, although now that I knew it was there I couldn't take my eyes off it. The last few notes of "Gimme a Little Kiss, Will Ya, Huh?" came to a close and Heinz made his way through the dancers to the band leader. I was openly watching by this point, and in my peripheral I could see that Redvers was as well. Heinz tapped the lanky blond man on the shoulder, and after a brief discussion, Heinz passed the paper in his hand to him. With a nod, the musician shuffled the paper into the stack of music on the podium in front of him and Heinz took his leave, meandering back through the crowd to the bar where he immediately ordered another drink.

"Well," I said under my breath. "What do you think that was all about?"

"I don't know, but it looks like I don't need to bother searching Brubacher's room right now."

I nodded. "You'll have to wait until he's had a chance to

secure whatever that was." I turned my gaze to him. "How do you intend to get in there, anyway?"

Redvers' eyes lit with amusement. "I won't have any trouble." My eyes narrowed at the confidence in his tone, and he continued on. "I have a uniform."

I heaved a sigh. "Of course you do."

The next morning I awoke early, thinking I might finally find Redvers still slumbering in bed beside me, but I was once again alone. I had no idea how he functioned on so little sleep.

Although it seemed we had endless days on board, I knew the truth was that our days were limited—it was already Sunday and we would dock on Thursday. I had much to accomplish if we were going to make progress in either of our cases, so I pushed myself out of the comfortable bed to get ready and within a quarter hour joined Redvers in the sitting room for breakfast.

Redvers was still in a robe and casually sipping his tea as I hurried through my toast and eggs. "No one is going to take that away from you, you know," he said. "You could take the time to actually taste it."

"I don't have time this morning." I scalded my tongue on the hot coffee and grimaced, then blew on the surface of the dark brew. "I want to stop by Vanessa's room this morning and see if she's awake before I go on deck and entertain Mr. Naumann." I added a slug of milk to my coffee to cool it down enough that I could bolt it back.

Redvers took another delicate sip and shook his head at me. "I'll discuss things with Dobbins while you do all that."

"Don't strain yourself," I said, eliciting a chuckle from the man. I gave a careless wave behind me as I grabbed my coat and hurried out the door. I saw Dobbins coming down the hall but didn't stop to chat with him. Redvers would both fill the man in and learn if Dobbins had anything to report. I called a quick good morning to our young steward and continued hurrying toward Vanessa's cabin.

There was no answer to my knock at her door and the cabin was securely locked. Actually, both doors were—I also tried the door to Vanessa's original suite on the slim chance Miles Van de Meter would suddenly open it, but there was no answer and nothing but dead silence from the other side.

When repeated knocking—then pounding—on the door to Vanessa's new suite failed to get a response, I heaved a sigh and headed up to the deck. I didn't want to be found breaking into the woman's room. There was entirely too much traffic in the corridors at this time of day to risk picking the lock, since I wasn't as quick as Redvers with the lock-pick set. I made a mental note to work on that when this trip was over.

I was scowling when I approached my chair, although when I caught sight of Heinz sitting and sipping a cup of tea— likely fortified with brandy again—I attempted to smooth my face into a pleasant expression. But I wasn't fast enough to avoid Heinz's observation.

"What is troubling you, Mrs. Wunderly? Is it some further news of your friend?"

I took a breath and blew it out again, feeling my eyebrows knitting together once more. I sat down and pulled the fur rug over myself to block out the brisk wind. "It is. I'm afraid she isn't answering her door this morning."

"Is that all?"

I questioned for a moment how much I should share with the man. It was useful for him to think my thoughts were completely occupied with Vanessa FitzSimmons. But was I being a disloyal friend by sharing too much with a stranger? And a suspected spy at that? Of course, that begged the question of whether Vanessa and I were even friends. The honest answer was no—I was an acquaintance who had personal reasons for my interest in her situation.

All this must have played over my face in some way, because Heinz smiled kindly at me. "I think perhaps it is your imagination getting away from you. You are worried for your friend, so you see trouble everywhere."

I grimaced. "Actually, I think she might be in real trouble." I proceeded to explain what I had seen with the switching of Vanessa's suite and her consequent drugging. Heinz frowned as my story drew to a close, and we were quiet for a moment. From the corner of my eye, I saw Dobbins step out on deck. When he saw us together, he made a show of checking his watch, then did an about-face and headed back inside. I hoped he and Redvers would make quick work of searching Heinz's room while I kept the man occupied. And while I wanted nothing more than to return to Vanessa's suite and bang on the door until someone answered, I now needed to keep Heinz talking.

I glanced at my companion, but it seemed that Heinz was occupied with his flask of brandy, topping off his tea, his face still thoughtful. Hopefully he hadn't noticed Dobbins.

As he slipped his silver container back in his pocket, I forced a smile to my face. "Enough about my friend. Let us talk about more cheerful topics."

The topic of the weather was quickly exhausted, and when I attempted to casually ask about Heinz's family he tensed and sent the volley back with a question about my own family. I chatted about my imaginary sister and our mother— none of it even close to true. I was glad I spent so much time reading fiction; it was easier to create my own on the spot. I only hoped I could remember what stories I had spun if the topic ever came up again.

Time and again, Heinz proved an expert at maneuvering around my subtle probes at the crack in his façade that he had shown the other night regarding his sister. I could not get him to even refer to her again, let alone tell me anything about the woman. I was going to have to put some real time and energy into getting the man to trust me, but I wasn't entirely sure how best to go about it, and I didn't have unlimited time in which to do so. I had to admit that with my attention being pulled into two directions, I was not at my sharpest.

Not that I would ever admit as much to Redvers.

Our conversation fell into a natural lull and I shifted restlessly in my chair. I wasn't getting anywhere with Heinz and I wasn't making any progress in learning what was happening with Vanessa either. The realization made me feel itchy to do something, anything, that would bring me closer to some answers.

"Is something the matter, Mrs. Wunderly?"

"I . . . I was thinking that perhaps I should try Vanessa's room again."

Heinz studied my face for a moment, and I braced myself for some further remarks about my worry being unfounded, but I was surprised once again—perhaps I had changed his mind with the story of her room being switched. "I will come with you."

But this chivalrous offer was the last thing I wanted. "Oh, that isn't necessary." I was already standing and folding my blanket. Once I'd said it out loud I couldn't bear to sit still any longer.

Heinz mimicked my movements, except he casually tossed his blanket onto the chair for someone else to fold and return. "No, it is better for you to have company. I can see that you are truly worried about your friend. And from what you have told me . . . well, I think that something is not right."

I looked at him for a moment before giving my head a little shake. I didn't know how to properly dissuade him from accompanying me. Could I ask Vanessa the questions I needed to ask with Heinz there? And should I be admitting to this man that I was investigating things? But I didn't have time to come up with a convincing excuse before Heinz offered me his arm.

I reluctantly took it. It looked like Heinz was going to meet Vanessa after all.

CHAPTER TWENTY-THREE

I directed Naumann to Vanessa's room, the suite where I had helped her into bed the night before. My knock at the door elicited the same response as it had that morning—silence. I put my hand to the doorknob and gave it an absent twist, but this time it turned easily. I stared at it for a moment in surprise before looking up at Heinz.

"It wasn't open when I was here earlier."

"That is not a good sign." A frown creased Heinz's forehead. "I will go first."

I gave a small shrug and let the man precede me into the sitting room. Peering around the doorway, I could see that the room was empty, but the door to the bedroom was closed. Heinz was moving steadily toward the door, so I hurried to catch up, stopping him with a hand to his arm.

"I should go first."

He looked as though he was going to argue, but then gave an abrupt nod, realizing it was more proper for me to enter the woman's bedroom than for him to do so.

"I will be right on the other side of this door if you need me," Heinz said.

I almost rolled my eyes.

The room was dark, the curtains closed tight over the

porthole. I flicked on a light and took in the room at a glance. There was nothing or no one that shouldn't be there, so I poked my head back through the doorway and told Heinz that things were fine before I quietly closed the door behind me. Vanessa was still sound asleep on the bed, a damp patch on the pillow beneath her cheek where she had been drooling. It was a picture at odds with the elegant woman I had seen up until now. I sat next to her on the bed and shook her shoulder.

"Vanessa."

She gave a quiet moan in response but didn't wake up. I picked up a glass on the bedside table and peered at the crusty residue in the bottom. It appeared to be the one the doctor had given to her the day before, but I didn't remember bringing it into the bedroom when I'd helped her to bed. Of course, Montgomery could easily have returned and given her another draught. In fact, I rather hoped that was what had happened, since Vanessa had been asleep for well over twelve hours—a single draught shouldn't have had such long-lasting effects. It reinforced my uncomfortable feelings about the crew, and I shivered as I remembered Benson's threat to drug me into submission as well. Would Dr. Montgomery continue to administer draughts and keep Vanessa insensible until we docked in New York?

I shook the woman a little harder and her eyelids finally fluttered to half-mast. "Vanessa. You need to wake up."

"I don't wanna. . . ." she murmured, but I was insistent. Finally, she was able to crack her eyes and drag herself up into a reclining position, propped against her pillows.

"I'm going to order you some coffee." I moved to the door as her eyes fell closed once again. Opening the door, I stuck my head outside and saw Heinz sitting casually in one of the armchairs.

"Is your friend all right?"

"She's having a hard time waking up. Can you order some coffee?"

"Certainly. And I think I will order some tea for myself. Would you like anything?"

I couldn't imagine sitting and having tea in the midst of this, so I just shook my head.

"Very well." Heinz moved to the phone and lifted the receiver.

I returned to Vanessa's room and found her still sitting up but with her eyes firmly shut. Her mouth was slightly ajar, as though she had fallen asleep again.

"Vanessa. You need to wake up. I have questions for you."

"Mmm. Why?"

"Because I need to know some things. Do you remember the doctor coming back to your room? After I left yesterday?"

Vanessa wobbled her head from side to side in what I took to mean no. Although I wasn't surprised she didn't remember anything, even if Montgomery had come by again. The way she had been drugged, I suspected the band could set up in this room and she would have slept through it.

"How about when you booked these suites? Did you book this trip for yourself?"

Vanessa gave her head yet another little shake, this time a slight frown bunching her brows. "Miles did. I gave him money." Her voice was still thick with sleep and I doubted she would remember any of this conversation. Hopefully she was telling the truth, although in her state, I doubted she had the fortitude to lie. This might actually be working in my favor.

Frustrated, I looked around the room, my eyes falling on her dressing table. Two keys. I stood, leaving Vanessa slumped against her pillows, and picked them up. They looked nearly identical, but holding them up I could read the numbers—one was for the room we were currently in, but the other was for the suite Vanessa had occupied previously. The one she had been moved out of, causing her current predicament.

Slipping the key for the other suite into my pocket, I stepped into the sitting room just as the knock on the door came. Heinz answered and admitted the waiter with his tray full of beverages. The young man deposited his load on the table, gave a short bow, and departed.

"Shall I pour a cup of coffee for your friend?" Heinz asked.

I crossed the room, shaking my head. I didn't want to risk letting anyone else fix a drink for Vanessa. I couldn't trust anyone on this ship, especially not Heinz Naumann.

I gave him a strained smile. "I'll do it. I know how she likes it." This was a lie, of course. I wasn't even sure if the woman cared for coffee, but I needed to get some caffeine into her system to wake her up. I poured the strong brew, leaving it black, and carried it back into Vanessa's bedroom.

Vanessa was still sitting up but was asleep once more, and I shook her, perhaps a little harder than strictly necessary, but she roused a bit and her eyes opened to narrow slits. Under normal circumstances, I would have marched to the doctor's office and questioned his use of such strong sedatives on a patient, but I wasn't sure even Redvers could keep me safe from the crew if I decided to confront any of them again.

I forced some of the caffeinated beverage into Vanessa, helping to hold her up while she drank. Eventually she was able to manage on her own, although she was still groggy.

"When did you get here, Jane? And how did you get in?" The coffee cup was clutched between her two hands, but I kept an eye on it in case it tipped one way or the other.

"The door was open." I checked the small clock. "And

I've been here for at least an hour." It had probably been less than that, but near enough. "My friend is in the sitting room. Let me tell him that we are fine and he can get on with his day." Vanessa mumbled something unintelligible but took another drink.

I went back into the sitting room, half hoping that Heinz had already gone. I was disappointed to find that the man was patiently drinking his tea and paging through a magazine he had found.

"American tastes are quite different than what is found in Germany."

I gave a forced little chuckle. "I can imagine." I came to stand behind the chair opposite his and rested my hands on the back. "Thank you so much for your help, Mr. Naumann. But I think I have it from here. She appears to be more alert. The coffee is certainly helping."

Heinz stood and nodded, but there was a gleam in his eye. "I must insist that you call me Heinz, Mrs. Wunderly." He cocked his head slightly and I could tell he expected me to respond in kind. It was impossible not to—despite everything, I still rather liked the man. Especially since he had immediately accepted my story about Vanessa and offered his assistance.

"Then please, call me Jane."

I nearly took it back when I saw the spark of triumph that crossed his face, but it was quickly wiped away and Heinz politely took his leave. As he left, I came close to reminding the man that I was married, but instead I heaved a sigh and locked the door behind him.

I could hear movement behind Vanessa's bedroom door, and I called through instead of reentering. "Do you need any help in there?"

"No! Thank you, Jane. I'm going to take a bath and get cleaned up. Is there any more coffee?"

Her voice sounded stronger and I breathed a small sigh of relief. "Yes, it's out here in the lounge."

"Excellent. Thank you."

I could hear the water in the bathroom starting to run, and I nearly excused myself entirely when I remembered the key in my pocket.

There was no time like the present for a little snooping.

CHAPTER TWENTY-FOUR

I poked my head into the hall and checked both ways to ensure that Heinz had well and truly gone on his way. There
was no way I was going to let the man catch me searching a
room—that was well outside what he would expect from the
role I was playing. The role of a concerned friend and dutiful
little wife.

The last was a real stretch of my acting abilities.

I let myself into the suite next door—the room I had originally met Vanessa in. Everything was pristine, as though no
one had been there at all. I looked around the sitting room
and saw nothing out of place. Walking through the bedroom,
I inspected the attached bathroom, but it had been wiped
down and was sparkling clean. There wasn't even a stray hair
that I could see—nothing that would indicate anyone had
been here, let alone a man who was now missing.

With a sigh, I stepped back into the bedroom. I checked
every drawer and beneath the bed, but came up with absolutely nothing. During my search, I noticed that the bed and
dressing table were bolted firmly to the floor—same with the
table and desk in the next room, although none of the chairs
were. I hoped we would never experience the need for those
precautions in person—it looked like a good storm could

send furniture flying. My stomach gave a little lurch at the thought.

The bedcovers on the double bed were pulled tight, as if it had never been slept in. I sighed and sat on it out of spite; whoever was perpetrating this elaborate ruse deserved to have their handiwork messed up. Especially since they had obviously gone to some effort—not a single thing appeared out of place.

Miles Van de Meter wasn't hiding here. Or at least he wasn't any longer.

I went back into the drawing room and took another look around. I pulled up the cushions on the love seat and looked beneath, finding nothing but a few crumbs. I did the same with both of the armchairs, but came up with exactly nothing. The only clue was that there were absolutely no clues.

Feeling slightly defeated, I returned to the suite next door, slipping into the sitting room and taking a seat in one of the upholstered chairs. I only had to wait a few moments before Vanessa made an appearance. She looked better than she had when she first woke up, but there were still dark circles under her eyes from too much sleep.

Vanessa sat in the chair across from me, pouring herself the last remnants of the coffee. She added some cream from the little pitcher and regarded me over the top of the cup. I was sorry that she appeared to have regained some of her composure—I was less likely to get straight answers from this version of Vanessa FitzSimmons. But I had to try.

"Have you seen the key for the other suite?" I wanted to hear her answer before I admitted that I had already found it and used it.

"No, I haven't seen it. Have you?" Her voice was quiet and had a tone of defeat to it, but it was hard to tell whether it was entirely genuine. Of course, it was difficult to tell whether anything with this woman was entirely genuine.

I paused for a beat before I shook my head, the key burning in my pocket. I wasn't sure why I didn't want to admit that I had found it lying on her dressing table in plain sight. I could pretend that it was to avoid causing her further upset, but the truth was I wasn't certain I could trust the woman before me. Had she possessed both keys all along? Yesterday I would have sworn the answer to that question was a resounding no, but after my search next door, I was no longer sure.

On the other hand, anyone could have snuck into Vanessa's room while she was passed out cold and left the key on the table. Dr. Montgomery had most likely been back in her suite to administer more drugs—was he the culprit? Or had Miles himself slipped in and left the key to cast more suspicion on Vanessa's story?

I had too many questions, and very little trust for anyone around me. Even the person I was supposed to be helping.

I made my excuses and told Vanessa I would check on her later. She seemed grateful for my help, but she also seemed to be looking forward to having some time alone. I understood how she felt.

Redvers wasn't in our suite, so I went hunting for the man on deck. I preferred to look for him there before I started haunting the gymnasium and indoor squash courts. This time I was in luck—I found him just finishing up a tennis game with another passenger. He was wiping sweat from his brow with a small towel.

"Good game, old boy," his dark-haired companion called from the other side of the court as he exited the area. A large net enclosed the entire playing space to keep balls from flying directly into the Atlantic, never to be seen again.

"Jane! What are you doing up here?"

"Looking for you."

"Well, you have excellent timing. I was just about to head back to our suite—walk with me."

I matched his leisurely stride, and couldn't help my awareness of just how much time the man appeared to be spending at leisure—although I couldn't be upset about the results. The exercise was certainly doing him a world of good. But it was annoying that I was spending my time today investigating, while he cavorted about playing sports. Didn't he have several rooms he needed to search?

"I'm glad you're enjoying yourself." I couldn't keep the irritation from creeping into my voice.

Redvers' eyes sparkled. "Oh, I am. And never fear, dear wife, I'm learning plenty. That chap was John McIntyre. You remember him, don't you? The radio operator. It's his time off and he was looking for a match. He also promised to send messages to shore for us at no charge if I won." He grinned cheekily. "Which of course I did."

I sighed. "Well, that's handy."

Redvers sobered. "It is actually. I need to ensure the man is discreet—he sees everything that comes in, and I need to make certain any messages we receive stay between us. They're coded, but even still." Redvers held out a hand for me to precede him in the small corridor. "I also had him send a telegraph to New York." Redvers nearly bumped into me as I stopped and turned to him with a raised eyebrow.

"I wanted to see if we can learn anything more about Vanessa FitzSimmons of the New York FitzSimmonses."

My lips tipped up in a slight smile at his using Vanessa's own words from when we first met the woman. It did sound quite pretentious.

"And before you can say it, it is not because I'm trying to prove that we shouldn't believe the woman. I simply think we can work better if we have all the facts." His voice rumbled quietly from behind me as we continued down the hall.

I nodded, deciding to hold my tongue until we were safely alone in our suite. I would fill him in on everything—including my burgeoning doubts about Vanessa—but I needed to make certain we wouldn't be overheard. Although I did appreciate that he'd immediately tried to assuage my worries, letting me know we were still on the same team. It was especially important to me now that I was having some second thoughts about Vanessa FitzSimmons and her relationship with the truth.

Once inside our room with the door closed securely behind us, I filled Redvers in on how Heinz had insisted on accompanying me to Vanessa's room. He frowned as he dug through his trunk for a change of clothing.

"Are you sure that was wise?"

"No, but I couldn't see any way around it. And hopefully it will deflect suspicion from me. If I'm caught up in my friend's troubles, I can't be worried about what he or anyone else is up to. At least I hope that's what he'll think." I didn't mention how I hoped more than ever that Brubacher was our spy—although it seemed unlikely that either of them was innocent after their exchange the evening before. Heinz's flirting still made me uncomfortable, but everything else about the man made me want him to be found innocent.

Redvers nodded. "I'm going to take a bath. We can continue this discussion when I'm finished." His smile turned into a wicked grin. "Unless you want to continue it in there?"

I flung the cushion from the chair at him as he laughed and headed out of the room.

When the man was appropriately dressed again, I filled him in on how both doors had been locked when I first knocked, but Vanessa's was open when I went back with Heinz. It had obviously been unlocked at some point while I was on deck, but I had no idea by whom—although it couldn't have been Vanessa. She'd been far too difficult to wake.

Then I filled him in on finding the second key and my fruitless search of the other suite.

"None of it bodes well. The key could easily have been left by anyone if the door was unlocked." He looked at me shrewdly. "But you have some concerns about Vanessa now."

I sighed and shrugged. It didn't make a lot of sense, since he was correct—anyone could have left that second key. But it had somehow planted seeds of doubt in my mind about Vanessa all the same. Could she have had both keys all along? Was she simply a gifted liar?

"Let's see what we find out from my contacts in New York," Redvers said.

After lunch, I spent the afternoon watching a silly play about life at sea put on by several members of the ship's crew—although thankfully neither Dr. Montgomery nor Officer Benson was anywhere in sight. Several of the passengers were pulled in to play minor roles, and it was good fun with lots of laughs. It was the perfect distraction from all the worries tumbling around my mind.

By the time I returned, Redvers was dressed in evening clothes and frowning at a piece of paper in his hand.

"What's that?"

"McIntyre just dropped it off." He passed the paper over to me. "It's the report on our Mrs. FitzSimmons."

"Already?"

"Apparently, there wasn't much digging that needed to be done. She's often in the society pages." His tone sounded regretful and I felt a little drop in my stomach as I perused the investigator's response.

According to the brief, staccato report, Vanessa FitzSimmons was a minor heiress—not on the level of a Vanderbilt or Rockefeller, but with enough money to live a luxurious existence. The family had made their money in shoe polish, and Vanessa frequently graced the society pages with her outrageous exploits.

"It sounds like she's an attention seeker." I looked up from the paper with its concise statements about the woman in question.

Redvers nodded but said nothing else, and I sighed. He had come to some conclusions but was going to let me get there on my own.

I continued reading to the end. "It doesn't look good for her, that's for certain," I said. "Although there doesn't seem to be any mention of insanity in her family. Did you specifically ask that question?"

Redvers nodded. "And there is no indication of that."

I sat down heavily in the remaining armchair, wondering idly if Dobbins would return its partner now that Redvers wasn't sleeping in the sitting room. "From this I might assume that she married simply for the attention. Or made the man up." I shook my head. "But I did see her husband that day. Or at least, I saw a man with her. A man that I haven't seen any sign of since."

"It's a large ship, of course. And there's the issue of our time docked in Cherbourg."

I nodded and traced the pattern on the arm of my chair with one finger while I thought. "Could she have hired someone to play the part of her husband?" I asked.

Redvers took a seat in one of the wooden chairs at the table, turning it to face me.

"It's something to consider. Although that still doesn't explain why we haven't seen any sign of him. Nor has anyone else."

I was quiet for a long time, my finger continuing its track on the pattern, the fine upholstery fabric smooth beneath my fingertip.

"What are you thinking?" Redvers finally asked.

"I'm weighing whether this is an elaborate scheme on Vanessa's part to get attention, since that seems to be her calling card." The report had given bare sketches of a few of her more infamous exploits—appearing at galas wearing next to nothing, drunken bathing in public fountains. And since it was a teletype, the report was brief—there was probably much more to be learned. It didn't look good and raised even more doubts in my mind about Vanessa.

He nodded, still saying nothing.

"Although what it says here"—I waved the paper in my hand—"is by and large innocent. Shocking, sure, but nothing truly harmful." I explained how the woman had been drugged to the gills and difficult to wake. "I'm not sure this is the same thing. Would she want to pull off a scheme that might actually harm her or at the very least keep her locked in her cabin?" I shook my head. "And as I said before, she was genuinely frightened when her room was switched. It would be difficult to pull off such a convincing act. *Something* is going on." I studied Redvers' handsome face for a moment. "What do you think?"

"I'm inclined to agree with everything you just said. And just to be clear, I believe your instincts about her reaction to the switched rooms." His dark eyes locked with mine. "But I also think we need to be cautious in believing everything Mrs. FitzSimmons tells us."

I nodded. I couldn't argue with that.

"Have you seen Dobbins today? Has he learned anything about either Vanessa or Heinz?"

At my use of Naumann's first name Redvers' eyebrow inched up and I felt my neck getting warm, but I held his gaze.

"No, I haven't spoken with Dobbins. I left a message for him that I wanted to meet with him, but I haven't seen him since this morning." Redvers gave a small shrug. "I'm sure he's busy with other guests and will get back to me shortly. I did give him a bit of a list."

I nodded and went to get changed for dinner.

CHAPTER TWENTY-FIVE

Instead of going to the main dining room, Redvers and I enjoyed a quiet meal at a table for two in the à la carte restaurant. It was a welcome change from the constant playacting I had been doing. Instead, I was able to relax into the man's company and simply be myself for a few hours.

Afterward, we followed the other first-class guests into the lounge where the night's shipboard entertainment was a piano player of some renown. "Is the band playing tonight?" I asked.

Redvers shook his head. "They have the night off." Frustration laced his voice, probably since their night off would delay his search of Brubacher's room yet again.

The lounge was full, and there was not a single empty table to be had this time, so Redvers and I found a spot to stand at the bar. It was actually a decent vantage point, since we could take in the entire room without appearing obvious about doing so. Upon inspection of the assembled guests, I was surprised to see Vanessa out of her room, seated alone at a small table near the middle of the lounge. A glance around told me that Dr. Montgomery was also on hand, watching her closely from his post against the back wall. Before I could make my way over to her and see how she was feeling, none other than Heinz Naumann approached her, and with a little bow, joined her at her table.

"Well, this can't be good," I muttered.

Redvers had his eye on the pair as well. "No. It can't."

Vanessa seemed on guard, but Heinz was using all of his considerable charm and I could see a smile start to play at her lips. I didn't think it would be long before Heinz had the woman laughing and eating out of his hand.

I turned my attention back to the pianist, but periodically glanced around the room so I could keep tabs on Vanessa and Heinz. Every time I looked in their direction it seemed that their chairs had moved just a little bit closer together. Perhaps it was simply to be able to hear one another better, but I doubted that was the case.

"She's a newlywed," I whispered in exasperation to Redvers.

"Well, we haven't really proved that." He was leaning against the bar, one arm casually tucked behind me, his breath tickling my ear.

I glared at him, and he chuckled, ignoring the scene behind us entirely. "You're going to hurt your neck if you keep craning it around like that. Besides, don't you think you're being a bit obvious?"

I gave him a little kick to the leg, although it lacked any real power, and he winked at me. The man was difficult to ruffle when he was truly enjoying himself. And he was usually enjoying himself when he was giving me a hard time.

After the first set of songs, the crowd started mingling and chatting once more. I let myself turn around again only to find that both Vanessa and Heinz were gone. I had a brief moment of hope that they'd left separately, but I knew it was unlikely.

I sighed. Why couldn't things be simple for once?

"Perhaps we should take another look at Naumann's room,"

Redvers whispered into my ear. "There's no time like the present." I finished the last sip of my drink, placed it on the bar, and followed him from the lounge.

"You really think this is the best time to do this?" I felt certain we would be caught. Or worse, we might walk in on something untoward. And hadn't Redvers searched the room just this morning?

But the man walked with purpose in the direction of Heinz's quarters. When we reached Naumann's suite I fully expected Redvers to pull out his lock-picking set, and I started to angle my body to hide him from view, but he gave a low chuckle and pulled a key from his pocket. I didn't even bother to ask how he had come by it—I simply followed him into the room and bolted the door from the inside.

"Didn't you already do this today?" I asked again.

Redvers shook his head. "Dobbins volunteered to do it, but I haven't heard from him since."

A quick glance around told me that the suite was unoccupied. "How did you know that Heinz and Vanessa wouldn't come back here?" It seemed unnecessary to mention that we both assumed they were together.

"A man like Naumann would never bring someone back to his room if he could help it. He'll always go to her suite." Redvers was already conducting a careful search of the sitting room.

I wasn't sure about the philosophy behind that, but I quickly got to work as well. "Are you expecting to actually find anything here?" I asked quietly.

"No, but we need to be certain." The man was inspecting the false fireplace to ensure Heinz hadn't found a clever hiding spot. I ran my hands along the bottom of the desk and pulled each drawer out. There was nothing to be found but the stationery provided by the ship. I checked beneath each drawer as well, but found nothing attached to the bottoms. I wiped a wrist across my forehead to remove the light sheen of sweat that had broken out there—it wasn't from anything but nerves. No matter how many times I had found myself searching a room over the past six months, I had yet to get used to the danger of being caught. It was exhilarating, but still terrifying.

Redvers moved into the bedroom and did the same quick, exacting search there while I worked behind him, ensuring that the room looked precisely as it had when we came in. I suspected that Heinz would still know that his things had been gone through, but I did what I could to minimize the evidence. Redvers went into the bathroom while I smoothed the bed covers and he came out a minute later, shaking his head.

"Nothing." With a last glance around the bedroom, he herded me to the door, and after listening for any sounds in the corridor, he ushered us back outside. I waited until we were on the next deck to speak.

"Now what?"

Redvers smiled, his one dimple winking. "Well, we may as well search the luggage room while we're at it."

We stopped at our suite where Redvers changed into the crew uniform he had "somehow" come by. He refused to tell me where he'd gotten it from—I assumed Dobbins had provided it, but I could tell Redvers didn't want me getting any ideas about where I could get one of my own. When he came out of the bedroom I gave him a quick once-over, noting that his pants were too short—as well as the jacket sleeves—but it would provide cover for us as long as no one looked too closely.

I followed him down the little-used staircase at the back of the ship, descending several decks until we were in an area adjacent to the third-class accommodations that was utilized only by the crew. I could feel my heart rate increase in proportion to my anxiety, but no one gave us a second look—for

all appearances I was simply a passenger being led somewhere by a helpful crew member. All the same, I kept my
head down and followed Redvers closely.

We stopped before the luggage room door and paused to
let a steward pass us by. He gave Redvers a brief nod before
shooting me a curious look, but continued down the corridor. Once he was out of sight, Redvers opened the door,
which I was surprised to see was unlocked, and we stepped
inside. There were no windows to aid us this time, so I stayed
close to Redvers and his flashlight. It was a creepy room at
night, racks of trunks and hatboxes stacked along the wall
and on large rows of shelves down the center of the space.
Everything cast strange shadows in the glow of our meager
light and I tried to keep my imagination at bay. All the same,
I had one hand on Redvers' strong back and was doing my
best not to step on the heels of his shoes.

"It should be arranged by cabin," Redvers murmured,
leading us down another aisle and flicking his light over the
numbers painted on the front of the rough wooden shelves.
We finally located Naumann's large trunk, a brown affair
with nothing at all on the exterior to indicate whom it belonged to. Completely inconspicuous.

"Help me with this," Redvers said as he handed me the
flashlight, and tugged the large trunk to the edge of the shelf.
I put one hand up to help him steady it, but he was able to lift
it to the ground on his own, despite its bulky size. It landed
with a muffled thump, and we both froze, but there was no
further sound except for our own ragged breathing. After a
moment, Redvers turned back to the trunk, pulling his lock-
pick set from his inner pocket, and went to work on the small
brass lock.

It was only the work of a few moments before Redvers
had the top open, and we peered inside. There wasn't much
to be seen—just a few pieces of clothing that the man obviously hadn't needed while he was on board. With a grunt,

Redvers sorted through them until he reached the bottom while I held the light. His face was cast in deep shadow, but I could see the moment of triumph when his hand found something of interest.

Redvers pulled the item up, and I turned the light on what was a small, gray, hardcover book. "Is that all?" I'd hoped for something more exciting than a little reading material.

He turned it over and we both caught sight of the title: *Life of Christ,* by Giovanni Papini. A quick flip through the pages revealed nothing interesting, and Redvers thoughtfully slipped the book back where we had found it. It was a strange title for a man like Heinz to have with him—he didn't seem at all interested in religion. Not to mention I'd have thought anything the man brought along with him as reading material would be written in his native language of German.

Redvers took more time to run his fingers over the seams of the trunk to ensure there were no hidden compartments before we sealed it back up—unlocked now, of course—and hefted it back onto the shelf. It scraped along the wooden racks, and this time when we froze, we heard something outside the door. We stood there, still as statues for several moments, but when there was no further sound, Redvers finished moving the trunk back into place and we headed to the exit. I led the way out with the flashlight and I noticed that Redvers didn't feel the need to follow as closely as I had on the way in.

More's the pity. I enjoyed any excuse to be near the man.

We were several decks away from the luggage room and nearly back to our suite when I could no longer contain the question that had been bothering me. "Why did you put the book back?" It was a strange little tome for Naumann to have, and I was hoping that it had some sort of significance. It would be disappointing to end a night of searching with nothing to show for our trouble.

Redvers gave his head a little shake and kept his lips sealed until we were safely ensconced back in our room. "There is nothing in the book we actually need. It's enough to know what the book is."

It was my turn to shake my head. "You're going to have to be more explicit than that."

"I agree with you that it's unlikely the book is innocuous. It isn't the type of thing a man like Heinz brings on a trip for a little light reading, especially since I recall the man saying he was agnostic. Not to mention, it would most likely be in German if it was his."

I made a noise of agreement. That was what I had decided also.

"But if Naumann is our man . . ."

"Which we haven't proved yet," I interjected.

Redvers rolled his eyes but continued. "Then it might be the key for a book cipher."

"A book cipher?"

"Each party has the same book, and when codes are sent back and forth they are broken using the book. It's impossible to break unless you know what book the parties are using."

"Why would they pick such an obscure book about religion? Why not something more commonplace? Like the latest popular novel?"

Redvers shrugged. "It has been a popular title among some sets. And my guess is that the other party chose the book. Maybe even passed Naumann his copy on board, and he stowed it in his luggage for later."

I thought for a moment. "That can't be what Naumann handed off to Brubacher."

Redvers shook his head. Naumann had given the band leader several papers, but nothing as substantial as a book. Not while we were watching, anyway.

"A drop would have been much safer anyway, rather than

handing the man something with an entire room of people watching."

I nodded, but had other questions. "If Heinz stowed the book away, does that mean he wasn't expecting to need it on board?" I sat down in the armchair.

Redvers made a noise and took a seat at the table. "It might mean that. But more importantly, it might also mean that his contact is here on board." I raised an eyebrow. "Naumann didn't have it with him before," Redvers explained. I didn't bother to ask how he knew that.

"Could Brubacher be the contact?"

"It's possible." Redvers sighed. "I really need to get into that man's room."

"They have the evening off," I reminded him.

Redvers cocked his head speculatively. "Since I'm already dressed, I may as well head down and see if Brubacher is actually in his room."

"And if he is?" It seemed like a risky proposition.

"Then I will make up an excuse and leave."

"Don't you think you'll be recognized?"

He shook his head. "There is so much staff on board this ship, I think they won't look twice at me."

I couldn't imagine a scenario where this man wouldn't attract a second look, even in disguise, but he had his mind made up already.

"Just be careful. We still have more time to do a search."

He nodded. "I will be."

I awoke early the next morning—alone, as usual, even though I hadn't gone to sleep that way—and entered the sitting room to find Redvers fully dressed and ready for the day. He rang for breakfast to be delivered, and while we waited I peppered him with questions.

"What did you find?"

"How do you know I found anything?"

"It's the smug expression on your face. Come on. Fess up."

Luckily, he decided to stop toying with me. It was the safest course of action for him since I hadn't had my morning coffee yet.

"I did a thorough search."

"Where was he? His room was empty?"

"Nearly the entire band was engaged in a low-stakes card game in the crew dining room."

"Were you seen?"

Redvers shot me a look. "Are you going to let me talk?"

I bit my tongue and gestured for him to go ahead.

"I didn't find any sign of another book on religion. And I'll take a look this morning, but I don't think the crew have luggage in the storage room, since they're limited to what they can travel with. It might be different for the musicians, but I doubt it." He paused and shifted in his chair and I had to restrain myself from prompting him again. "The only thing I did find was several sheets of music with the name H. Naumann listed as the composer. It was mixed in with the other music."

"What?" I'd heard the man, but couldn't quite believe my ears.

Redvers just looked at me.

"Do you mean to tell me that Heinz is a musical composer?" Snatches of remembered conversation suddenly came back to me. Naumann and I had had a lengthy conversation—well, it was more like a lecture from Heinz—about music. He hadn't mentioned writing any himself, but it made a strange sort of sense that he would, given his rabid interest.

"What kind of music was it?" I was curious about this aspect of the man I'd spent so much time chatting with, but there was no way that I could ask Heinz about his music without revealing how we'd come across it.

Redvers shrugged. "I can't read music, so I couldn't say."

I gave a mock gasp. "There's something you can't do?"

"Don't let word get around."

I smirked, then thought through the implications of Redvers' find. "Well, I suppose that rules out our band leader as Naumann's contact." I frowned. "Does that rule him out as our spy?"

Redvers looked askance at me. "I hate to tell you this, but it's looking more and more like our only viable suspect is your Heinz Naumann."

"He's not *my* Heinz Naumann." I almost added that if I didn't know any better Redvers sounded a bit jealous, but I held my tongue. "What about Van de Meter?"

Redvers shook his head. "We can't even prove the man is still on board the ship, let alone that he exists in the first place. I think with the sudden appearance of *Life of Christ*, Naumann is our likeliest candidate."

It was disappointing that Heinz was our likely culprit, to be sure, but I wasn't devastated by the fact. The appearance of the little book was fairly damning, and I accepted that Redvers was probably correct.

That sorted, my mind pinged in a different direction. "Where do you suppose Vanessa and Heinz disappeared to last night?"

"Perhaps they went for a walk on deck."

My incredulous look spoke for itself.

"Very well. I know what we're both thinking. And it does complicate matters somewhat. But perhaps we can use it to our advantage."

I was about to ask just how he thought we could do that when a knock came at our door and the waiter came in with our breakfast tray. As he set it on the table, Redvers took the opportunity to question the man.

"I say, have you seen our steward by any chance? Mr. Dobbins? I left a message for the man that I wished to speak with him, but I haven't heard anything from him. I'm becoming quite put out at the poor service."

I knew this last part was merely for effect. Redvers wasn't put out so much as he was worried. It turned out he had every reason to be.

"You haven't heard, sir." The young man fiddled with the stripe running down the side of his pants. "Mr. Dobbins was found this morning. I'm sure another steward will be assigned to you very quickly."

Redvers and I both sat up straight. "Found? What do you mean, found?"

The lad cleared his throat nervously as he took a step backward toward the door. I didn't blame him for wanting to escape—Redvers looked very intense.

"His body was found in the Turkish bath early this morning. He's dead, sir."

CHAPTER TWENTY-SIX

Redvers and I both muttered some curses, shocking the poor waiter even further before we allowed him to flee. I gave the steaming pot of coffee one sad glance before I hurried back into the bedroom to change into a day dress. Redvers and I both were ready to bolt from the room in record time.

"They're not likely to let us in, you know." My voice was breathless from keeping up with the pace that Redvers was setting as we raced through corridors and down multiple flights of stairs. As always, I was impressed by his unerring sense of direction—he invariably seemed to know exactly where we were going.

Redvers said nothing, but the grim and determined set to his mouth spoke volumes. I couldn't help a little smile—I would hate to be the man who stood in Redvers' way this morning.

There were few passengers out since the sun was just starting its ascent into the sky, but I muttered apologies to the few early risers we nearly ran down in our haste to get to our destination on the F-deck. As we entered the cooling chamber of the Turkish baths, I took a brief moment to take in the stunning room—yet another on this extraordinary ship. It certainly brought to mind our time in Egypt—the delicately carved teak, the "Cairo curtains" disguising the portholes yet letting light filter through, and the pierced brass Arab lamps hanging from the ceiling were all reminiscent of décor I saw at the Mena House, and for a moment I was transported back. But here the walls of the room were covered with large blue and green tiles, offset by the warm teakwood, and contrasting nicely with the patterned tile floor. Canvas chairs for recovering from the steamy baths were scattered around the room, where I guessed the attendants would bring cooling drinks to the lounging guests. It was incredible to me that this type of facility—not to mention the swimming pool and gymnasium—was available on board a ship. It was a large ship, but a ship nonetheless.

After my brief moment of reverie, I hurried to catch up with Redvers as he passed through the cooling room and into the baths themselves. The décor here was similar—beautiful tiles, but slightly more utilitarian to withstand the steam from the pools. A group of officers including the captain stood in a semicircle around one of the small baths—I counted four men in total. Even from where we stood near the entrance, I could see past their legs to where Dobbins's body had been pulled from the water and now lay in a growing puddle on the tile floor.

Redvers cursed under his breath, and I looked over at him, tearing my eyes away from the body of our steward stretched out on the floor. I knew he'd been hoping the waiter was incorrect about the identity of the dead man, just as I had been.

At the sound of our footsteps crossing the room, one of the officers turned and put out both arms. "You can't be in here right now." I was relieved that none of the men appeared to be Officer Benson. The last thing I needed was yet another run-in with that man.

Redvers merely glared at the officer until he faltered and turned slightly toward the captain, standing at the front of the gathered men. "Captain," he called softly.

The captain turned and at the sight of us breathed out a gusty sigh. "You two. Head back to your cabin. There is nothing for you to see here."

"This man was our steward."

"That may be true, but he isn't any longer. Someone else will be assigned to you."

What we needed here was a distraction so that Redvers could get a quick look at the body without admitting to his true purpose on board the *Olympic*. It wouldn't do to reveal ourselves to these men, especially since we had already determined that not even the captain was worthy of our trust.

I stepped closer to the group, then put a hand to my head and feigned a swoon, nearly toppling the captain over and knocking him into the other three men like a set of well-dressed dominoes. It was a silly ploy, but effective. Several cries went up, and the men nearly tripped over each other in an attempt to catch me before I hit the floor—although it was ultimately Captain Bisset who broke my fall. Redvers had enough time to move around the men and give Dobbins a quick once-over while the men fussed over me and the captain lowered me to the ground. Through narrowed eyes I could see Redvers inspecting Dobbins's head and pushing aside the clothing around his neck.

"I'm so sorry," I said faintly. "I've never seen a dead body before." I made my voice wavery, as though I might weep at any moment. "It's just so distressing." It was in fact distressing, but I was more than able to stand my ground at such a sight. It wasn't the first time, although I always hoped it would be the last.

I heard one of the officers tell another to call for the doctor and the man took off at a trot out of the room. I tried to call after him and tell him it wasn't necessary, but the captain patted me on the arm with rather a lot of force and told me not to talk. I shielded my eyes with one hand, but peeked through and saw that Redvers had nearly finished his inspection. With my other hand, I pushed myself up to a seated position, causing the two men to flutter a bit more while telling me that I shouldn't strain myself. Really, it was quite insulting how little the men thought of the female constitution. Finally, the second mate turned to see what Redvers was up to, and why he wasn't attending to me.

"I say, get away from there, sir. You need to get control of your wife."

I kicked out a bit with my leg, catching the man in the shin, then gave a little moan, as though it had been involuntary. I was pleased to see the man wince and lean down to rub the spot with his hand.

After a beat Redvers dutifully came over and pushed his arms beneath my own, helping me up to standing. "I'm sure she's fine now, gentlemen. No need for the doctor. You know how women can be. I'll just get her back to our room." I thought about kicking Redvers as well, but I simply let him half carry me out of the room instead. Through partially shuttered eyes I could see that the men looked doubtful, but they let the two of us go.

Once outside in the corridor, Redvers let go of me and gave me a wide grin. "Well done, my dear. I was able to see everything I needed to."

I glowed from the praise—and the term of endearment—but I could hear voices coming down the hall, and I gave Redvers a little push in the opposite direction. The last thing I wanted was to be sedated and locked in my room like Vanessa FitzSimmons. And I suspected that was the first thing the doctor was going to insist upon in order to "recover my nerves." We slipped around a corner just in time to avoid being seen.

CHAPTER TWENTY-SEVEN

Since I thought our room was the first place the doctor would come looking for me, I requested that we head to the café in order to have our breakfast, despite the platter of food in our suite that was surely cold by now. I had the start of a headache that I knew was from a lack of coffee, and my stomach was rumbling despite having just seen poor Dobbins's body stretched out on a cold tile floor.

The café was about half full when we arrived, and Redvers requested a secluded table, tossing an arm around me and giving the hostess a wink. She fluttered her lashes at him and led us to a corner neatly tucked behind a large potted palm.

"Was that entirely necessary? She might have just given us the table."

Redvers grinned at me. "Jealous, little wife?"

I wrinkled my nose at him and waited until after we had placed our orders before interrogating him about what he had seen when he inspected Dobbins. This wasn't the first dead body I had seen, but that didn't change how much it affected me. I was saddened to my core that the young man's life had been cut short.

"Did you get a good look at Dobbins?" At his nod I continued. "What did you see?"

"There didn't appear to be any blows to the head, but

when I moved his collar I could see there were definitely some marks to the back of his neck—it looked like the start of bruising."

"As though someone held him under."

"Precisely."

I took another sip of coffee. "Do you think the doctor will notice the same thing?"

Redvers shrugged and toyed with his teacup. "Who's to say? I'm surprised the doctor wasn't already there when we arrived, to be honest."

Looking back on it, it was a bit strange that the crew hadn't immediately called the ship doctor.

"Do you know what the protocol on a boat is?"

"A ship."

"That too."

"I'm not sure." Redvers looked up and stopped talking as the waiter delivered our food. He flicked his napkin onto his lap and, once the man was out of earshot again, he continued. "There are no police on board to investigate. I would imagine that one of the officers would assume the role and look into things."

I nodded. "And if they see the same bruises you did, they would have to assume it was no accident."

"Our question is, why was he killed? Because of the matter that brought us here?"

I suddenly felt stricken with guilt. "Or because I asked him to look into what was happening to Vanessa FitzSimmons."

Redvers nodded, his face serious.

I poked at the eggs on my plate, suddenly not very hungry at all. It was going to be a difficult task to uncover exactly what had brought about Dobbins's untimely end.

Redvers grimaced. "It's going to be hard to get information about the crew without someone on the inside." It sounded heartless, but I knew he was just being practical. Redvers was sorry about Dobbins's death, but we also needed to figure out our next steps. "I haven't revealed myself to the captain. I'm wondering whether I'll have to now."

"Is that usual? I would have thought the captain would be told up front."

Redvers looked thoughtful as he drank his tea. "Normally, yes. Especially after something like this. But Captain Bisset hasn't exactly made a good impression. I'm not sure what to make of the man. Especially given what we suspect about his . . . extracurricular activities."

I knew he was referring to the suspected smuggling. I hoped Redvers had put the photos I'd taken in a safe place.

"And I haven't forgotten that the man seemed to know my real identity. The only person who should have known that was Dobbins." Redvers frowned, then smoothed his face as he continued to muse. "Bisset is nearing retirement." That was surprising to me. He wasn't a young man, but he certainly didn't seem old either. "But he has a clean background otherwise. No mishaps with any ships, other than that one incident during the war, and a good safety record." He gave his head a little shake before pouring himself another cup of tea, adding milk and several spoonfuls of sugar. "But it bothers me that the doctor wasn't there with the body. I hope Bisset isn't going to try to cover things up."

I agreed. From the beginning Bisset had been unhelpful, refusing to order his crew to do anything to aid Vanessa FitzSimmons. I knew the captain had shown us the manifest only to stop us from asking further questions, and after seeing that the doctor hadn't been called immediately at the discovery of a body . . . well, I thought Redvers had every right to be concerned that Dobbins's death wouldn't be handled well either.

Redvers' gaze had drifted behind me, but now it sharpened on me again. "You should go back up to the deck and pretend everything is normal. Talk with Naumann. See if he knows anything about Dobbins's death."

Heinz Naumann was a carefully closed book—I hoped I would be able to tell if the man was lying when it came to whether he'd heard about Dobbins's demise.

It struck me that Heinz might have been the orchestrator of it.

I tried to keep a pained expression from my face. "You think it might have been Heinz who killed Dobbins?"

Redvers raised a dark brow. "You don't?"

I drank some more coffee while I considered that. True, it didn't bode well for Heinz that we had narrowed down our field to merely him as the likely spy and we had asked Dobbins to search Heinz's room just before he was killed. It was impossible to know if Dobbins had managed to finish that task—or whether he'd been caught in the act—since we hadn't seen the steward since he'd been given the instructions. On the other hand, killing a man over a room search seemed extreme. A spy had to assume that his things would be gone through at any time, didn't he?

"No, I don't." I shook my head to punctuate my point. "Killing a man over a simple room search? It's too extreme of a response. I think this has to do with whatever is happening to Vanessa."

"Is that simply because you like Naumann?" Redvers had a twinkle in his eye.

I narrowed my eyes at him. "No." I said. "I'll admit that spending time with him isn't exactly a chore, but I truly don't think he had anything to do with Dobbins."

Redvers sobered, his dark eyes on mine. "Just be careful with the man."

I wasn't sure if he meant with my emotions or with my person, since he believed Heinz was our culprit. Then I cleared my throat, remembering how easily Heinz had led me out onto the night-drenched deck. "What will you do?"

"I'm going to send some messages to shore and report on

this development. Then I'll see if any of the officers will talk to me about Dobbins. Learn what I can about his death and what they plan to do with his body."

"I would avoid the first mate. He isn't likely to give you any help."

Redvers shot me a winning smile and my heart skipped a beat. "But he hasn't met me yet."

I doubted Benson would be as charmed as I was.

CHAPTER TWENTY-EIGHT

We went our separate ways and I headed up to the first-class deck to see if Heinz was soaking up the sea air. It was an overcast day, somewhat gloomy, and I found that it matched my mood after the morning's discovery.

As I neared my chair I could see that someone was already occupying it, and chatting merrily with Heinz. I nearly stuttered to a stop when I realized that someone was Vanessa FitzSimmons. After seeing them together the night before, I shouldn't have been surprised, and yet somehow, I was.

"Jane!" Vanessa waved one hand at me. "Come join us. I'm sorry, I know I've taken your chair, but I think you can sit in this one." She gestured at the empty chair on the other side of her. "It doesn't seem to have an owner." Vanessa was clearly unwilling to give up my seat.

I smiled stiffly and glanced at Heinz, who had a distinctly triumphant gleam in his eye. It left me wondering why—because two women seemed to be fighting for his attention? Or for some other reason? For the first time I wondered if I had misjudged the man. We had already established that he was likely working on behalf of his home country, willing to carry secrets back, but I had never considered how far he might be willing to go for those loyalties.

Or what he was capable of.

After exchanging some pleasantries about the morning and the poor weather, Vanessa and Heinz went back to their earlier chat, which seemed to include which casinos on the Mediterranean were the best and which were the most stacked toward the house.

It only took a few moments before I stopped listening entirely. I had zero interest in gambling, and after a beat they'd stopped trying to include me in the conversation anyway. I stared out over the open sea instead, watching the gray waves collapse in on themselves as I huddled into my wool coat.

"Jane." Vanessa's impatient voice broke through my reverie. "What are you thinking about? You seem quite unlike yourself this morning."

I turned my head and gave them a wan smile. "I'm afraid my steward was found dead this morning." My eyes flicked between the two, but I was mostly concerned with Heinz's reaction. His face did crease in a grimace at my pronouncement, but he quickly resumed his devil-may-care air. I wasn't sure what to make of his reaction, although it didn't seem to be one of guilt.

"Is that all? I'm sure they'll assign you a new one shortly. It's nothing to be worked up about."

I stared at the woman for a beat, wondering how someone could be so heartless. Before I had chalked her callous nature up to shock from her ongoing trials, but that couldn't be the case here. In fact, it was rather shocking to me how cavalier she was suddenly being about her missing husband—flirting with the first handsome man to come along. Perhaps Heinz wasn't the only one I had misjudged.

"Now, Vanessa." Heinz glanced at me and back at the striking redhead. "A man lost his life."

Vanessa paused for a moment, then rolled her eyes. "Yes, very well. I suppose you're right."

A slight furrow between Heinz's brows told me he wasn't

terribly impressed with Vanessa's attitude either. Heinz tried to shake it off and resume their conversation, but the same spark wasn't there. After a few beats, he stood and excused himself, kissing Vanessa's hand before offering his fur rug to me as he left, as Vanessa already had her own. I took it gratefully, covering myself up to my neck with the thick warmth.

"You must think me terribly cruel," Vanessa said to me once Heinz had disappeared from sight. "And here I am flirting with another man." She sighed and twisted her wedding band around her finger while gazing in the direction Heinz had gone. "I hope I haven't driven him away as well."

"I'll admit I'm a bit taken aback." There was no sense in trying to hide my feelings about the matter. They were written on my face.

She attempted a careless shrug, but her shoulders stayed tensed and her hands continued their nervous movements in her lap. "I'm simply trying to distract myself. And it never hurts to flirt with an attractive man. I thought . . ." Vanessa trailed off and I watched a series of emotions flit across her face. "I thought that perhaps if Miles knew I was toying with another man that he would finally reveal himself."

"You believe he's still somewhere here on board?"

Vanessa's voice rose an octave. "Of course I do! He has to be here somewhere. He couldn't have just disappeared." She paused, a hitch in her voice. "But I don't know why all these other things are happening to me. If he knew about them, why wouldn't he come forward and help me?" She glanced around anxiously now, and I wondered whom she was looking for, but I kept my thoughts to myself on that matter.

But I couldn't hold my tongue on another. "Have you considered that it might be Miles"—I paused, considering how to phrase things—"who is behind these strange things?"

Vanessa's entire body tensed and her voice became quiet. "I can't imagine he would do something so cruel. Even if it was for my money."

Her response made it seem that she had at least considered the possibility. If Vanessa were to be deemed insane, Miles would control her wealth. But I decided not to press the issue. Instead I nodded and we fell into an uneasy silence.

I understood her reluctance to believe she had married someone capable of playing such cruel tricks on her—who wanted to admit they'd been taken for a fool? And Vanessa certainly wouldn't want to believe that someone married her only for her money.

And yet while Heinz was with us she had displayed none of the anxiety she was now apparently feeling. Was she trying to smoke Miles out like she said, or was she actually afraid her husband would suddenly appear? Just how good of an actress was Vanessa FitzSimmons, and was *she* the one playing games?

It hurt my head to contemplate the possibilities. Then I remembered that I had seen her maid, Rebecca Tesch, going into a crew member's cabin. But when I mentioned it, Vanessa just gave a brittle laugh.

"Oh, well done, Rebecca. I'm glad someone is having fun aboard this ship."

"You think she's simply having fun?"

"Certainly. I'm sure she's met some handsome sailor and is having an on-board tryst. Good for her, I say. We girls should have a bit more of that in our lives. Especially before we get back to the States and it's all rotgut booze and people hounding our every step."

This wasn't the response I expected. From the exploits I'd read about in the report Redvers showed me, I'd assumed Vanessa was seeking out attention from the papers, but now it sounded as if she resented being followed about town. But why would one jump into a fountain if they weren't looking for attention? It was hard to know what version of Vanessa was the real one.

But more than that, her explanation for Rebecca's excursion didn't ring quite true. Whatever Rebecca's reasons were for venturing into the crew area, it was hard for me to accept that it was something as innocent as a shipboard romance.

Vanessa and I were still sitting in silence, both of us watching the ocean pass by, when Dr. Montgomery found us.

"Mrs. FitzSimmons," the doctor said, causing Vanessa to jump in her seat. Well, my seat. She hadn't seen the man coming as I had, and her face twisted into an unattractive grimace. "Would you care to take a walk around the deck with me?"

"No, I really wouldn't. But I suppose you're not actually offering me a choice, are you?"

The doctor smiled pleasantly, despite Vanessa's obvious rudeness, and with a sigh, she stood, dropping the rug on the chair. Montgomery's pleasant demeanor never changed as she reluctantly took his arm.

"I'll see you later, Jane." She glared fiercely at the man beside her, before turning back to me with a meaningful look. "We will meet in the lounge later for a drink."

I agreed, but gave a shiver as I watched the doctor lead her away. I hoped he was simply checking on her welfare and hadn't come to drug her back into oblivion. It wasn't as if she was causing any trouble at the moment—we had simply been sitting quietly. Either way, I was deeply uncomfortable with the doctor's presence, especially since there was little I could do to help Vanessa at this point without putting myself in danger as well. I needed to be seen as a levelheaded woman, not a "hysteric" who needed to be managed. I was already on thin ice after my performance in the Turkish bath this morning—the last thing I needed was to bring more attention to myself.

But I resolved to check in with Vanessa later, despite my mixed feelings about her.

Since both my companions had gone, I decided to focus on figuring out what Rebecca had been up to. I stood and neatly folded my rug, placing it back on Heinz's chair before making my way to the entrance leading to the crew quarters. I paused before the set of stairs that I had followed Rebecca down and stood for a moment, listening. I didn't hear anyone below, but I was feeling especially cautious after my last trip down these stairs.

Once my foot hit the floor, I scurried forward toward the door I had seen Rebecca disappear through. The monotonous gray closed in around me as I stood before the door I believed was the correct one. Unfortunately, they all looked the same, with only a painted number on each to tell them apart. I glanced up and down the empty corridor, and then back at the stairs, trying to judge whether I was at the right place. With a shrug, I raised my hand and gave a quiet knock.

Nothing.

I knocked again, with a little more force this time, but there was still no answer. With another glance around to make sure I was alone, I pressed my ear to the door to see if there was someone hiding within, but was met with nothing but dead silence. I took a step back and bit my lower lip. Should I stay and risk being seen? Or should I simply come back in a few hours and hope that the occupant would be inside?

My decision was made for me when I heard several pairs of feet coming down a set of stairs at the far end of the drab corridor. I turned on my heel and nearly ran back up the stairs I'd come down, stopping only when I was back outside. I pressed one hand to my chest to stop my racing heart, and did my best to appear casual. It was unlikely that I was pulling it off.

I paced the nearby corridor, the difference between the crew areas of the ship and the décor for the passengers all the starker now that I had seen below. I was about to give up and go back to my suite when I heard the unmistakable voice of

Eloise Baumann booming from the deck above me. I couldn't make out what she was saying, but my first instinct was to ensure that I stayed well hidden.

Yet as I thought about it, it occurred to me that Eloise was a busybody. Perhaps she had some gossip that I could use—or perhaps I could ask the right questions and have her gather information for me. I squeezed my eyes shut and pursed my lips. The last thing I wanted to do was put myself directly in her path, but right now, it seemed like the best plan if I had any hope of learning something useful.

With a sigh, I flouted all my instincts for preservation, and headed straight for the quicksand.

CHAPTER TWENTY-NINE

I caught up with Eloise and her put-upon sister, Margret, just before they entered the women's lounge.

"Mrs. Wunderly!" Eloise's voice drowned out everything around her and I made a conscious effort not to cringe, forcing a smile to my face instead. "I hope you will join us for tea. We have had quite the trying morning."

I nodded agreeably and followed the women to their table, doing my best to ignore the stares from the other patrons. Eloise certainly made an entrance wherever she went, both with her booming tones and her appearance. Today she was outfitted in an outrageously orange dress festooned with feathers that was drawing as many stares as her inability to modulate her voice.

Eloise barreled over whatever the hostess was trying to tell us—most likely that a member of the waitstaff would be with us shortly—and ordered an elaborate tea service for us. I shot the young woman an apologetic look, but she didn't seem to notice. I watched as she marched away and spoke to another member of the staff.

"Very rude," Eloise announced. "She didn't seem at all interested in taking our order."

I didn't bother to mention that she wasn't the one who was supposed to take it. Or that she hadn't even let us look at the menus before deciding what we were having. Any sort of reply would have been wasting my breath.

Eloise opened her mouth—most likely to continue complaining—but I managed to head her off for once. "What was so terrible about your morning?" If I could move the conversation in a different direction, perhaps I could bring up Dobbins in a natural way.

It turned out I didn't need to spend my time on calculations.

"Our steward was found dead this morning!" Eloise's face was filled with outrage.

My eyebrows went up in surprise. Poor Dobbins. I didn't realize he had also been servicing Eloise and the Goulds. The man must have had his hands full even without our tasks.

I was about to mention that we had shared a steward when Eloise continued on. "I went and spoke with the captain as soon as he didn't show up this morning. The poor service on this ship is quite shocking, actually, and I'm sure Captain Bisset wants to be kept informed of how his important passengers are being treated."

I stifled a laugh at Eloise's opinion of her status on board. A glance at Margret told me that she shared my opinion on how ridiculous her sister's statement was.

"Then the man made me wait for quite a long time. I understand that he had to attend to the body, but really. I've never been so insulted. I told the young man that I would be going back to my suite and that he could come and find me when Captain Bisset returned. Honestly. I couldn't believe he expected me to sit and wait as though my time wasn't incredibly valuable."

This was going down a path that I didn't need to hear about, so I jumped in with a quick redirect. "What did the captain say about your steward?"

"That he's dead, of course." Eloise pinned me with a hard look. "Are you not listening, Mrs. Wunderly?"

"No, of course I am." I shifted in my seat despite the fact that I had done nothing wrong. "I just meant—"

She cut me off. "We will be assigned a new one immediately. I told him that had better be the case." Two members of the waitstaff hurried up to the table and deposited fine china cups, a large pot of tea, and a plate of small sandwiches. They moved away just as quickly, before Eloise even had time to draw another breath. I couldn't help a small smile, and my eyes met Margret's across the table—once again it seemed she was thinking the same thing.

"What do you think they will do with the body?" This came from Margret, and my mouth nearly dropped open in shock. The woman never spoke, but she had asked exactly what I wanted to know. It was as though she could read my mind.

"According to the captain, he's to be buried at sea first thing in the morning."

I might have gasped, but it was lost in Eloise's continuing narration of what else the captain had told her. I tuned out for a moment—it was nothing to do with Dobbins, and everything to do with Eloise's exacting standards and Captain Bisset's reassurances that everything would be made right. I almost felt sorry for the man.

Almost.

But the person I most felt sorry for was Francis Dobbins. I supposed I knew that men who died at sea were buried in that manner, but there would be no gravestone, no burial plot for his family to visit. I made a mental note to ask Redvers if Dobbins had family back on land and how they would be notified of his passing.

But then my mind moved on to practical matters. If they were burying him so soon, it was unlikely that any further examination of the body would be done. Had Dr. Montgomery already seen Dobbins? And had he noticed the marks on his neck that Redvers had discovered? Surely if he had, they wouldn't be tipping the body overboard so quickly. Although, I supposed they had no real place to keep a body on board the ship.

Still, it all felt quite hurried to me.

I tuned back in to Eloise's monologue. "And Captain Bisset told me that two people came into the room where the body was this morning and caused quite a scene. Can you imagine? I don't know what on earth would possess someone to go into a room that has been closed up."

I nearly argued that there had been no indication that the room was closed, but I kept my mouth shut. Eloise Baumann did not need to know that Redvers and I were those very same people. I could only imagine the talking to I would be in for—or the questions about what we were doing. I suspected that underneath all the bluster and talk, Eloise was no fool. We did not need her working out that Redvers and I weren't precisely what we seemed and then broadcasting it for all to hear.

I continued nodding at what I thought were the appropriate times and looked toward Margret. She was studying me with a speculative look in her eye, but she quickly busied herself making a second cup of tea.

Before I had time to think about what that could mean, I was called to attention by her sister. "Don't you think, Mrs. Wunderly?"

I had no idea what the question was. "I'm quite sure you're right, Miss Baumann."

She beamed and I breathed a small sigh of relief. I figured it was the safest way to go—the woman loved hearing she was right, that much was clear. Margret's mouth tipped up in a smile, and I knew she wasn't fooled in the slightest. My own smile mirrored her own, but I had to wonder about the quieter of the two sisters. I had seen more flashes of personality today than I had previously.

What was going on in Margret's head while her sister held court?

When I had gotten as much information as I was going to from the women, I excused myself with a false promise to take tea with them again the next day. I sincerely hoped I wouldn't need to do so. Taking a meal with Eloise was more painful every time I sat through it, although at least I had some useful information to show for my troubles today.

Once back in our suite I breathed a sigh of relief at the deafening quiet. I sat in the upholstered chair and let myself soak in the stillness. I hadn't yet decided what my next step would be when the door opened and Redvers let himself into the room.

"Back so soon?" Redvers' voice was threaded with amusement.

"I could say the same about you. Shouldn't you be off doing something?" I couldn't quite remember what tasks he had assigned himself.

"Trying to get rid of me?" He chuckled, then grew quiet as he studied my face. "At least Naumann hasn't tossed you overboard."

"No, but Dobbins is about to be." Redvers' eyebrow went up in question and I explained what I had learned from Eloise about his imminent burial at sea.

"Damn. The captain refused to see me, so I hadn't heard anything about that."

"He's probably had his fill of complaints from the passengers today."

"Perhaps."

I sat up from my slouch and looked at him. "You think it's something else."

Redvers shrugged. "It's just a feeling I get. Something isn't quite right with the man." He had mentioned that fact several times, and I knew it was bothering him that he couldn't place what the trouble was. Redvers liked to deal in tangibles—background checks and facts. He was more unsettled by "just a feeling" than I was.

I was learning to trust my feelings again.

Pushing thoughts of the captain aside, I moved on to my own morning. "Well, I wasn't able to make any headway in figuring out where Rebecca disappeared to down below."

Redvers took the seat opposite me and a speculative gleam lit his dark eyes. "Perhaps we should trade for the time being. I'll try to find out who's staying in that room, and you can learn more about the captain."

I couldn't help my smirk. "I feel like I've already done your job for you." My grin widened at his answering glower, then I became serious. "Frankly, it's a good idea for you to try to figure out who's staying there. I'm nervous to try again—Benson wasn't thrilled to see me down there the last time. I'm not sure what would happen if I get caught again."

"I'm sure nothing serious would happen to you."

I couldn't be as certain, especially after seeing the aftermath of Vanessa's treatment. I still had an uneasy feeling about the doctor coming to fetch Vanessa from the deck. But it was a good idea for Redvers to try the door again. There was little chance he would be drugged and stashed away if *he* proved inconvenient. Redvers could move around the ship with more impunity, and as a man he would be treated much less harshly for breaking the rules and entering a crew area.

"Vanessa is convinced that Van de Meter is still on board somewhere. I haven't the faintest idea where the man could be hiding if that's actually true."

Redvers agreed. "It does seem unlikely that he would be able to hide this long without being discovered by the crew if he's a stowaway."

"Unless he has a room under a different name." I didn't know why we hadn't considered that possibility until now.

"It will be hard to find him if that is the case."

We wouldn't be able to locate him by name, but what if there was another way? "If he's going undetected, that means he's pretty much confined to his room, correct? How can we find out if there's someone taking all their meals in their room?"

Redvers' eyes lit with appreciation. "The kitchen staff. You're a genius, darling."

My face flushed with pleasure, and I tried to hide it by quickly turning back to business. I didn't want him to know how much his simple words could affect me, especially since I wasn't sure whether there was any deeper meaning behind them. I hated to admit that I hoped there was. "I'll take care of talking to the kitchen staff." I paused. "I'll also try to track down Rebecca and see if I can get an answer from her about what she's lying about and why."

"You think it's a good idea to confront her about it?"

I shrugged. "I may as well try."

"You'll have to venture down to the second-class deck to find her," Redvers said. "Then we'll meet back here for dinner?"

I nodded, filled with new determination. The clock was ticking on our time aboard this ship, and we had entirely too many questions to answer before we docked.

CHAPTER THIRTY

I headed directly to the kitchen area while Redvers made plans to infiltrate the crew deck. I wished him luck—better luck than I'd had at any rate. I went through the main dining room to the very back where I came upon a large set of double doors that led to the kitchen. As I peered through the crack and watched the staff bustle around the large room beyond, I contemplated who would be the best person to pump for information.

But the decision was taken out of my hands. The door swung open, nearly striking me in the process.

"I'm so sorry, ma'am. I didn't see you there. Behind the door." It was a gentle rebuke, and the short, round man who stood before me in his smart uniform smiled kindly as he said it. Then something in his eyes shifted slightly as he looked me up and down.

"I know, and I apologize for being in the way. I just had a question for someone on the kitchen staff, but I couldn't decide who best to ask."

The man looked at me speculatively, his waxed moustache twitching ever so slightly as he took my arm and gently guided me away from the door. His hand lingered just a second too long. "Perhaps I can help you. My name is Josiah Waters. I'm the head steward here on the *Olympic*."

I gave him my best smile, despite my discomfort with the man and the way his eyes stayed on me. "It's a pleasure to meet you, Mr. Waters." I fidgeted with the wedding band that came with our cover story. I was unaccustomed to having anything on that finger anymore, and now I toyed with the shiny gold band. "I'm just wondering if you might have some information . . . about a friend of mine." The way I said "friend" made it obvious that the person I sought was more than a friend. "I wouldn't want my husband to find out." It was a gamble taking this approach, but it was the first one that had come to mind, especially since the man seemed less than a gentleman himself. "I met another guest and he was such a good dancer, but I haven't seen him since."

Waters nodded in an understanding fashion. "A good dancer is hard to find, ma'am."

I agreed enthusiastically. "And my husband, well, he's not always so graceful on the dance floor." I could only imagine what Redvers' reaction would be if he heard me ascribing all my terrible dancing abilities to himself. I almost giggled at the thought, but restrained myself. Waters nodded sympathetically, so I rushed on. "I wouldn't want you to think the wrong thing."

"Of course not." But the gleam in his eye told me otherwise.

"But I . . ."

"Say no more, ma'am. But how can we help you find your dancing partner?"

I described Vanessa's husband for Waters and he listened with a slight frown on his face. "But you see, I haven't seen him since that first night. And I have checked everywhere. So, it occurred to me that perhaps he has taken ill and is confined to his room."

The light went on in Waters's blue eyes. "Ahh, I see."

I nodded. "Can you tell me if anyone is taking their meals in their room?"

The steward glanced around him, then studied my face for a moment. I worried that he was going to demure and refuse to answer me, but he surprised me. "No, ma'am, not in the first-class cabins, at least. There is an elderly woman who is taking her meals in her suite, but no one else who has been doing so consistently. Plenty of breakfasts delivered to the rooms, but not so many lunches or dinners."

I nodded, feeling defeated that my clever tactic had not turned up any more useful information. As much as I would have rather hurried on my way, I took another stab. "What about the second class?"

Waters shook his head, light from the overhead fixture gleaming off his bald scalp. "If he was traveling second class it is unlikely he would have been dancing with you."

"I suppose that is true." I considered that for a moment. It would have been smart for Van de Meter to book himself into another class for the trip if he planned to disappear. It would make finding him more difficult, since there was not much mingling between the classes.

A spark lit Waters's eyes at my downcast expression. "But I can check with the staff in the other kitchens."

"You would do that?" He reached out and took my hand. I flinched at the unexpected contact but smiled, despite the fact that his clammy palm made my skin crawl. "I can't tell you how much I appreciate the help."

"I hate to see a maiden in distress. Where shall I leave word for you?"

I paused, but ultimately gave him my room number. It wouldn't be difficult for him to learn the information anyway, and at least I wasn't staying there by myself. He promised to send word once he had spoken with the others. I thanked him again and he gave me a moist kiss on my hand before I was able to pull away and take my leave.

I felt disgusted by the entire interaction. I'd used his lecherous nature to get what I wanted—information—but it left me feeling more than a little soiled. At least I didn't have to promise anything in return, and I would do my best to avoid any further run-ins with the man.

Although I hadn't come away with nothing. At the very least I knew Miles Van de Meter wasn't secreted away in a first-class cabin. I'd managed to narrow the field a little. And hopefully Waters would come back to me later with some information that would narrow it even further.

I decided to swing past Vanessa's room to check on her before beginning my search for her maid and had my hand raised to knock when I heard a familiar rumbling voice just behind me. "I thought I might find you here."

I dropped my hand and turned to find Redvers leaning against the wall, hands tucked casually into his trouser pockets. My heart skipped at the sight of him, as it usually did. But I covered it by grabbing his arm and pulling him down the hallway away from Vanessa's room. I wasn't even sure she was there, but I didn't want to risk her overhearing us if she was.

"Did you learn anything?" I whispered.

Redvers fought an amused smile. "I did."

I waited for a beat. "And are you going to tell me?"

He winked, then finally spilled. "I found the occupant of the room." He shrugged. "It was the fourth mate." I couldn't help the defeated sigh that escaped me. "I asked him about Rebecca's visit, and he admitted that he was having a bit of a romance with a second-class passenger, and described her perfectly." Redvers gave a little snort. "He begged me not to say anything, since it's strictly against the rules and he could lose his position."

"It's a wonder he's willing to do it at all in that case." It also occurred to me that if the man could lose his job, he was unlikely to simply give up his secrets to a complete stranger. So why confess to Redvers? "And how did you get him to admit to all this?"

Redvers waved a hand. "I can be very persuasive." I narrowed my eyes at him. "And I may have threatened him with exposure. I suggested that I had proof."

I shook my head. "That poor man. He didn't stand a chance."

"He did not. His name is Lee Schnell, incidentally." Redvers and I continued walking. "And we shouldn't feel too sorry for him if he's in the habit of seducing young women on board."

I shrugged. "Unless they want to be seduced." I firmly believed women had as much agency as men in such matters. My mother had instilled a deep sense of equality in me from the beginning—even if my memories of her had begun to fade, that never would.

Redvers' deep voice dropped into an even deeper rumble, one I could feel in my chest. "Some women want to be seduced, eh?"

I felt electricity tingle up and down my spine, but I casually slapped his arm and continued walking, ignoring the heat rising in my face. Redvers' attentions felt entirely different than my interaction with Waters—in all the best ways.

"Did you learn anything else from Schnell?"

Redvers looked amused at my abrupt question, but he went along with it. "Not really. He was just another clean-shaven officer in a blue uniform." He mused for a moment. "Schnell seemed a little older than usual for such a low rank, but perhaps he came to the field later in life."

My mind was already moving forward, thinking about the likelihood of Rebecca having a fling with a member of the crew. It didn't seem like something the serious young woman would be interested in, but stranger things had happened. Vanessa had certainly given her the freedom to do so during this trip—maybe the girl was simply taking advantage of her free time to have a bit of fun before going back to her full-time duties as a maid.

I still needed to talk to the girl though.

"Do you think that's necessary?" Redvers asked.

I realized I had said that last bit out loud, and I looked up at Redvers. "I do. There's still the matter of her lying about the trunks anyway. I want to talk with her and see if I can get a sense of what's true and what isn't."

Redvers shrugged one shoulder. "It's up to you. I'm not sure it's worth the time, especially since she's unlikely to come clean about any of it." I gave him a dark look, since it was a sentiment entirely too close to his earlier dismissal of the case as a whole, and he held up his hands in surrender. "But of course, I bow to your instincts."

"Good," I said, my voice light. "It's about time."

He chuckled, but after a few paces turned serious. "We need to figure out what happened to Dobbins."

I nodded. I just wasn't sure how we were going to go about doing that.

Chapter Thirty-one

The next morning, I dragged myself out of bed far earlier than I wanted to, but Redvers had learned that Dobbins was to be cast into the sea before the sun came up. It made sense, since the captain wanted to avoid the passengers seeing any of the proceedings, but I was resentful of the time of day and the fact that we had been woken by a brisk alarm.

I also resented how little progress we'd made the night before. Both Vanessa and her maid were nowhere to be found, and I was more than a little worried.

I threw water on my face in lieu of drinking my usual carafe of coffee and headed out to the sitting room. Redvers greeted me with an overlarge grin and I nearly growled in response. It was far too early to be that jovial.

He, of course, simply laughed at my surliness.

But we both sobered as we headed toward our destination. I had done my best to securely pin my burgundy felt cloche, but the chill morning wind was doing its level best to send it to the ocean's deep. Along with poor Dobbins. I pulled my coat more snugly against my throat as we descended the stairs to the second-class deck. Redvers led me toward the rear of the boat where the quiet ceremony was to take place.

"Do you think they're going to let us join them?" My voice was whipped away to the west by the wind.

"No, we'll try to stay out of sight."

I nodded. We descended several more stairs until we came to the back deck. There a set of stairs led up again to the lifted platform at the very rear of the ship. We quietly ascended and then came to stand behind a large white air duct. From there we could see the proceedings, but masked by the dim light we wouldn't necessarily be seen by the captain and his men. A canvas bag in the shape of a body lay at Captain Bisset's feet, and even from where I stood I could see that the top of the bag was stitched closed. A man clutching a Bible stood to the other side of the body; I assumed he was the ship chaplain.

"Interesting," Redvers murmured. I tore my attention away from the proceedings and turned to see where he was looking. He was gazing behind us and gave a slight nod to the deck above. I squinted and could see Heinz Naumann standing against the railing of the first-class promenade. Only a few yards away Eloise Baumann and her sister also stood, the first rays of sun breaking through the cloud cover and illuminating Eloise's elaborately feathered hat that she was forced to clutch with one plump hand.

"Do you think they know each other?" I whispered.

Redvers shook his head. "I'm not sure."

My eyes fell to the deck below, and I could see the outline of another person standing at the railing, leaning forward to see the ceremony just starting behind us. "I think that might be Rebecca Tesch." Redvers followed my gaze and made a noise in the back of his throat. "I wonder what she's doing out here." I also wondered how she'd been managing to avoid me.

"I wonder what any of them are doing here."

We turned our attention back to the burial, and watched as the chaplain read some words of scripture. Dobbins's body in its canvas coffin was lifted by several burly members of the crew and placed on a long wooden plank. The chaplain's words were lost to the wind, but as he wound down and closed his black leather Bible, the men tipped the board up. The bag slid slowly at first, gaining momentum as it descended, then left the board entirely and disappeared from sight. I couldn't hear the splash, but I imagined the sound and found myself wincing. The ship's horn let out three soulful blasts in Dobbins's honor, and with that it was over, the ship's crew moving to disband and return to their duties.

We quickly turned behind us, but the figures we'd seen before had already disappeared.

Since we were already on deck we swung by the telegraph office. Redvers' new friend McIntyre wasn't on duty, but there was a small envelope with several messages waiting for Redvers. He pocketed them and we returned to our suite where I immediately flopped into the chair.

Redvers raised a brow. "You aren't going back to sleep?"

I was too tired to come up with a quip. "No." I didn't think I would be able to get back to sleep after seeing what we had. I needed some time to process both Dobbins's burial and why the others had come out to witness it. "But I do need caffeine. Do you think the café is open yet?"

"I think in about thirty minutes."

I nodded. "How do they ensure that the body will . . . stay down?" It was an indelicate question, but I was definitely curious.

"They weight it down."

I nodded again. "It was a very perfunctory service." Altogether it had taken less than a quarter of an hour.

Redvers shrugged and came to sit across from me, crossing one long leg over the other. "Dying at sea is something these chaps understand is a possibility when they join. Of course, they aren't usually murdered on board. Still, it's customary to simply say a few words as they respectfully send them off on their final voyage. But that's about the extent of it."

I didn't bother to ask how Redvers knew this. He was a font of knowledge on many subjects. "The other question is obvious. What was everyone else doing there?"

Redvers' foot bounced against his knee. "I can tell you what I think Naumann was doing there."

"If he was responsible, do you really think he would show up to see the man buried? It seems entirely too obvious. It would be much smarter to stay indoors and pretend he had no knowledge of the thing at all."

"I never claimed the man was smart."

I rolled my eyes but didn't bother to answer that. "It's interesting that Eloise and her sister decided to attend. I thought their only interest was how quickly they would get a new steward assigned to them." Although I was no longer sure if I should be painting Margret with the same brush as her brash older sister. After yesterday it seemed that perhaps the woman was more perceptive than I had credited her for. Of course, she might have simply come because Eloise badgered her into it. I could see how it would be easier on the whole to go along with Eloise's plans rather than argue with the woman.

I still didn't believe Heinz was responsible for the murder, despite Redvers' feelings to the contrary, although I had to admit I didn't have any better explanation. I might have blamed Miles Van de Meter himself, if it weren't for the fact that there had been no sign of the man since I had initially seen him on deck during our departure. Was it possible he had somehow disembarked at Cherbourg after all?

"What are you thinking about?" Redvers' amused voice broke into my thoughts. He had removed the envelope from his pocket and was perusing the telegrams.

"Where on earth Miles Van de Meter has gone to."

"I completely forgot to ask if you learned anything from the steward."

I grimaced, remembering how dirty I had felt coming away

from that conversation. "There was nothing of interest in first class but he said he would check second and third. In case Van de Meter is traveling below."

Redvers noticed my reaction, setting his foot on the ground and leaning forward, the messages forgotten for the moment. "Did something happen with the steward?"

I shook my head, then ran a tired hand over my eyes. "Not really. Just your run-of-the-mill lech." I put up a palm to stop Redvers from whatever he was going to say next. "It's fine. Nothing I can't handle."

Redvers grumbled, but subsided back into his chair. I appreciated that he was ready to come to my defense, but if he tried to step between me and every man who made my skin crawl with a few lewd looks we would never accomplish anything.

I changed the subject. "I need to go find Rebecca. Do you remember what room Dobbins said she was in?"

To his credit, Redvers never blinked at my abrupt transitions. "I do. She's in D61. Are you thinking of trying again to find her this morning?"

"I am. Especially after seeing her at the burial." I nodded toward the messages lying near Redvers' hand on the little table. "Anything interesting in this morning's reports?"

Redvers nodded. "They've figured out what it is that Naumann is after."

I was still the tiniest bit reluctant to accept that Naumann was our man. "Are we absolutely certain that Brubacher is in the clear?"

Redvers looked amused. "Yes. His background came up clean. Not only that, but his family left Germany a generation ago because of disagreements with the government. It's unlikely he would work for them now."

I sighed. "Very well. Naumann is our man."

"He is. And it appears that he's traveling to the United States to steal some plans for a rocket."

"What kind of rocket?"

"Robert Goddard—a professor at Clark University—has been secretly developing a liquid-propelled rocket and he ran some launches recently that were quite successful. All very hush-hush of course. But it appears the Germans caught wind all the same, and we would like to stop them from getting that type of technology."

I didn't understand the details, but it sounded like a significant advance. It also made a great deal of sense in terms of our mission. The war wasn't so far in the past that anyone was willing to take a chance on letting the "huns" make progress toward another one. Now that we knew who the culprit on board was and what he was after, we could hopefully stop him from getting his hands on the designs once we arrived in the U.S.

"Excellent." I checked my watch. "Do you think we should head to the café now? It must be nearly open."

Redvers chuckled and pushed himself to a stand, securing the messages back in his pocket. "Heaven help anyone who comes between you and your morning coffee."

I gave him a dazzling smile. "You *are* a fast learner."

Chapter Thirty-two

After eating a hearty breakfast and fulfilling my caffeine needs, I was still tired but feeling more prepared to face my tasks for the day. I checked on our deck chairs, but Heinz Naumann was nowhere to be seen—I wondered if he had gone back to bed after rousing himself so early to watch Dobbins's burial. Either way, I decided not to waste my time waiting for the man.

My first priority was finding Rebecca Tesch. I made my way down the large main staircase, traversed down a long hallway, and located the staircase for the second-class passengers—not quite as luxurious as the first-class staircases, but still quite fine with its carved wooden posts and diamond-patterned carpet. I found Rebecca's cabin, but there was no answer at my knock on the door. I had a sense of déjà vu from the day before when I stood before the fourth-mate's quarters, waiting for an answer that never came. At least this time I wasn't concerned about being escorted away.

I knocked again, louder, with the same result. But today I was not going to be dissuaded. After pausing a beat to decide where the young woman might have taken herself off to, I strode off in search of Vanessa FitzSimmons's erstwhile maid.

I finally found her in the second-class lounge. It was the

third place I looked, after the second-class passenger deck and the dining room. All were quite beautiful spaces with carved wood and spacious design, although the difference in elegance between the first class and below was still notice-able. Still, it seemed quite a comfortable way to make the voyage. Although I did have to wonder how the third-class passengers fared on the decks even further below.

Rebecca was seated at a two-person table, reading a beaten-up and dog-eared hardback—*The Red Lamp,* by Mary Roberts Rinehart. I took the seat across from her without saying a word, and I could see from the look she gave me from be-hind her book that she was considering whether or not she could ignore me entirely. I smiled patiently.

"I can wait all day."

With a sigh Rebecca lowered the book, but refused to put it down completely.

"Good book?" I asked politely, but Rebecca refused to an-swer me. "Very well. I have quite a few questions for you, and I expect you to start telling me the truth. Or this will in-deed be your last week of work with Mrs. FitzSimmons."

Perhaps the threat was unnecessary, but I had arrived ready for battle and with no tolerance for nonsense, espe-cially after combing the deck for the woman. Not to mention the fact that a man was dead and it was possible that my questions had led to his demise. I didn't have the time or pa-tience to play games with silly girls who thought they might outsmart me.

Rebecca quietly closed her book and set it on the table, folding her hands on top of it. She gave a single nod and I got right to it.

"Why did you lie about the trunks in Mrs. FitzSimmons's room?"

Rebecca refused to meet my eyes. "I can't tell you that."

"But you admit that you were lying."

She didn't say anything, looking out across the room, as though she might find salvation from some other quarter. But no one was coming to her rescue.

"Very well. We'll come back to that."

Now Rebecca looked at me, her eyes soft and worried. "Please, miss. I'm . . . I don't want any trouble. For myself or for Mrs. Vanessa. She's a nice enough lady, but we're both in some hot water."

"What kind of hot water?" Beyond what I had already seen.

But Rebecca just shook her head, eyes damp.

"Is someone threatening you? You can tell me if they are. We could protect you."

At my words the girl's shoulders stiffened and I thought I was finally getting to the heart of things. But no matter how I prodded, the girl's lips remained sealed on the matter.

I tried a different tact. "Why did you go down below to the crew quarters? Who were you meeting with?"

"It started with just a bit of romance. A little flirting." Then a grimace of distaste crossed her face.

"But it became something else?" I asked.

Her voice turned mechanical. "I was having a little romance with a crew member. That's all, ma'am. Just a bit of fun."

Perhaps it had started as a bit of fun, but somewhere along the way it had obviously turned sour. Was he the one now threatening Rebecca? Because it was obvious from her discomfort that someone was. But what was he threatening her for? Favors of some kind? My mouth soured at the thought. I hoped the kind of trouble she had gotten herself into wasn't the kind that ended with a baby on the way.

"Has he hurt you in some way? Please tell me what's going on, Rebecca."

"I never meant Miss Vanessa any harm." She just shook her head again. "But you should stay out of this, ma'am. For your own good." With that, Rebecca grabbed her book and hurried from the room. In her speed, she failed to notice that the scrap of paper she had been using as a bookmark had fluttered to the floor in her wake. I stood and retrieved it, but when I looked up, she was long gone.

I turned the paper over and quickly read the words written in a bold hand, all capital letters: *Be on deck. 4am. See what happens when you disobey.*

I suspected I was holding the reason why Rebecca Tesch had turned up to see Dobbins's burial that morning.

CHAPTER THIRTY-THREE

I wandered back up to the first-class promenade and my deck chair, thoughts swirling. Was the threat from the fourth mate—the man she had met with in his quarters? Or were these two completely separate issues? Had Rebecca gotten herself mixed up in something more, or was this all because of Vanessa FitzSimmons's missing husband? The girl had lied about the trunks, and was now being threatened by someone, that much was certain. I wished she hadn't run off before I'd had the chance to learn more answers—although I wasn't sure she would have given me any. The girl was certainly frightened of someone or something.

I'd slipped the paper she dropped into the inner pocket of my wool coat so that there was no chance I would lose it. Despite the sunshine, the wind had a chill to it, so I stopped by the rug room and rented myself one. Then I headed to my assigned deck chair, noting the empty seats on either side, shook out my rug, and huddled beneath it. I tilted my face into the sun, uncaring about the freckles that would most likely result, and allowed myself a moment to soak up the unusually sunny day.

We had very little time left on board. On the one hand it didn't feel like enough, yet on the other it felt like an eternity, especially when faced with the vastness of the water stretching out around us. I looked forward to being back on solid land as much as I looked forward to solving the various mysteries surrounding us.

"Mrs. Wunderly! It's quite shocking that you have no hat on. You're going to get freckles!"

I had allowed my eyes to close while I enjoyed the warmth on my face and now I reluctantly opened them to find Eloise Baumann and her sister standing before me. I nearly sighed out loud at the interruption, but I restrained myself and patted my windswept hair instead.

"Yes, I hadn't planned on coming on deck and I quite forgot my hat."

Eloise's lips were pursed and I steeled myself for the forthcoming lecture, but she surprised me by changing the subject.

"I see you were out early this morning. I can't believe your husband would take you to see such a morbid affair."

I didn't mention that she had also been out on deck to watch the very same thing. I glanced at Margret and caught her rolling her eyes.

My mouth opened to respond, but Miss Baumann steamed right over me before I could make a sound. "We were there to pay our respects."

"Of course," I murmured.

"And, of course, I will need to report back to my circle of friends what a burial at sea looks like."

I raised my eyebrows at this. I wasn't sure a group of society ladies absolutely needed a play-by-play of the man's brief ceremony before being laid to rest at the bottom of the ocean. It seemed gauche.

"We've been assigned a new steward already." Eloise sniffed. "We'll see if this one is up to snuff." That was certainly news, since I hadn't met the new steward yet. Then she cast a disapproving eye at me before continuing on. "You should get inside before you get any more sun, Mrs. Wunderly. I'm sure your husband wouldn't approve of you being out here without proper covering. Just think of what will happen to your skin."

This coming from a woman who had one hand firmly clamped to the overlarge hat on her own head to keep it from tearing off and flinging itself into the ocean beyond. It appeared to be even larger than the one I had seen her wearing this morning, and I wondered just how many enormous chapeaux the woman had brought on board.

"You know, you're absolutely right, Miss Baumann." I stood, folding my fur rug and placing it neatly on my chair. I would return it to the rug room later. In the meantime, I forced a smile at Eloise. "I would hate to get sun spots."

"More than you already have."

My lips narrowed, but I kept enough of my smile in place that she seemed convinced that I was heeding her obviously excellent advice. In truth, I just wanted to escape below to my suite where I could think in peace. It was really too bad that I couldn't continue to enjoy the small bit of sunshine we'd had on this trip.

"Come, Margret. We need to find our own chairs. I think they're up here around the corner. . . ." Her voice faded off into the wind as her sister dutifully followed behind her. Just before she turned the corner, Margret turned and gave me a quick wink before disappearing. I shook my head in shock before heading down below.

I had no idea what to make of that woman.

Back in my suite, I carefully removed the note from my pocket and placed it on the coffee table. I shed my coat and took a seat, then proceeded to stare at the note for a long time. I hadn't come to any better conclusions by the time Redvers returned, and I was glad for the interruption.

"What do you have there?" Redvers covered the small space in several strides with his long legs and picked up the paper that I had been contemplating.

"Rebecca Tesch dropped it."

"On purpose?"

I shook my head, and Redvers put the paper back on the table, then took the seat opposite me. Now we were both contemplating the threatening note.

"Did you learn anything from her?" I could feel Redvers' dark eyes on me and I looked up.

"No, I'm sorry to say I did not." I reported everything Rebecca had said and how I felt that her story about a shipboard romance still rang false.

Redvers frowned. "I didn't get the sense that the fourth mate was lying, but perhaps I need to speak with him again."

"Do you think he's the one who sent the note? I was wondering if this was two separate issues, or if he's the one threatening her."

"If he's the one threatening her, then he's most likely the person who killed Dobbins," Redvers said. "And I can't imagine what his motive for that would be. Killing someone is an extreme reaction to being caught having a fling with one of the passengers."

"I'm just not convinced that's what's happening here," I said.

"What do you think is happening?"

"I have no idea."

"Well, that's very helpful."

I stuck my tongue out at him. "I don't see you coming up with any better theories."

He paused, building suspense. "As a matter of fact . . ." I held my breath in anticipation of some great reveal. Some new clue that would point us in an entirely new direction. "I don't either."

I deflated. That was not what I wanted to hear.

I cast back for what Redvers had said he would try to do this morning. "Did you learn anything from Dr. Montgomery?"

Redvers crossed his ankle over his knee and leaned back. "He's an interesting chap, our Dr. Montgomery."

I cocked my head. "How so?"

"I don't think he's entirely on the side of the captain and crew. He seemed genuinely regretful about having to drug Mrs. FitzSimmons." I made a noise in the back of my throat and he continued. "Dr. Montgomery also doesn't agree that Dobbins's death was the accident the captain is claiming it is."

I leaned forward in my seat. "Really?"

"He was asked to examine the body, but when he pointed out the marks I had noticed on the man's neck, Captain Bisset told him that those were not to be mentioned in his report. It wasn't a request—it was an order."

"Why would the captain want to cover up the fact that Dobbins was murdered? Is that why the burial happened so quickly?"

"No, apparently those always take place immediately, so that bit was quite normal. But the fact that the captain has ordered his crew to treat it strictly as an accident isn't normal at all."

"You don't think Bisset had anything to do with Dobbins's death, do you?" The idea seemed quite shocking. I didn't care for the captain or his attitude toward women, but it was a far cry from murder.

"It's hard to say. Naumann is still my top candidate, but it seems the field is widening."

It was a little irritating how Redvers was sticking so strongly to his belief that Naumann was guilty. Well, he was guilty of something—sedition—but not necessarily of murder. I still didn't believe the man was responsible for that.

"Did the doctor have anything else to say?"

"He doesn't believe that Vanessa's husband was ever on board. He thinks it's just a cry for help."

I couldn't help but roll my eyes at that. "I suppose I'm just another hysteric as well."

Redvers shrugged apologetically, then continued. "I did learn something from your kitchen steward."

My eyes widened. "You went and spoke to him?"

"I didn't want you to have to follow up with the man." His lips tightened. "I was quite clear that he shouldn't be interacting with other men's wives in such a manner."

I knew I wasn't actually Redvers' wife, but I couldn't help the flush of pleasure at his words. It made me wonder if my feelings on the subject had really done such a complete turnabout. Would I enjoy being Mrs. Redvers Dibble?

I certainly wouldn't enjoy the last name.

But there were other aspects that I would certainly enjoy. Unaware of the direction my wayward thoughts had turned, Redvers had continued on, then stopped when he realized I wasn't listening.

"Jane?"

"Hmm?"

"Did you not want to hear about what the steward had to say?"

"Oh! Of course. My apologies. I just . . ." I didn't want to explain where my thoughts had gone, and I felt my face getting warm.

Redvers looked amused. "I was just saying that the steward did in fact talk to the other kitchen staff. There is no one matching Van de Meter's description sequestered in their room."

"Could he be simply in second- or third-class and taking his meals as normal?"

"It would be chancy. Vanessa has been doing regular circuits of the ship—even belowdecks—from what I've been told by the doctor. They've tried to dissuade her, but she won't be stopped. Unless they keep her drugged and locked in her suite."

She hadn't mentioned that to me, but considering everything else about the woman, it was hardly strange. It also occurred to me that I hadn't seen Vanessa since Dr. Montgomery had led her away the previous morning. We had intended to meet for a drink, but never did. I felt a rush of guilt for not having remembered to check on her; she wasn't my responsibility and yet I still felt I'd been remiss in not stopping by. Had something happened to her?

"Has he been keeping her drugged?"

"The doctor seemed reluctant to, but it also sounds like he's getting a fair amount of pressure from the captain and the first mate to do just that."

I was fairly certain my face looked as though I had sucked on a lemon.

"I agree." Redvers shook his head. "I think the woman is getting the short end of the stick."

It felt like the first time Redvers had come down firmly on Vanessa's side, and I was relieved.

"What are our next steps with Naumann?" I didn't want to lose track of our original purpose.

"Remain friendly with him. We need to continue to track him. And we should also start thinking about who his contact on board might be. Remember that the book appeared in his luggage after we set sail. So, someone on board here delivered it to him."

I sighed. That seemed a monumental task. It could be anyone, really.

"I'll probably give his room another thorough search," Redvers mused.

"Do you really think searching his room is going to give us his contact? I don't think he'll have it written down in a notebook for you to conveniently find."

"No, of course not. I'm sure he's simply got the name memorized."

"And he hasn't spoken about meeting up with anyone when he arrives in the States."

"Have you asked him directly?"

"No. But now that we're getting close to the end of our voyage, I'll ask him what his plans in America are." Although it was unlikely he would tell me the truth.

Redvers nodded. "We haven't much time left."

I was about to reply when there was a knock at the door. Redvers stood and opened it to find Heinz Naumann himself standing on the other side.

"Mr. Wunderly." He nodded at Redvers, then took a single step into the room. "Mrs. Wunderly. Have you seen or heard from Vanessa . . . er, Mrs. FitzSimmons recently?"

I shook my head, again feeling a wave of guilt for not checking on the woman.

Naumann's blue eyes looked troubled. "I can't find her anywhere and she's not answering her door."

CHAPTER THIRTY-FOUR

Perhaps there was no real cause for alarm, but my instincts warned me otherwise. Without another word I stood and walked past both men out into the hall. I waited long enough for Redvers to close up after us, but then continued at a hurried pace toward Vanessa's suite.

When I reached the room—the suite she had been moved into—I tried the door and found it locked. I knocked loudly, but there was still no response. I looked to Redvers. He paused and glanced at Naumann, and I nodded and pulled a couple of pins from where they had been holding the sides of my hair in place. I was about to set to work when Naumann stepped forward.

"Please, allow me."

Redvers and I shared a look of shock, as Naumann took the pins from my hand and went to work on the door. It was a mark of how truly worried he was that he would perform such a task in front of us—especially since he had the door open in a very short period of time. All my doubts about his identity were quickly smothered. Only someone quite practiced at the art of lock picking could have opened the door that quickly.

Although I had to wonder why he hadn't done this earlier

when he stopped by this room. Was it because he wanted witnesses to what we would find?

In a panic, I rushed through the newly opened door and into the bedroom within. Her pale body lay quite still in her bed, and I choked back a sob. There was no blood that I could see and no obvious signs of trauma, but she didn't look alive either. I rushed to her side and pressed a hand to her neck, searching for a pulse but not finding one. I put my face to her nose and could just barely feel an exhale of air on my cheek. I lifted her lifeless wrist and pressed my fingers to her pulse point there, and was able to pick up a weak beat. I gave her face a little slap, but there was no response.

I looked behind me to where the men stood in the doorway, unsure of what to do. "Help me get her into the bath. And make it cold. One of you run and get the doctor."

The two men shared a look between them and, without words, Naumann elected himself to fetch Montgomery. Redvers came forward and scooped the woman up in his arms, following me into her private bathroom. He gently placed her in the tub as I turned on the cold water—not too cold, but brisk enough to give her system a little shock. At the feeling of chilly water pooling around her legs, Vanessa's eyes began to flutter, but still failed to open.

I hadn't even noticed that Redvers had left the bathroom until he returned with a pill bottle. "It looks like she took all of these." I glanced at the vial in his hand, but couldn't concentrate on reading the label.

"What are they?"

"Sleeping pills." He shook the empty container. "They are prescribed to her."

I turned off the taps, not wanting to completely soak the woman, and continued trying to wake her. Once the danger had passed, I could deal with whether she had taken them

230 Erica Ruth Neubauer

herself or whether it had been someone else's idea. But right
now Vanessa was far from out of the woods.

Mercifully the doctor arrived quickly, with Heinz in tow. I
didn't trust Montgomery, but neither did I know what else to
do—at the moment he was our best bet for keeping Vanessa
alive. The doctor shooed the other men out of the room, and
asked me to stay while he administered ipecac to get the pills
out of her stomach.

"Will this work?" I asked worriedly.

Montgomery's voice was grim. "It will have to."

We managed to pour some of the foul-smelling liquid
down her throat, helping her to swallow. Within moments,
she was retching and getting the poison out of her stomach.
It was unpleasant to watch, but I was glad there was something to get up—at least the pills hadn't completely dissolved
into her system.

An hour later the doctor and I emerged from Vanessa's
room. Redvers and Heinz were both sitting awkwardly in the
outer room, neither speaking to the other.

"She's asleep now, but I think she will wake up this time,"
I said. "We got quite a bit of it out of her stomach."

Heinz shot a look at Redvers before turning to the doctor.
"Do you think she took them all?"

The concern in Heinz's voice gave me pause. Just how
much time had the two been spending together?

"It certainly looks that way." The doctor paused. "I'll stay
here with her and keep her monitored. I suggest you all . . ."
He trailed off. He didn't have any suggestions for what we
should do after finding a woman nearly dead in her suite. I
didn't either.

"Thank you, Doctor." Heinz gave a little bow and excused
himself from the room. Redvers and I waited a beat and then
did the same.

"What now?" Redvers asked once we were in the hall.

"I would like a bath." I felt sweaty and wrung out from helping the doctor with Vanessa. Redvers nodded in understanding and led me back to our suite.

We didn't discuss what had just happened, but it was certainly the only thing I was thinking about.

Chapter Thirty-Five

Ilay soaking in the small tub, grateful once more that our suite had its own private bathroom. But I couldn't scrub the images of Vanessa's still form from my mind. I didn't always like her, but I certainly didn't want to see her dead. Redvers had already told me to avoid blaming myself for not checking in on her sooner, but it was hard not to. We were lucky to have found her when we did, and I couldn't help thinking that if I had stopped by last night or earlier this morning, I could have stopped her. I didn't think this attempt on her life was simply a cry for help—it had been far too thorough.

With those thoughts swirling, I stepped from the tub and went into the bedroom to pull on a new dress, a green floral number with a black tie at the neck. I smoothed my now-damp hair and stepped back into the sitting room where Redvers was waiting patiently.

Before he could speak, I started in. "Well, I think we need to concentrate our efforts on what brought us here in the first place. Let's come up with a plan to search Naumann's room again. Or maybe figure out who his contact on board is." I didn't want to talk about what had just happened. Not yet, at any rate. I needed some time to think about Vanessa

FitzSimmons—and why she had been driven to take her own life. Or make the attempt, at any rate.

Redvers' eyebrows shot straight up. "Vanessa's maid was threatened. You don't think . . ." At my steely look he shook his head instead of finishing his thought. "Very well. We can talk about it later."

I was relieved, but I knew the man wouldn't let it drop for long.

Instead of focusing on how long he would give me to avoid the topic, I decided to tick off on my fingers what we both knew and still needed to learn. "There's no longer any doubt that Naumann is our man." Redvers nodded and I moved to the next finger. "But we need to find out the name of Naumann's contact."

"Since it looks like the drop was made on board, they are likely a passenger," Redvers said.

"Or a member of the crew." I paused and gave that some thought. "Have we completely eliminated Brubacher? Could he be the contact?"

"It's unlikely. But we'll keep an eye on him."

"We also need to find out if the fourth mate is the one threatening Rebecca." I frowned. Could Schnell have killed Dobbins? Over his job? It seemed an extremely unlikely possibility.

"I can't fathom the motive though."

Neither could I. I had seen most of the other officers of the ship, but it occurred to me that I had never seen the fourth mate. "I've never seen the man. Why is that? Aren't they supposed to rub elbows with the passengers?"

"I asked him that, actually. He was sick for the first day or so, some kind of stomach bug, and then because the others had to pull his shifts during that time, he's been doing all the night watches to make it up to them."

"And then he sleeps during the day."

"It would appear so."

That made sense, although I would still dearly love to interrogate the man about the nature of his interactions with Rebecca Tesch. Something didn't feel right there—their stories matched up, but in a way that was entirely too pat. It just didn't seem as though Rebecca was telling the truth, although with as many lies as that girl had told me so far, it was nearly impossible to untangle what was truth and what was fiction. The only tangible thing I had from the girl was the sinister note she had dropped.

"If the fourth mate isn't the one threatening Rebecca, it's most likely Vanessa's husband doing it. But we aren't certain that he's still on board." I made a noise of frustration. "Unless he's been hiding in one of those funnels the entire time, I don't know where he could be."

Redvers snorted.

I was quiet for a moment, thinking through what else we needed to answer. Even though I didn't feel comfortable with the story of the romance between Rebecca and Schnell, the fourth mate, it was beginning to seem like a separate issue. Although one I still wanted to check out when I had the chance to talk with the girl again.

Which led us back to Vanessa's husband. "If Van de Meter is the one threatening Rebecca, then he's likely the one who killed Dobbins." And in that case, there was plenty of motive, especially since I'd helped kick up a fuss to find the man. I felt a pang of guilt—what if my questions had led to poor Dobbins's demise? Had Van de Meter killed the steward to keep from being found? I only wished that the ship had been thoroughly searched when Vanessa had first asked for it to be done. If it had, Dobbins might still be alive. "I would also dearly love to know what Captain Bisset is up to."

Redvers' face darkened. "So would I."

*   *   *

Redvers wanted to conduct a few more searches, but we decided to save them for after dark. There was entirely too much staff about during the day, and the night shift was sparser of personnel—and led by the fourth mate, apparently. I made a mental note to go out at night and try to get a look at the man so that I would have a face to put with the name.

But for the time being, I decided to head up to the deck and see if I could find Heinz. There was no time like the present for asking him about his plans once he got to America. I was hoping that with all that had happened he would be more susceptible to opening up. While I was busy with that, Redvers would radio to shore and report to his superiors.

I pulled on my heavy wool coat and added a thick scarf before I headed above. It was another sunny day, which felt entirely at odds with the awful scene from that morning. It felt wrong to enjoy the weather somehow, and I concentrated on the brisk wind instead of lifting my face to the warmth.

I could see that Heinz was already in his chair when I approached, and he was drinking directly from his flask instead of pouring it genteelly into his teacup. It seemed he was as affected by the morning's events as I was.

He glanced over at me as I took my seat, then resumed his staring over the water and taking the occasional nip. "Have you heard anything?"

I shook my head. He grimaced but didn't say anything else.

I studied his profile curiously. "I didn't realize you and Vanessa had become so close."

Heinz nodded and was quiet for so long that I didn't think he was going to speak again. Then he gave me a quick glance and turned his gaze back out over the ocean. The waves had light whitecaps today, whipped up by the wind.

"Vanessa . . . in some ways she reminds me of my sister Helga." A bittersweet smile twisted his lips. "Helga is . . ."

Heinz seemed to search for the word in English. "Fragile. She is fragile in the mind."

I nodded my understanding, wondering if his sister had suffered a similar episode to what we had just witnessed.

"Where is she now?"

Storm clouds rolled over Heinz's face. "She is in a facility. It is owned by the government." He turned and his blue eyes met mine, pleading with me to understand. He wouldn't say it in so many words, but his story, combined with his earlier comment about how he did everything because of his sister—it didn't take much for me to conclude that he was being controlled through Helga.

"Will they hurt her?"

He shook his head. "Not as long as I do what I am supposed to." He took a longer drag off his flask, then gave it a little shake to see how much was left. Without looking at me, he held out the silver container, and this time I took it. A shot of whatever he was having was exactly what I needed. I took a hearty sip, and the apple-flavored brandy went in sweet but burned all the way down. I returned it to him and he screwed the cap back on, but didn't put it away.

"Are you meeting someone in America? After you land?" It was now or never, as honest as the man was being with me. I knew he was giving me far more than he should, even though what he was saying wasn't much.

He shook his head sadly. "That I cannot say."

I nodded. I hadn't really expected him to answer, so I would have to find out some other way.

We were both quiet for a long time, until finally Heinz stood and offered me his hand. "Come. Let us go see if she is awake yet."

I let him pull me up and followed him.

CHAPTER THIRTY-SIX

Dr. Montgomery answered the door almost immediately when we knocked. He gave a small, tight smile and let us into the outer room. "I assume you've come by to check on the patient."

"I need to speak with her." I looked meaningfully at Heinz, willing him to understand that I wanted to speak to her alone, and he nodded.

Montgomery shrugged. "You can try, but I'm not sure she's awake enough to actually communicate."

Heinz and I shared another look, and he stayed behind with the doctor while I went into the sun-bright room. Obviously, the doctor was trying to keep the woman awake, because the shade that usually covered the porthole was pulled aside and fresh sea air was pouring in through the opened window.

I sat on the bed next to Vanessa and studied her face for a moment. It was still pale, but had a bit of pink back in the cheeks, so she looked less like death personified. I reached out to touch her arm and her eyelids fluttered.

"Vanessa?" My voice sounded loud in my own ears.

She murmured and I tried again. This time she managed to come around a bit and blink her eyelids open to half-mast.

"Jane."

"How are you feeling?' "

Vanessa frowned, her eyes drifting shut again. "No. I didn't take those pills."

I sighed. It was obvious to me that she wasn't awake enough yet to have any sort of conversation.

At my sigh her eyes drew open to slits. "No, Jane. Miles . . . he was here." I frowned and she continued on. "He . . . was the same but different. And . . . he had a gun."

Now I was certain that the woman had been dreaming. Perhaps she'd been having a nightmare and convinced herself that she should take the entire bottle of pills to escape.

"He made me take them." Her voice was weaker again, and her eyes had drifted closed once more.

I sighed and patted her on the shoulder. "Just get some sleep, Vanessa. We can talk about this later."

I went back out into the sitting room and met with stares from both men. Heinz looked expectant while the doctor simply looked tired. I shook my head at Heinz, then turned to the doctor. He had saved the woman's life, so some of my suspicions about the man had eased. I couldn't imagine that he would do something to harm Vanessa when he had worked so hard to keep her alive.

"Thank you for taking care of her."

"It's my duty." He shifted on his feet.

My eyes narrowed slightly. "Well, yes, but I appreciate it nonetheless."

"I mean to say, I've been ordered to stay with Mrs. Fitz-Simmons until we dock. I'm not to let her out of her cabin."

"You reported this to the captain?"

Montgomery shrugged. "I had no choice, I'm afraid."

I was frustrated that he would report Vanessa's incident to Bisset. I knew the doctor was suspicious of the captain and his motives on board this ship—he'd said as much to Redvers, so I had hoped Montgomery might keep this quiet. Although, perhaps it was for the best that Vanessa had constant supervision. That way she was unlikely to cause herself further harm until she was on shore and could get some real help.

Heinz excused himself and went in to see her. I suspected he would be spending the remainder of the afternoon with her, so I took my leave with a reluctant promise to return when Vanessa was feeling a bit more awake.

Although from Montgomery's expression when I said it, I worried that keeping a watch over Vanessa wasn't the only thing he had been ordered to do. I wondered if he had been ordered to keep her "sedated" as well.

Frustrated and needing some time alone to think, I headed to the lounge. The plush wool carpet muffled my footsteps and I took a seat in a lavishly upholstered chair beneath one of the sparkling crystal chandeliers hanging from the ceiling. The room was fairly empty, as many of the passengers were off enjoying the other amusements on offer. A waiter appeared at my side almost instantly and I ordered a gin rickey, then sat pensively, looking for a few moments of peace to think.

That wasn't to be.

"I'm surprised to find you here." Redvers' voice didn't sound surprised, but it also didn't hold a trace of judgment.

"It's been a day. It's been quite a trip, actually." I could hear the weariness in my own voice.

He nodded and sat himself across from me, setting his Scotch on the rocks down on the table. I smiled—I should have known he wouldn't let me drink alone.

Redvers let me get halfway through my drink before he started asking questions. "So, what happened?"

I turned the glass on the table and watched the condensation make designs in its wake while I quietly related the conversation I'd had with Heinz on the deck. Redvers' face remained impassive, although I could tell he was soaking up every word. Then I described what Vanessa had told me in her still-drugged stupor.

"You don't believe her?"

I shook my head. "She was obviously still heavily drugged. The more I think about it, the more I'm sure it was just a nightmare. It probably seemed quite real to her, but there's no proof Van de Meter is even still on board." This completely contradicted my earlier insistence that I had seen Vanessa's husband when we pushed away from the dock, but no one had seen the man since. I was starting to believe I had been completely taken in by the woman and her desire for attention. She was just a fragile woman who needed help—much like Heinz's sister Helga.

Much of this I said out loud to Redvers, who simply sipped his Scotch and watched me work through things. Despite everything, I truly appreciated the man's ability to stay quiet and simply listen. When I finished with my self-recriminations over my gullibility he took another sip, set his glass on the table, and leaned forward on his forearms.

"Jane." I could barely look at him, so I took another sip of my refreshing drink instead. While I'd talked the ice had melted down and it was now more water than gin. "I would love to be able to tell you I told you so."

I snickered. He *would* love that.

"But I do believe you were right all along. And I don't necessarily think Vanessa is lying about seeing her husband."

I flapped a hand in frustration, nearly overturning my drink. "But where is he?"

He shook his head. "I don't know. But I think it's likely that if he threatened Rebecca, and possibly killed Dobbins, then he also might have tried to kill his wife."

"But why?"

"My guess is for the money. If he can make it look like

she's gone mad and killed herself, he's free to show that marriage certificate and collect her fortune."

"But why go to the trouble of making her look crazy?"

"Because it will look like a suicide, and he'll be able to collect. He can't inherit if he murders her. But if he makes it look like she went slowly insane and ended her own life, he certainly can."

When explained that way, it made sense. But it was still just conjecture—especially since we couldn't find the man.

"Why kill Dobbins?" I was curious what Redvers thought Van de Meter's motives might be.

"Dobbins might have found him. Or saw something he shouldn't have."

I processed that, hoping that it would somehow make me less responsible for the man's death.

"I trust your instincts, Jane." Redvers' brown eyes held mine and warmed me far more than gin ever could.

"I just don't know what to think about anything right now." I felt sorry for a German spy, which I never thought possible. And I was beginning to doubt whether I had even seen Vanessa's husband like I had insisted all along. Was it possible I had seen some other couple on the deck that day? Had the men been correct all along in assuming that Vanessa was an unstable liar? I hated to think that was the case, but I didn't feel certain of anything—except how I felt when I was with Redvers. That was surprising considering my terrible track record with marriage, but hugely comforting at the moment.

Then a new concern struck me. What would happen when this voyage was over? How could I make certain that I was able to work with Redvers again?

CHAPTER THIRTY-SEVEN

I didn't have much time to contemplate the issue of our future before Redvers lifted his empty glass and tilted it side to side. "One more?"

I gave a reluctant smile. "One more." I held up a stern finger. "But just one. We need to be on our toes."

Redvers returned minutes later with our refreshed drinks and I was able to relax and simply enjoy his company. We talked about topics that had nothing to do with what was happening on board the ship and I came away from the lounge feeling much better than I had when I entered. We went to dress for dinner, and after a light meal of roast capon and vegetables, we returned to the lounge to enjoy the band, although both of us abstained from alcohol now, sipping club soda instead. We had plans for the evening, and we couldn't afford to be sloppy and get caught.

It was late by the time most of the passengers had either retired for the evening or the men had sequestered themselves in the gentleman's lounge to gamble the night away, and I had to stifle a series of yawns. I was just thinking about ordering a cup of coffee when Redvers leaned over and murmured, "Ready?"

Just like that, I was wide awake.

We walked arm in arm to the exit, then turned and walked

up a flight of stairs that took us to the upper promenade, for all the world looking like a couple out for a casual stroll. In the freezing cold. My shawl wasn't doing anything to keep me warm tonight, and without a word Redvers took off his jacket and wrapped it around my shoulders. I breathed in the smell of pine and soap, grateful for both the comforting smell as well as the warmth.

We continued our casual stroll until we neared the captain's office. A quick glance showed that it was dark inside.

"How can you be sure the man is in bed? He's the captain after all."

"In exchange for some monetary compensation, the steward at his table had no problem making sure the captain's drinks were a little stronger than usual. I've been assured Bisset was quite sauced when he went to bed." This was whispered in my ear before he bent in front of the door and put his lock-picks to work. Within moments we were standing in the outer chamber where his secretary greeted passengers. Redvers was prepared to work his magic once more, but the inner door to the office was unlocked.

"It seems foolish to leave this open," I said as I closed the door behind me, sealing us into the pitch-dark room. Redvers flicked on a tiny flashlight and made his way to the wall where he pulled aside the curtain covering the porthole there. Moonlight streamed in, and Redvers turned his flashlight back off, then quickly set about rifling through the captain's desk.

He glanced up at me. "Listen at the door and tell me if anyone is coming."

I rolled my eyes but did as he said, huddling in his jacket. I watched as he efficiently searched the desk, then the small wooden filing cabinet.

"Anything?" I wasn't sure what I expected—that Captain Bisset left incriminating evidence out in the open? It was highly unlikely.

Without so much as a glance in my direction, Redvers turned his attention to the squat green safe tucked in the corner. He bent before it and placed his ear against the door, turning the knob, this way and that. I held my breath, waiting to see whether the man was also a safecracker.

I learned new things about him all the time.

It took an excruciating amount of time, but finally the door popped open with a soft click. I took a deep breath and abandoned my post to look over Redvers' shoulder as he pulled out the ship's log, then a dark green book. He reached in further, pulling out a sheaf of papers under which sat another green book. After a quick glance at the paperwork, he put the stacks back inside, adding the second green volume to the first one he had laid near his feet.

"What are those?" I pointed to the books.

Redvers quickly flipped through the ship log, and then set it aside. "It should be records of any cargo the ship is carrying." Redvers opened the first, and I could see lists neatly annotated with dates and weights in their proper columns. Satisfied that things appeared to be in order, Redvers set that book aside as well and picked up the second, the one that had been stuffed further back in the deep well of the safe.

Here everything was written in code, with dates, weights, and numerical amounts recorded, but it was impossible to tell what the numbers signified.

Redvers ran his finger down the encoded column. "If I had to guess, I'd say we were correct—the captain is doing a bit of smuggling."

"But what?"

"He makes this run to America regularly; and what are Americans burning for right now?"

"Decent booze." And people were paying a pretty penny for it. "Where would he be stowing that though? That Customs wouldn't find it?"

"There's any number of ways. Hidden compartments, inside other shipments, a couple of greased palms. But this explains why the man didn't want anyone searching the ship too strenuously. It also explains the picture you took of him on the dock at Cherbourg receiving that envelope."

Redvers put the ship log back in the safe along with the legitimate book, but tucked the coded book under his arm.

"What are you going to do with that?"

"I'm not sure yet. But my guess is that it will come in handy."

We swung by our suite to deposit the stolen logbook. Redvers slipped the slim tome beneath the mattress—it wouldn't hold up to a thorough search, but it would serve for the time being. In the meantime, I couldn't stop thinking about how many crew members would have to be in on the operation for the captain to smuggle efficiently.

"How many men do you think are working with him?"

Redvers shrugged, smoothing the covers back into place and looking over at me. "Only a very reliable handful is my guess. He wouldn't want to risk anyone spilling the secret, but he would need men to move the goods."

I thought about likely suspects, and recalled how unfriendly the first mate had been in all my interactions with him—but especially when I was found somewhere I wasn't supposed to be. "I would wager that the first mate Benson is in on it."

Redvers cocked his head. "That's a fair bet, actually."

I looked around. I wasn't ready for bed, now that adrenaline from our search was coursing through my veins. We'd been successful once tonight—what else might we get done? "Now what?"

Redvers looked amused. "I don't think there's much else we can accomplish tonight."

I mentally ticked through my list. I could go see how Vanessa was faring, but I decided to put that off. Heinz was probably with her, and I didn't want to be in the way. At least, that's what I told myself. The truth was that my doubts about the woman had left me feeling less than eager to see her again.

I needed to speak with her maid Rebecca and try to get the girl to tell the truth for once, but it was late and I didn't want to disturb the girl's roommate. That was a task that could wait until tomorrow.

With a sigh, I agreed that it was time for bed. Not that retiring for the evening was any great hardship now that Redvers and I were sharing one.

In fact, it wasn't long before I completely forgot that I'd wanted to get a look at the fourth mate that night.

CHAPTER THIRTY-EIGHT

The next morning, I awoke feeling full of optimism. We had started to pry open some of the cracks in our troubles—we now knew why the captain was behaving badly, and we had solid confirmation that Naumann was our spy, even if we didn't know who his contact was quite yet. But even without the contact's name, we had the code book, so any messages sent between Heinz and the contact could be broken by Redvers' people.

If we could just learn who had caused Dobbins's untimely end, I would feel as though we had accomplished much of what we were meant to. I ignored the little voice in the back of my mind reminding me that Vanessa FitzSimmons was still in a world of trouble, since her missing husband was a strong suspect for our killer. But I was still unsure of how much trouble she'd brought on herself, and her claim that Miles made her take the pills made me uneasy. I told myself that the doctor was with her, and probably Heinz as well, shushing the voice that insisted what she really needed was a friend.

The voice was harder to ignore when a note was delivered by our steward just as I was enjoying my morning coffee.

Please stop by and see me. —V

"Are you going to go see her?" Redvers was dressed in a charcoal suit with matching vest and looked completely at ease as he sipped his tea from the dainty china teacup.

"I don't know. I'm pretty tied up this morning."

Redvers' eyebrows spoke volumes, and I shifted uncomfortably in my seat. "I have to see Heinz on deck this morning."

"It's not terribly necessary, actually." Redvers shrugged. "We know he's our man, and we even know what book he and his contact are using."

I pursed my lips. "That feels like a weak excuse to simply give up now. What if he tells me something important?" Redvers said nothing, but I could feel his eyes on me, so I blew out a breath and studied the ceiling. "Very well, I'm not anxious to visit her again."

"Even after what we talked about yesterday?"

"Even then. And I'm sure she's in good hands with Dr. Montgomery." I returned my attention to my coffee and took a sip, ignoring the fact that I still didn't trust Montgomery wholeheartedly, and until this latest episode would have been entirely uncomfortable leaving her in his care. "And Heinz! He seems quite taken with her and has been checking on her frequently. We have very little time left on board, and other matters to worry about."

Redvers had to concede that point. "Once we land it will be impossible to learn what happened to Dobbins."

"So, what can we do about it?" I asked.

"I think we can put that logbook to some use."

"Where is that, by the way?"

Redvers looked smug as he crossed his ankle over his knee. "It's somewhere where they will never think to look for it."

I realized he must have snuck out before the sun came up in order to hide the thing away. "Are you going to tell me where?"

He shook his head. "It's better if you don't know." He

looked for a moment as though he wanted to say something else, but he remained silent.

"Is there something else you're not telling me?"

"Yes, but I'm saving it for later." He gave me one of his charming smiles—probably to soften that blow—but I narrowed my eyes at him. When my continued scrutiny failed to elicit any sort of reaction from him, I finally shrugged. I wasn't sure exactly what he was keeping from me or why, but I decided not to let it bother me. I had other things to concern myself with.

But it turned out those other concerns were keeping themselves from me as well. I sat in my usual deck chair, miserable in the gloomy cold, and waited for over an hour before I accepted that Heinz wouldn't be joining me that morning. I then went in search of Rebecca in her room and everywhere I could think of on the second-class decks, but couldn't locate the woman anywhere. I was a little concerned, especially after the threat she'd received. Although it was possible that she really was having a fling with Fourth Mate Schnell and was hidden away somewhere with him.

Feeling desperate to make any sort of headway, I hunted through the café and the ladies' lounge for Eloise and Margret. But they were nowhere to be found either, and I wasn't *quite* desperate enough to locate their room. I'd hoped they might have some scrap of gossip for me, but it looked as though they'd disappeared with the rest of them.

It was late afternoon when I returned to our suite, thoroughly discouraged and more than a touch cranky.

"No joy?" Redvers asked. "You look out of sorts." He had removed his jacket and appeared to be writing a letter at the small desk, shirtsleeves rolled up to reveal tanned forearms.

"None. It seems everyone has disappeared." I frowned.

"Although I'm quite concerned that I couldn't find Rebecca Tesch anywhere."

Redvers turned around fully and a frown creased his brow also. "Nowhere?"

I shook my head. "I scoured the second-class decks and checked everywhere she could conceivably be. I couldn't find her anywhere. She could be with Schnell of course, but that doesn't feel quite right either."

"Hmm." From the tone of his voice, I could tell this news worried him just as it worried me. "I can't see Schnell continuing to risk it now that I've spoken to him."

What he didn't need to say out loud was that the threat Rebecca had received didn't appear idle—someone had taken out Dobbins, and it was likely that the note's sender was the culprit. I only hoped they hadn't decided to eliminate Rebecca from the equation as well.

Redvers checked his watch. "Perhaps it's time we spoke to the captain."

"If we can find him," I muttered, still thoroughly out of sorts.

Redvers smirked. "I don't think that will be a problem."

Redvers was, as usual, correct. Captain Bisset was sitting behind his desk when we were ushered into his office. I glanced around. It looked much different in the daylight, as opposed to when we were snooping around in total darkness.

The captain was rubbing his temple with one hand, and I guessed that he was still nursing a headache from the night before. "What do you lot want now?" the man growled.

Redvers calmly took a seat in one of the chairs in front of the desk, casually crossing his legs as I slowly lowered myself into the other.

"We've come to discuss your smuggling operation."

My eyes popped open wide—I couldn't believe he had led with that. The captain put on a good show, but I could see that some of the ruddy color had left his cheeks.

"I don't know what you're talking about, and you can both leave my office immediately." He opened his mouth, most likely to call out to his secretary to have us removed, when Redvers smoothly interrupted him.

"I wouldn't recommend that. You see, I have your logbook." Redvers smiled. "Not to mention photographic proof of you accepting bribes."

A choking noise came from the captain's reddening face, and then he nearly spat at us. "I will have you arrested."

Redvers shrugged, the picture of a gentleman on holiday without a care in the world. "Now, I think we can work something out. I don't particularly care about smuggling per se—the Americans deserve their liquor as much as anyone else—but there are some things that we *do* want."

Bisset's lips worked but nothing came out. It almost looked as though he was chewing on his own tongue—he was certainly mad enough. Minutes ticked by before he finally brought himself to speak.

"I could have your rooms searched and find the book. And the photographs. Without proof you have nothing."

Redvers smiled. "Do you think I'm foolish enough to hide anything in my room?" He shook his head as though the man had told an amusing anecdote. "They are somewhere you'll never find them. And frankly, you don't have the time or resources to locate them before we dock."

I wondered where on earth he had put the book and the photographs, or whether he was bluffing. I studied his face, and his calm seemed genuine. I gave my head a little shake and continued to enjoy the show—the captain had barely spared me a glance since I had walked in. I may as well have been invisible.

"What do you want?" Bisset finally ground out.

Redvers' mouth split into a wide grin, and I couldn't help a little smile myself. We were just getting started.

CHAPTER THIRTY-NINE

"First of all, we want this ship searched for Rebecca Tesch, one of your second-class passengers."

The captain looked incredulous. "Why? Why would you want to search for a woman in second class?"

"Because we're afraid that something might have happened to her." Redvers thought for a moment. "In fact, we would also like to see inside the quarters of the fourth mate. I think he's been having a fling with her."

The captain sank back in his chair. "Is that all? Who cares if the man is having a bit of fun?"

Hadn't Schnell been worried about losing his job if the captain found out? This response from Bisset was miles away from that. "Because there's quite a bit more to it than that," I interjected.

The captain didn't even look at me, just continued gazing steadily at Redvers. "I won't have you waking the man when he's off watch." Redvers was about to say something when Bisset held up a hand. "But I'll let you in once he's gone back on duty."

I sighed since that would be sometime after midnight, now that Schnell had taken all the late-night watches. Probably all the better to flirt with the young ladies during the day. I mentally kicked myself for not having gone on deck to talk to the man the night before—it had completely slipped my mind.

Redvers considered the captain for a moment, then conceded the point. "Very well, but in the meantime, I would like a search of the rest of the ship to be conducted in order to find her."

Bisset shrugged. "Is that all?"

"Not hardly. I would also like to know why you've dismissed the fact that Dobbins—one of your own men—was murdered on board this ship and you continue to call it an accident."

At this Bisset looked slightly abashed, but he quickly covered it up. "Look, Mr. Dibble." He was back to using Redvers' real name instead of calling us the Wunderlys. It led me to wonder once again who had tipped him off. "What I put in my official report is none of your concern. It's very likely that the man just had an unfortunate accident."

"And the bruises on his neck? Indicating that he had been held down in the water?"

"Well, you can't prove that, can you? Now that he's been properly buried."

The man had us there. I was shocked at his flagrant disregard for his own crew member and that feeling was reflected in Redvers' face as well. The captain's voice softened. "His family will be well compensated. It does them no good to believe he was murdered. Let me handle this in my own way."

"Are you doing anything to find his killer?"

Bisset tugged at his beard. "Like I said, let me handle this my own way."

I couldn't stop my eyes from rolling. I doubted the man was doing anything to bring justice to poor Dobbins.

"Finally, there's the matter of Mrs. FitzSimmons."

It was the captain's turn to roll his eyes. "That woman is a liability and completely unstable."

"We would like for you to stop sedating her."

"There I can't help you. And it's for her own good, man." Bisset shook his head. "You can think what you like, but I do not want a society woman committing suicide on my ship. It's truly for her own safety that Dr. Montgomery stay with her and keep her calm."

I put my hand on Redvers' arm. "He might be right," I said softly. I didn't want any harm to come to Vanessa, but perhaps the best thing *was* for her to stay sedated. She'd had a series of shocks—real or imagined—and once we were on dry land it would be safer for her. I made a promise to myself that after this chat with the captain I would stop by and visit her instead of avoiding her as I'd done all day. I would ensure she was being taken care of and that Dr. Montgomery was doing what he was supposed to.

Redvers looked at me, then gave a brisk nod to the captain. We stood to take our leave and Bisset stood as well, clearing his throat uncomfortably.

"What do you plan to do with that log?" he asked. "And how did you get into my safe?"

Redvers looked steadily back at him. "I have no intention of turning it over to the authorities if that's what you're worried about. Although, I can if I must." The captain had started to look relieved but stiffened again. "Once we've landed it will be returned to you. As long as what we've discussed is taken care of."

I noticed that Redvers hadn't addressed the captain's second question. Or where he'd learned Redvers' real name.

Bisset gave a brisk nod.

Redvers smiled. "We'll see you this evening then. To conduct that search of Schnell's room."

The captain looked as though he wanted to say something else, but changed his mind and watched us leave instead.

We returned to our suite to dress for dinner. The evening's affair was a fancy-dress ball, with a costume ball on the following evening since it would be our last night on the ship. I couldn't think of anything I wanted to do less than attend a ball, but I put on the finest gown I had been provided with and stepped into the outer room to find Redvers dressed in a beautifully cut black tuxedo. I suspected that my eyes lit up at the sight of him.

I distracted myself with other matters. "Do we have time before dinner to stop by and check in on Vanessa?"

Redvers checked his watch. "Not quite. Perhaps we can after we finish our meals—before the dancing starts."

I groaned. I had hoped we could avoid the dancing since we had so many other things to worry about.

After an uneventful dinner in the à la carte restaurant, Redvers and I made our way to Vanessa's suite instead of following the stream of well-dressed passengers making their way to the ballroom. At our knock, Heinz Naumann opened the door and frowned upon seeing us. "She asked you to come many hours ago, Mrs. Wunderly."

I winced, both at his calling me by my formal name and because he was correct—I had been avoiding her all day. But I refused to make excuses for myself and simply nodded instead.

He stepped aside to let us in and we found Dr. Montgomery just coming out of her bedroom. "Ah, I'm glad to see you've stopped by. She's been anxiously waiting for you." This last was directed to me.

"Is she awake?" I wondered just how "sedated" the man was keeping her.

"She is. I've given her something to keep her calm, but she's definitely awake."

I nodded and, taking a deep breath, crossed the room and pushed open the door. Vanessa was propped against her pillows, the golden glow from the lamp on her side table bathing her face in warm colors. She looked much better than the last time I had seen her, that much was certain.

"Jane. I was starting to think you had abandoned me entirely." Her words were slow but clear.

The guilt in my chest sat even heavier. "I haven't abandoned you." It was all I could manage in response, since the truth was that I nearly had.

"I told you that Miles was here."

I sat on the edge of her bed. "Are you sure it wasn't a dream, Vanessa? You've had quite a hard time."

She moved her head gently side to side, her eyes never leaving mine. "I didn't try to kill myself. It was Miles." She put her hand on mine, and I glanced down at her elegant hand. "Please believe me."

I rolled around several responses before deciding on honesty. "I am trying to. But I have to admit it's . . . difficult."

Vanessa closed her eyes and nodded once.

I jumped back in. "Have you seen your maid today?"

Her eyes opened again and fixed on me. "I haven't seen her in several days, actually. Why?"

I didn't want to alarm her, so I just shook my head. "No reason."

But Vanessa wasn't fooled and a spark of fear entered her eyes. "Please try to find her." I was surprised by her genuine concern for the girl, especially when she'd seemed so callous toward other members of the serving class, like Dobbins. This woman was like shifting sand—you could never quite get your stance.

"Promise." Vanessa held my gaze until I gave her the answer she wanted.

I went back out into the sitting room where the men were waiting for me. Heinz came forward immediately and pulled me aside. "Did she tell you about her husband?" His voice was low and I had to lean in to hear him.

"She did." I glanced behind Heinz to where Redvers and the doctor were both frowning at us.

"I don't trust the doctor. But I worry for Miss Vanessa, so I will stay with her."

"That's very good of you, Heinz." I pulled back to look at him, and he did in fact appear worried. "I'll stop by later tonight to check in on you both again."

He nodded and we rejoined the other two men.

The hours until we could go into Schnell's room seemed to crawl by. The last thing I wanted to do was attend the ball, but Redvers convinced me to make an appearance rather than wear a hole in the carpet of our sitting room. I argued that it was better than leaving him crippled by dancing with me, but he was intractable on the issue.

Even being swung around the room in a waltz—while crushing Redvers' toes—couldn't break my increasing sense of anticipation and the crawling anxiety I was feeling. I hoped that Rebecca would be turned up by the search the captain had promised, but I felt in my gut that it wasn't likely. I had done my own thorough search of the areas she might have been in, and unless she was somewhere she wasn't meant to be, she had disappeared.

Redvers limped only a little as he led me back to the sidelines. "Shall we get a drink?"

I shook my head. I wanted to keep my head clear. I looked up at him and saw that he was frowning at something over my shoulder, and turned. "What are you looking at?" The only familiar thing I could see was Douglas and Margret Gould and their insufferable relation, Eloise. I turned back around quickly and hoped I hadn't been spotted. While I had sought them out earlier in the day, I no longer needed to subject myself to Eloise's blather for information.

"Perhaps we could move over there." I indicated the other side of the room with my head, hoping to be out of the line of Eloise's fire.

Redvers' lips pursed. "I'd rather we stayed where we are."

I frowned at him, thinking it a strange response, and watched as his eyes flicked around the room repeatedly but continued to return to the Goulds.

"Is there something you aren't telling me?"

"No. Why ever would you think that, my dearest?"

I frowned at his obvious attempt to distract me, when he offered me his arm and ushered me to the other side of the room just as I had just asked him to. I didn't even bother to inquire why he had suddenly changed his mind, and instead let my frustration be known by giving him a pinch on the arm. He grinned at me.

Perhaps it was time for a drink after all.

Midnight finally rolled around, and the majority of the passengers were still enjoying themselves at the party, the energy becoming more frenetic the closer we got to shore. Redvers and I hurried to Captain Bisset's office where we waited impatiently for the man for nearly fifteen minutes before he decided to turn up. We followed Bisset to the crew deck I had been escorted from, and waited while the man sorted through his keys, finally locating the correct one.

"I'm sure you won't find anything. . . ."

The man's words trailed off as we stepped inside Schnell's room. It was dark, so the captain flicked on the lights, revealing the form of Rebecca Tesch bound and gagged and lying upon the small bunk.

CHAPTER FORTY

In a panic, I pushed past both men and rushed to Rebecca's side, where I was relieved to see that she was very much alive and struggling against her bonds. The first thing I did was pull down the cloth gag covering her mouth before I set to work at untying her hands. Words came pouring out of her mouth as soon as it was uncovered.

"He's gone for Vanessa. He called the doctor and told him there was an emergency somewhere else to get him to leave her alone and then he went to her. I think he's going to do something."

"How long ago was this?" Redvers asked as he pulled the last of the binding around her ankles free.

Rebecca massaged her wrists, trying to get feeling back into her hands. "I don't know exactly. I've been here for several hours . . . so maybe twenty minutes ago?"

Redvers and I were already halfway out the door when she gave us this last bit of information. We left the captain tending to the girl while we rushed off in a desperate attempt to get to Vanessa before Schnell did, knowing full well we were probably too late already. Bisset called something after us about sending help, but neither of us responded.

I was out of breath when we reached Vanessa's room, the door closed but unlocked. There was no one inside, but a quick glance around showed an envelope propped in plain view on the desk. I snatched it up and tore the flap open, quickly skimming the letter's contents while Redvers read over my shoulder.

"It's a suicide note. Says she can't live with herself after all the deception." I said this aloud even though Redvers was reading the exact same thing I was.

"I doubt she's the one who wrote it."

"Agreed." I was trying to think quickly. "What would be the best way to get rid of a woman in another suicide attempt? Especially if the first one failed." We shared a look and without a word we raced out into the hallway, headed for the open air.

"Where do you think?" I gasped along in his wake.

"Probably the rear. The least amount of people around."

We scrambled down the multiple stairs to the second-class deck, then out a door onto the outside promenade, which was ominously empty. Most of the passengers had either retired for the night or were enjoying the fancy dress ball—one of the last gasps of fun before we docked in New York. Schnell had timed this well, picking a night when there were likely to be no witnesses on deck. Redvers and I hurried down the outdoor staircase and back up, just as we had the morning of Dobbins's burial at sea.

I could only pray we were in time to stop another one.

I nearly slipped on the stairs going up, but managed to catch myself on the railing and continued hot on Redvers' trail. He barreled between the pair of white air ducts, then beneath the raised watch platform, coming to a screeching halt just beyond. He stopped so quickly I almost ran into the back of him, but I put out a hand and stopped, chest heaving.

We had found them.

"Schnell," Redvers said, and the clean-shaven man with a gun stepped slightly sideways to see us while keeping his weapon trained on the two figures who stood before him—

Vanessa and Heinz. Vanessa, draped heavily over Heinz's arm, was obviously still suffering from the effects of the sedatives Dr. Montgomery had given her.

"Miles Van de Meter!" I exclaimed. His beard was gone, but there was no mistaking the man who had stood with Vanessa that first day on deck as we pulled away from the Southampton pier. Redvers glanced at me, and I could feel all the pieces clicking together as a bitter smile twisted Van de Meter's lips.

"One and the same." The brass buttons of his fourth-mate's uniform gleamed in the dull yellow glow from the light on the bridge behind us. "Although my real name is Lee Schnell. I thought a more hoity-toity name would get me farther with her crowd. And I was right, wasn't I, darling?" This he said with a wolfish grin in Vanessa's direction that sent a shiver down my spine with its maliciousness.

He gestured with the small black pistol for us to join the others, and we slowly moved in that direction, Redvers doing his best to shield me with his own body. As we approached, Heinz nodded with his head toward Vanessa and then myself, and I understood that he wanted me to take her. I hoped it was because he was looking for an opportunity to get the jump on Schnell; maybe between Heinz and Redvers we could find a way to gain the upper hand.

"I must say I'm glad you were too stupid to put it together."

He was speaking to our entire group, but I took it rather personally. I was too busy accepting Vanessa's weight from Heinz to answer the man, but it was just true enough to make me spitting mad. Redvers hadn't seen Vanessa's husband on deck—or hadn't noticed him—and he was the only one who had spoken to Schnell. I obviously would have known it was the same man immediately, which is why he ensured I never got a glimpse of him.

It explained so much else as well. Why we couldn't figure out where Vanessa's husband was hiding on the ship, or why he wasn't listed on the ship manifest. He wouldn't be since he was a member of the crew. And of course he hadn't given Vanessa his real name, which is why Redvers' people couldn't find any background information on him.

I was sagging with Vanessa leaning heavily on my left side, but I sent a verbal shot at the man anyway. "You can't get away with this now. There are far too many witnesses."

He shrugged casually. "We're getting closer to shore. I'll figure out a way to explain the disappearances. Or I won't." He chuckled. "There's nothing to tie this to me, and pretty soon I'll have enough money that it won't much matter if they do. I'll be long gone."

"Except for Rebecca." She could tie it all to Vanessa's husband.

"Who?" Schnell frowned a bit.

"Vanessa's maid," I said with a touch of impatience. "I'm not sure why you didn't kill her also."

He sighed. "I was planning on disposing of her after I finished with Vanessa. One body at a time. I have to time them just so. I just didn't expect *my wife* would have an extra man in her room." Schnell shot a dark look at Heinz, who took a single step forward before stopping when the gun wavered on him. "Although perhaps I shouldn't have been surprised. My wife is quite the whore."

Vanessa was silent at my side, not bothering to contradict anything Schnell was saying, although I could feel her shivering in her nightgown. He hadn't let her grab anything to cover up with, although I supposed he wouldn't since he was planning to simply throw her overboard.

"And why kill Dobbins?" Redvers' voice came from my right, picking up my thread of questions.

Schnell rolled his eyes briefly, but it wasn't long enough for him to lose his focus on us, and his gun never wavered. "That fool caught me going into her room." Schnell chucked his chin at Vanessa slightly, then gave a shrug. "He was a liability."

Vanessa started trembling even more, if that was possible. I wasn't sure whether it was due to shock, her husband's words, or the effect of the drugs, but I didn't dare take my eyes off the man with the pistol to find out how she was doing.

It would have been a wasted effort anyway, since Vanessa chose that moment to collapse to the deck beneath us.

CHAPTER FORTY-ONE

In the beat that it took everyone to realize what had happened, chaos broke out. I dropped to the deck beside Vanessa while Redvers used Schnell's momentary distraction to rush directly toward the man. Heinz was a few beats behind Redvers since he paused to look at Vanessa before joining the fray.

At least, I believe that's what happened. I was checking Vanessa's head and saw the blur of Redvers' jacket from the corner of my eye when I heard the first shot and threw myself over Vanessa's body. When I looked up, Redvers was tumbling to the deck and Heinz was just reaching Schnell, at which point they began grappling for the gun. Another shot cracked out, but once Redvers went down, I had eyes for no one but him.

"No, no, no, no, no . . ." I repeated aloud, over and over, while I scuttled across the moisture-slicked planks to where he lay. He was so still that I feared the worst. I began patting him everywhere to see if I could find a wound while words tumbled freely. "Please don't be dead. You can't be dead. I didn't get to tell you that I love you." The fact of my love had never been more obvious to me and was now crushing me with fear for his life. When I took a breath and managed to actually look at the man, I could see that his chest was still rising slightly. "I'll do anything. Just don't be dead."

I heard a distant splash behind me and a cry from Vanessa. When I turned to look, both Heinz and Schnell had disappeared. A glance at Vanessa showed her pushing herself to her feet and making her way unsteadily to the railing.

"Careful!" I shouted to her, worried that she too might find her way overboard. She was close to the small gap in the railing where the men had disappeared, but I could see she had a white-knuckled grip on the painted rail as she peered into the darkness below.

When I turned back to my inspection of Redvers, he had one hand to the side of his head and one eye squinted up at me.

"You love me? Then you'll agree to marry me."

I was so relieved to hear his voice that I threw my arms around him, causing him to wince as I bumped his head in my enthusiasm. "You're alive! Yes!" Moisture dampened my face and I realized I was crying in relief.

"Of course I am, although I don't think we can say the same for the other two." Both Redvers' eyes were trained on the railing behind me where Vanessa stood shivering in the cold. His eyes met mine once again and he said quietly, "You agreed. I'm holding you to that."

His words barely registered. He was alive, but I was still concerned that he was grievously wounded. "I thought you'd been shot. Are you certain you haven't been?" I cast anxious eyes over his person looking for the growing red stain I was convinced I would find at any moment.

Redvers patted his coat, much as I had done moments earlier, but he came up with his finger pushing through a round hole in the fabric.

"Missed me." I gasped in relief and he continued. "Clobbered me in the head with that pistol though, which was deuced hard."

If I'd been in a calmer frame of mind, I might have asked which was harder—the pistol or his head. It was probably a toss-up.

I wiped my face, relief making my limbs feel like India rubber. Then Redvers pushed to his feet and extended a hand. I grasped it gratefully and he pulled me up—I wasn't sure I would have been able to do so on my own with all the adrenaline coursing through my veins. We cautiously made our way to Vanessa FitzSimmons where she stood staring over the rail.

"They're gone," she whispered.

Even if she had immediately run for help, I doubted we would have been able to save either man. The sea was far too cold, and the ship was moving at a steady clip away from where they went in. Besides the fact that either one of them might have been dead before hitting the water—I had no idea where that final shot had gone.

Redvers removed his coat and draped it over Vanessa's shoulders, then gestured with his head for me to lead her back inside. Redvers stayed on deck, searching the dark water for any glimpse of the men, life preserver now in hand, ready to throw at the slightest sign of them.

Vanessa and I had nearly made it inside when I saw the captain finally hurrying in our direction.

"There are two men overboard," I told him calmly.

He gave a start, then began shouting orders to the officer who trailed in his wake. By the time we reached the first-class corridor where Vanessa's suite was located, I could feel the juddering of the great ship coming to a halt.

I doubted they would find anything.

Vanessa was nearly catatonic by the time I got her back to her room. I ran a warm bath for her to take the chill off, but even after a long soak the woman couldn't stop shivering. I suspected the shock of the evening went far deeper than her lack of coat out on the deck. Dr. Montgomery finally gave her yet another sedative and she managed to still long enough to fall asleep.

Out in the sitting room, I stood for a moment, unwilling to leave her completely alone, but longing for my own bed. Montgomery noticed my hesitation and steered me toward the door. "I'll stay with her."

"I think the danger is past, but I don't want her to be alone."

"She won't be."

I nearly argued that she wasn't supposed to have been left alone before either, but I didn't have the strength to present a fight. With a nod, I let myself out into the corridor and returned to my own room where I dropped into bed, exhausted. The rest could wait until morning.

Chapter Forty-two

It was late morning when I dragged myself out of bed. I pulled on my robe and went into the sitting room, where a pot of coffee had already gone cold.

Redvers was writing at the desk and looked up as I came in. He was fully dressed and appeared as though he'd been awake for hours.

"Did you even go to bed?" I picked up the pot of coffee and considered drinking it cold, but set it back down with a sigh.

Redvers grinned. "I've already sent for another one."

"Bless you," I said with feeling.

"And to answer your question, I did catch several hours of sleep. You were already dead to the world by the time I got back, however."

"Speaking of dead."

Redvers nodded solemnly. "Both bodies have been recovered. They pulled them out not long after they stopped the ship."

Belatedly, I realized we were underway again. I was glad to have been wrong about them not finding anything—even though Heinz was a spy, he deserved better than to be lost at sea. After all, he'd given his life to protect Vanessa. In a way,

I thought he had given his life for his sister—the fragile woman Vanessa reminded him so much of. He substituted one for the other as he took Vanessa's tormentor overboard with him.

"Did Rebecca have anything else to say for herself?"

Redvers nodded. "Schnell attempted to seduce her, and when that didn't work, he simply blackmailed her into doing his bidding. I believe he worked out her family situation and threatened her mother and younger siblings."

"He really was a monster."

Redvers nodded. "She lied about his trunks, and when it seemed as though she would crack and tell you the truth, he began sending her threats. And when Dobbins went snooping in Vanessa's room, he caught Schnell instead, so Schnell drowned him."

I felt a pang of guilt that I was the one who had asked Dobbins to do that snooping. Perhaps if I hadn't, Dobbins would still be alive. But I was glad that Redvers had been wrong about the identity of the killer. Heinz was innocent—not that it mattered much now.

Redvers had become quite adept at reading my face. "It isn't your fault."

I turned sad eyes to him. "Thank you for saying so. But I can't help but feel responsible."

There was a knock at the door and a waiter brought in a breakfast tray, complete with a new pot of coffee. I set right in on making myself a cup while he cleared the old things away. When he had gone, we resumed our conversation, but it went in an entirely different direction than I had anticipated.

"When shall we get married?"

I blanched. "Excuse me?"

"Last night. You agreed to marry me. And I don't intend to let you weasel out of it."

Redvers calmly sipped his tea while I sat in stunned silence. I was hearing the words, but they weren't making sense quite yet.

"So when would you like to?" Redvers pressed on. "Perhaps there is a chaplain on board who could take care of things."

I thought back to the melee the night before. Had I agreed to marry him? And had his proposal been genuine? I had thought about it again last night as I collapsed into bed, but I'd assumed it was due to the bump on his head that he'd even asked.

"You were serious?"

"Very much so." His dark eyes searched mine. "I love you, Jane Wunderly. I want you to be my wife."

At his words, my stomach dropped, but in the very best kind of way. The look in his eyes left me breathless, and I could feel my skin itching with heat. I already knew what my answer was going to be, but I couldn't make it *that* easy for him. "If I agree to this, I want to keep my own last name." I couldn't imagine changing it to "Dibble."

"It's very unorthodox, but then my dear, so are you. Very well." He smiled. "I can't really blame you, to be honest. Wunderly suits you far better."

I'd fought tooth and nail after my first husband died to get my maiden name restored to me. I didn't want to give it up again.

But I did love the man seated across from me. That had been brought home clearly the night before as he lay on the deck unconscious. If anyone could change my mind about never wanting to marry again, this was the man to do it. And apparently he had, because I had just agreed to tie the knot with him. I waited for a feeling of dread, but it never came. Taking a sip of coffee, I realized that my heart was light—I was making the right choice by accepting his hand. And I knew he would be nothing like my first husband. The two were like night and day.

I was about to respond when there was another knock at the door and the captain barged in. He eyed the two of us, but quickly turned his attention solely to Redvers.

"Did you want to be present when we make the arrest?"

"What arrest?" I put my coffee cup down a little too sharply and the clank made me wince, but it hadn't broken. The captain ignored me, but Redvers looked slightly abashed.

"Can it wait until we're dressed and ready?" he asked the captain, glancing at my dishabille.

The captain grumbled, but I suspected it was really Redvers who was running the show at this point. Especially after blackmailing the man the day before. "I'll meet you on the promenade in fifteen minutes. We thought it best to do it before they go to any of the public areas."

Burning with curiosity—and more than a little irritation that Redvers had left me out of whatever was happening—I was already shutting the door to the bedroom so that I could pull on a knit dress and grab my wool coat. I also put on my burgundy cloche, hoping that it would hide my bed-mussed hair. I stepped back into the sitting room in under five minutes, and Redvers chuckled. He grabbed his own outer coat, a dark gray number, and we locked up our suite.

"Spill it."

"When I returned to the luggage room to hide the captain's logbook," he started, but I quickly interrupted him.

"Why did you go to the luggage room to hide it?"

He cocked an eyebrow. "Are you going to let me finish?"

I shrugged. "Maybe."

"I went back to the luggage room because I decided the most unlikely place to search for the book would be in someone else's luggage."

It was pretty clever actually. "How could you be sure that someone wouldn't require their trunk and then find it?"

It was his turn to shrug. "I bribed the steward. He was to report to me if the trunk was requested."

"Then what? I assume something happened while you were there."

"Not so much that something happened, but what I found." He paused and my curiosity nearly burned me with its intensity. Luckily for both of us, he continued. "The other copy of *Life of Christ*."

"The code book. Or so we assume." I pieced the rest together. "You think that person is . . . was . . . Heinz's contact." I was irritated that he hadn't told me, although I recalled that several times during the trip there had seemed to be something he wanted to say but stopped himself.

"I do."

It hadn't yet occurred to me that without Heinz, we would have that much more trouble discovering who his American contact was. I was truthfully relieved—despite my annoyance—that Redvers had already uncovered a solid lead. "Do we have enough to make an arrest? Just based on finding one book? I thought you said that it was a popular title."

"Oh, I think we'll be able to get what we need."

"Who is it?" I couldn't wait until we reached the deck. I needed to know now.

"You're about to find out." He gave me a smug grin and I pinched his arm. He really could be the most aggravating man.

CHAPTER FORTY-THREE

We arrived on deck to find that Eloise, Margret, and even Douglas had been boxed in by Captain Bisset and several of his crew members. They were attempting to enjoy the sunshine on their deck chairs, but the captain had them surrounded.

"What is this all about? Why are you blocking my sun?" Eloise bellowed, her indignance causing her ample bosom to shake. Margret looked quietly amused and Douglas was continuing to peruse a book, ignoring the entire thing. His ability to pretend nothing was happening was quite impressive.

"Douglas! How can you sit there reading? Do something about this." It seemed that Eloise had noticed the man's indifference as well.

He shrugged without bothering to look up. "It has nothing to do with me, I'm sure."

"Margret," I breathed out, taking in the scene before us. It would explain so much about her secretive nature and her forever amused expressions.

"Not quite," Redvers said, giving the captain a nod. His men moved forward and helped Eloise to her feet.

"Eloise?!" She was the last person I would have expected. Her mouth never stopped moving—which was a terrible quality in a spy. But I thought back to her many monologues

and how she never really seemed to say anything at all. And
how she talked about her mission work—the reason she had
traveled to England in the first place.

"If you'll recall, her father was a professor at Clark University."

"She never said which university."

Redvers shrugged. "It's enough of a connection. I'm sure
once we do some more digging back on shore, we'll find the
proof."

Margret overheard us talking. "Oh, there's no need for
digging. I'm quite sure I can give you everything you need."

My mouth dropped open in shock. I couldn't believe the
woman was willing to sell out her own sister, regardless of
her sins.

She gave me a sly smile. "I guess I'll have to learn how to
manage my own servants."

In the end, Margret gave us more than enough information to keep her older sister locked up until we reached shore.
Eloise was bitter that her father hadn't been recognized for
his similar accomplishments, and had no qualms about steal-
ing information from Goddard's experiments and selling
them to the German government. "To the motherland" as
she termed them. Margret had long suspected her sister of
being up to something, and had been quietly keeping watch.
We were grateful she had done so, although when I asked
why she hadn't turned her in sooner, she hadn't been able to
give a satisfactory answer. But if we were lucky, Goddard's
work could continue unimpeded—or stolen. Heinz was out
of the picture, but it was only a matter of time before someone made another attempt. Although Redvers assured me
that security measures would be put into place to prevent
something similar from happening again.

Redvers managed the paperwork for Eloise's arrest while I
checked in on Vanessa one more time. She had some color

back in her face, but was clutching the doctor's arm as he sat next to her on the settee.

"Thank you for your help, Jane. I know I didn't always make it easy for you."

I shook my head. I still felt guilty for how I had disbelieved the woman, falling into the same trap as the men had—thinking her nothing but an attention-starved socialite. I wasn't sure I would ever be able to shake that feeling of having so badly misjudged someone, as well as mistrusting my own intuition. I had been right from the outset, but had been fooled into doubting myself. It was a hard lesson to swallow.

"I'm sorry. That I didn't believe you when you said that you'd seen Miles. Er, Lee."

It hardly seemed adequate as far as apologies go and for all that I felt responsible for, but Vanessa smiled. "I understand why you didn't. No hard feelings. And you were there when it counted."

I couldn't agree, but her acceptance was very gracious. "What will you do when we get back?"

"I'm going to lay low for a while, I think. I've had my fill of adventure for quite some time. And of men."

I glanced at where she was still gripping the doctor's arm, but I didn't say anything. The woman had earned whatever small amounts of security she could find.

I stood to leave, but she stopped me. "Will we see one another again?"

I shook my head. "Probably not. We run in very different circles, Vanessa."

Vanessa smiled sadly. "But you never know."

I returned her smile, then bid them both good-bye.

Later, Redvers found me sitting in my deck chair, gazing out over the water. I was soaking up the last few rays of late afternoon sun, and feeling quite badly that the chair next to mine would never see its occupant again. Redvers carefully avoided sitting in Heinz's seat, taking the one on the other side of me instead.

"Another case successfully wrapped up."

I wasn't sure how successful we were since three men were dead, but I kept that to myself. "You know, once we are married, you're going to have to stop keeping things from me."

Redvers gave me a roguish grin. "We'll see about that."

I rolled my eyes at him.

"And when shall we find ourselves before the altar?" He reached over and took my hand in his.

I paused, then gave him a mischievous smile. "Oh, I think you should meet my father first, don't you?"

ACKNOWLEDGMENTS

First of all, a quick author's note—for plotting purposes, I had to make the voyage across the Atlantic a little longer than it would have actually been. A little creative license is necessary sometimes to make sure you can squeeze all the action in.

On to the good stuff.

A huge thank you to my readers. You make this possible.

Huge thanks to John Scognamiglio, my editor extraordinaire, as well as to Larissa Ackerman, my truly outstanding publicist. I'm so lucky to work with the two of you. Thank you to Robin Cook and to Sarah Gibb for her artistry. Further thanks to the rest of the Kensington team who work so hard to get books into your hot little hands.

Thank you to Ann Collette, my amazing agent who always makes me feel grateful that she chose me. I promise those four-hour conversations will happen once I have something interesting to talk about.

So much love and thanks to Zoe Quinton King, my dearest of friends and editor and boo. I'm so lucky to have you on my team both in my life and my career. I'm grateful for you every damn day.

Big love and thanks to Jessie Lourey, Lori Rader-Day, and Susie Calkins, who are the tater tots on my hot dish. (They make everything better. I'm not implying these lovely women are potatoes.)

Immeasurable thanks for the friendship, love, and support to Tasha Alexander, Shannon Baker, Gretchen Beetner, Lou Berney, Mike Blanchard, Keith Brubacher, Kate Conrad, Hilary Davidson, Dan Distler, Daniel Goldin, Juliet Grames, Andrew Grant, Glen Erik Hamilton, Carrie Hennessy, Tim Hennessy, Chris Holm, Katrina Niidas Holm, Megan Kantara, Steph Kilen, Elizabeth Little, Jenny Lohr, Erin MacMillan, Joel MacMillan, Dan Malmon, Kate Malmon, Mike McCrary, Catriona McPherson, Katie Meyer, Trevor Meyer, Lauren O'Brien, Brad Parks, Roxanne Patruznick, Margret Petrie, Nick Petrie, Bryan Pryor, Andy Rash, Jane Rheineck, Kyle Jo Schmidt, Johnny Shaw, Jay Shepherd, Becky Tesch, Andy Turner, Tess Tyrrell, and Bryan Van Meter.

Love to Naomi Fenske—sometimes goals are super easy to meet.

Katie and Trevor Meyer, I will road trip with you any day.

Thank you to the amazing booksellers and librarians who've supported this book and especially to the folks who hosted me for another virtual tour—I can't wait to meet you all in person. Special shout-outs to Charlotte and the crew at Mystery to Me, John and McKenna at Murder by the Book, Anne at Book Carnival, Daniel and Chris at Boswell Books, Anastasia at the Savoy, Barbara at the Poisoned Pen, Devin at Once Upon a Crime, Lisa and Laura at Barbara's Bookstore, and Dan Radovich at Barnes and Noble.

Sometimes the reason that you're lucky is that you've dodged a bullet.

Thank you and big love to my amazing family, Rachel and AJ Neubauer, Dorothy Neubauer, Sandra Olsen, Susan Catral, Sara Kierzek, Jeff and Annie Kierzek, Justin and Christine Kierzek, Josh Kierzek, Ignacio Catral, Sam and Ariana Catral, Mandi Neumann, Andie, Alex, and Angel Neumann. Special thanks and love to my dear friend Gunther Neumann, who is truly a rock.

And finally, all the love and thanks to Beth McIntyre. For 36 years of friendship and counting. (I hope that math is right, but I'm an English major. It's in the ballpark at least.) You are the wind beneath my wings. My love for you is like a red, red rose.